Eyes on You

Eyes on You

A Novel of Suspense

Kate White

An Imprint of HarperCollins*Publishers*

EYES ON YOU. Copyright © 2014 by Kate White. All rights reserved. Printed in the United States of America. No part of this book may be used or reproduced in any manner whatsoever without written permission except in the case of brief quotations embodied in critical articles and reviews. For information address HarperCollins Publishers, 195 Broadway, New York, NY 10007.

HarperCollins books may be purchased for educational, business, or sales promotional use. For information, please e-mail the Special Markets Department at SPsales@harpercollins.com.

FIRST HARPERLUXE EDITION

HarperLuxe™ is a trademark of HarperCollins Publishers

Library of Congress Cataloging-in-Publication Data is available upon request.

ISBN: 978-0-06-232669-0

14 ID/RRD 10 9 8 7 6 5 4 3 2 1

To Jody Gaylin, Amy Archer, and Lori Stone
Thank you, Thank you, Thank you

Eyes on You

Chapter 1

The shoes had made a nasty dent in my paycheck, but I wasn't sorry I'd splurged. They were Chanel, black-textured with a peep toe and a gold zipper up the back, really more of a booty than a stiletto. And not what you'd ever call "Fuck me" shoes—there was nothing about them that would make a guy want to bed you, unless he was the type who liked a razor-sharp heel at his throat. These were what you wore on your feet when you needed armor, when the night would include a few foes half-hidden among the friends and fans. They were the kind of footwear that said you could damn well take care of yourself.

"Fuck *you*" shoes, I thought. That's what they were. And I knew I might need them tonight. Because in TV there were always people who wished the worst for you.

As soon as I stepped off the elevator onto Bettina's floor, I could tell her apartment was packed. The din drove its way through the door, a babble of voices punctuated by ice clinking in glasses and bursts of laughter. Bettina had told me not to show until six-thirty ("The guest of honor must make an *entrance*"), and I was one minute ahead of that. I didn't want to seem all eager-beavery, but I also couldn't stand waiting any longer. I was about to be feted for the book I'd written, and I wanted to savor every second, especially because just two years ago, a night like tonight would have been preposterous to imagine.

The penthouse door swung open presto-like before I could even touch it. There was a guy right inside, wearing a collared black shirt, black pants, and gleaming, super-pointy black shoes. He smiled, beckoning me in. A twentysomething girl stood next to him, poured into a tight black dress and holding a clipboard. Big smile from her, too, as I stepped inside. The white walls of the entrance gallery popped with edgy modern art.

"Welcome, Ms. Trainer," the guy said, obviously recognizing me. "I'll let Ms. Lane know you're here."

"That's okay, I'll find her," I said. I wanted a few moments to take everything in and *relish* it all.

I moved down the hall, inching by a cluster of people I didn't recognize, and emerged into the enormous living room, nearly jammed with well-dressed guests. I'd been to Bettina's apartment a couple of times when I'd consulted for her, but always during daylight hours—for offsite breakfast meetings and once a luncheon we'd put together for a group of key celebrity publicists.

Though I knew the place was a jaw-dropper, with floor-to-ceiling windows facing the lower Hudson, I wasn't prepared for the magical twilight tableau in front of me. Hundreds of lights sparkled from buildings on the New Jersey side of the river, and inside, where every possible surface of the columned loft-style room was dotted with white votive candles. The air smelled of vanilla and some exotic fruit—maybe mango. Manhattan meets Madagascar, I thought. Just the kind of magic touch Bettina would concoct.

Pretty quickly, I started to pick out familiar faces—the major players from my book publisher; staffers from Bettina's website; colleagues from the new cable show I was cohosting; my TV and book agents; and fortunately, a few gossip columnists, whom I was counting on to create hype for the book.

I recognized more than a few boldface names, people Bettina had obviously coaxed or strong-armed into coming out on a Sunday night in summer. As expected, there were a few foes also, including Mina Garvin, the

TV critic who'd bludgeoned the show its first week on the air. But so what? I had the shoes for it.

I swung my gaze around the room, searching for my cousin's daughter, Maddy, who'd been working as my intern the past few months. This party wasn't meant for friends or relatives, but I'd asked Maddy to come in case I needed assistance. There was no sign of her, but to the far right, near a bar twinkling with glasses, I picked out Carter Brooks, my coanchor on *The Pulse*, holding court with the president of the network and a couple of other honchos. At six-three, Carter towered over the other men.

Off to the left, I noticed Vicky Cruz, aka "Cruz Missile," on the move through the crowd, her short red bob punctuating the room like the head of a giant kitchen match. Within a few seconds, she'd maneuvered her way into the all-male circle. She was known as a ballbuster, and she practically ruled the network as the host of its highest-rated show, yet in social settings with powerful men, she preferred to play the pussycat. I didn't like her show, and based on my limited contact so far, I didn't like *her*, but her success blew me away.

Simultaneously, several people spotted me and smiled, but before anyone had a chance to approach, Bettina zoomed over in my direction, parting the crowd like a speedboat through water. She was wearing a plum-colored dress with lips to match.

"Hello, darling," Bettina said, scratching her lacquered hair against each of my cheeks as she air-kissed me. "You look fabulous."

I liked Bettina, and I admired her fiercely—she'd built a monster Web empire, made a bloody fortune, and paid me nicely for consulting on how to turbocharge her celebrity coverage—but I also knew to keep my guard up around her. She made me think of a stray husky a college friend had adopted. He'd adored that dog, spent endless hours running and hiking with her, but refused to let her sleep in the same room with him. "Not with *those* eyes and teeth," he'd said. "I'm sure she's part wolf."

"Everything is amazing, Bettina," I said. "I can't believe you lured all these people out tonight."

"The key is for you to totally enjoy yourself," she said. "Tonight is all about *you.*"

I flashed a smile, knowing, not ungratefully, that Bettina's comment was part bullshit. She had her sonar continually set for excuses to entertain, to bring together powerful and influential people in a mix that hummed, sizzled, throbbed, and sometimes burst into flames. But I was delighted to be her excuse tonight. "I intend to totally luxuriate in the evening," I said.

"Why don't you mingle for a little while, darling? Sign books. Share some of those secrets you wrote about. And then, around seven-fifteen, I'll make the toast."

"Perfect."

Bettina snapped her fingers at a passing waiter, snatched a glass of white wine from the tray for me, and then motored off, parting the crowd again.

I indulged in a sip of wine, set to mingle. Tom, the executive producer of my show, squeezed through the crowd to offer congratulations, as did my book editor. At one point, I felt like I was being watched, and I let my eyes wander. Mina Garvin was staring at me, but she quickly looked away. It probably galled her that after a rough start five months ago, our show was now killing it in the ratings. Though she'd been right about how lame we were in the early weeks, her review had been especially mean—and *personal*, as if I'd hooked up with her husband or kicked her puppy in the head. Some people might have wondered why she'd been invited. Bettina once told me that her secret sauce for a good party included a few haters in the mix.

Someone squeezed my arm. It was Ann Carny, the PR director for the network. We'd become friends about four or five years ago, while working at another network, and she'd been a rock for me when my life had gone to hell. Now that we were ensconced once again at the same company, it had become easier for us to stay in touch.

"Hey there," I said, taking in her pale blue dress. "You look terrific."

Ann favored subdued styles, and the effect was always polished, elegant.

"Ditto," she said. "And what an amazing night. You must be so thrilled."

"I am. I can't believe the spread Bettina's put on."

"I don't mean just the party. You seem to own the world these days." Ann turned her head and pointed with her chin. At her direction, my eyes found their way to a huge shimmering canvas of irregular stripes in orange and black and red. Displayed on the rustic table beneath the painting were dozens of copies of my book, *The 7 Secrets Women Keep.* The front cover was bold and graphic; the back featured a huge photo of me in a tight red dress.

"Displaying them beneath that Sean Scully painting was a good idea," I said. "It will keep my ego in check."

"Oh, come on. Your book's great, and you should let your ego run wild tonight," Ann said. "You're even entitled to *gloat.*"

"Mostly, I just feel relieved. To be back on track again. Thanks, of course, in no small part to you."

"Sorry I can't do a celebratory meal with you later. I've had this dinner on the books for ages, and I'll have to split in a sec."

"No worries. Maddy's going to grab a bite with me, if I can find her. I haven't had time to be much of a mentor, so maybe I can play catch-up tonight."

"Speaking of egos running wild, here comes your coanchor."

I smiled in greeting as Carter approached me, conscious that there might be a few people checking us out right then. One of the factors that had made the show successful so far was the on-air rapport between the two of us. With Carter, that didn't involve much heavy lifting. At forty-one, he was still the quintessential bad boy—charming, at ease in his skin, and great-looking, with deep blue eyes, slicked-back brown hair, and the kind of full, sensuous mouth that bad boys seemed to have an unfair market on. And off-set he looked even better: no make-up or product gleam to the hair.

Because of our rapport, there'd already been a few unfounded rumors in the press linking us romantically, and Ann, in her work role, advised us to discourage them. It was okay for people to *wonder* if we were getting horizontal, but God forbid we were actually doing so.

"Congratulations, Robin," he said. "Do I get an autographed copy of the book tonight?"

"Of course," I said. "Though should I just sign my name? If I make it out to you, you won't be able to regift it."

Carter smiled. "Okay, so I accidentally gave someone a watch that said Lionsgate Pictures on the face. You ever gonna let me forget it?"

"I guess I'll have to wait until Christmas and see what you give me."

"Switches for being such a wiseass. Ann, however, is a different story." He glanced toward her and grinned. "I know it's only August, but I've already been perusing the Tiffany website with her in mind."

"Carter, I do spin all day long," Ann said dryly. "I don't need any from you. So tell me, have you read Robin's book yet?"

"Actually, I have," he said. "Robin gave me an advance-reader copy."

"Oh, come on, Carter," I said. He'd been hyping the book during the past few shows, but I doubted he'd done anything more than skim it. "Don't tease."

"I'm being serious. I finished it last night, and I thought it was terrific. Very smart." As he spoke, his eyes seemed to hold mine an extra beat.

"Thanks," I said. His comment had pleased me more than it should have. "I appreciate that."

"Of course, what I *should* have done is employ some of the wisdom from it."

"How so?" I asked.

He shrugged. "I got the boot the other night," he said. "From that woman Jamie I was seeing."

Carter sometimes shared a few details about his personal life, but it was always just surface stuff, chatter meant to charm you into thinking you knew him when that wasn't the case at all.

"Oh please, Carter," Ann said. "You've never been dumped in your life. I'm sure Jamie simply saw the handwriting on the wall." She glanced at her watch. "Oops, I have to fly. Good luck, Robin."

As soon as she edged away through the crowd, reporters and columnists began to push toward me, asking for comments. And then came people with copies of my book for me to sign. The guy in black from the door materialized with a holder stuffed with black Sharpies. I set down my evening bag and went to work. A couple of times, I scanned the crowd for Maddy—this was one of those moments when I could have used her help—but again, no sign of her.

As the last of the autograph seekers moved away, I was suddenly alone. I could tell my face was a little flushed, and my fuck-you shoes had started to pinch. It would be smart, I realized, to freshen up before the toast. I grabbed my purse from the table I'd set it on and made my way down a long back hallway to where

I knew a second powder room was located. It turned out to be empty. I slipped inside and closed the door. The party was instantly muffled, like the sounds from a ship that had just sunk beneath the sea.

The room was dim, lit only by pin lights in the ceiling and a row of votive candles on a long glass shelf. I exhaled slowly and took another breath. There was something about the mango scent from the candles that instantly relaxed me.

The party had gone brilliantly so far. At least a dozen bloggers and columnists had asked me for brief quotes about my book. They'd come tonight mainly for a chance to check out Bettina's legendary apartment, but as long as they plugged the book, I couldn't care less why they'd showed.

I turned toward the mirror and stared for a moment at my reflection. Though I'd be thirty-eight in early October, I knew I'd probably never looked better. Some of that was due to the haircut. For the launch of the show, the hairstylist I'd hired had suggested what she called a "choppy shag" that came to my chin and flattered my face in a way long hair never had. And though I'd had it styled tonight for the party—and my makeup done—it was easy enough to pull off myself.

At the moment, though, my hair was the only thing getting shagged. To some degree, that was *my* choice.

I'd had one brief romance this past winter, when I no longer felt so bruised from my divorce, but once I'd been hired for the show, I'd put every ounce of energy *there*. And that was the way it had to be. This was my chance to retrieve what I'd lost.

Except my marriage, of course. I might have felt gutted when everything unraveled, but there was no way I would ever want it back.

I popped open the latch on my evening bag, reached inside for my lipstick, and reapplied the deep red color. As I dropped the tube back in the bag, I made sure the folded notecard was tucked inside. It had the list of people I intended to thank during my remarks.

As soon as I re-entered the living room, the guy in black from the front door was back by my side, his expression expectant. "Ms. Lane is ready to give the toast now," he said.

"Great," I said. I snaked behind him toward the far end of the room, where Bettina was standing with her back to the view. She nodded to me as I reached the fringe of the crowd. Before stepping forward to join her, I pulled the notecard from my purse and set my bag down on a table. Bettina tapped her wineglass several times with her thick gold bracelet. The room went nearly silent, and people turned all their attention toward us.

Her toast was pure Bettina, all gushy and dramatic. She ran through my bio, how I'd segued from being a print journalist and frequent TV guest to a job as a celebrity reporter on the top morning show and eventually to host of my own cable show. Then, she exclaimed, she'd been lucky enough to nab me as a blogger and consultant before I was lured back to TV. She said she was thrilled for my success on cable's *hottest* program, and declared that my book blew the lid off what women really feel.

I tried not to cringe at the hyperbole and instead did what Ann had advised: I briefly let my ego run wild and lapped it up.

Then it was my turn. I didn't feel nervous, exactly—it had been years since speaking publicly had scared my pants off—but I felt a quick rush of adrenaline. I was in front of tons of heavy hitters, people who could slice and dice a person behind her back, and I couldn't help but feel exposed up there. Yet as I glanced around, I saw a sea of receptive faces.

I grinned and thanked everyone for coming. I quickly described the genesis of the book, how there are some parts of themselves that women felt too uncomfortable to share, even to their partners and closest friends. While I spoke, I unfolded the notecard in my hands. "I don't want to take you away for long from either the incredible view or that fabulous tuna tartare, but there are a few people I *must* thank individually."

I glanced down at the notecard and almost jerked back in surprise. It wasn't the right card. Or rather, it *was*—I could see the names I'd jotted down—but someone had scrawled words over them in thick, black Sharpie strokes: "You evil little bitch. You'll get yours."

Chapter 2

My heart lurched, and for a moment I felt suspended in time. I needed to read the names—I needed to read them *right then*—but I couldn't make them out beneath the menacing script.

I slowly folded the card, raised my head, and forced a big smile. I would have to wing it, partly from memory, partly from picking out faces in the room. I started by thanking the publishing team and worked my way from there. I faltered once, flustered, and pushed through. As my gaze swept across the room, I realized that the person who'd snuck into my handbag and left the message was standing somewhere in front of me.

When I was done, people applauded exuberantly, but it was hard to enjoy it.

"That was a wonderful toast, " I said to Bettina as the clapping died down and the crowd began breaking up into groups again. She squeezed my arm appreciatively and then was hijacked by a guest. Instinctively, I searched for Ann, then remembered she'd left forty-five minutes ago. I stepped closer to the window, turned my back to the room, and reopened the notecard.

Seeing the message again made me catch my breath. The heavy, ragged strokes nearly pulsed with rage. I tore the card into pieces and stuffed them into an empty cocktail glass on a table nearby.

Who could have done such a loathsome thing? In my job, I expected occasional barbs and left-hand compliments, but not *this*. Did someone have a grudge against me? Whoever it was must have acted when I'd been signing books. My purse had sat on the table unattended for at least twenty minutes. The person clearly had used one of the Sharpie pens from the holder.

I closed my eyes and tried to picture who'd been hovering around me at that point. It was all a bit of a blur. There was one person, though, whom I couldn't forget, someone who'd been in the immediate vicinity: the TV critic Mina Garvin. Was she pissed because the show's success had made her eat crow?

I needed to rejoin the mix before people began to wonder why I had my face glued to the window. I took a breath and spun around. And then there was Maddy, right in front of me, dressed in a low-cut black cocktail dress.

"Where have you *been*?" I snapped. I was totally rattled, I realized.

"Oh, I'm so sorry, Robin," Maddy said. She tossed her thick buttery-blond hair out of her eyes. "I was feeling kind of queasy, and I almost didn't make it. I got here when you were signing books, and I didn't want to interrupt."

"Are you okay now?" I asked, sorry for my tone a moment ago.

"Yes, better. I think it's just my period coming on."

"Have you had a chance to network a little? There are some amazing people here."

As I swung my head in emphasis toward the center of the room, I caught two men ogling Maddy's breasts.

"Oh, yes," she said. "I talked to a few producers from other shows. I figure the more contacts I make, the better it is for next year."

"Exactly."

"I'm just so glad it doesn't have to end," she said. Maddy was a rising senior at New York University, and I'd managed to extend her internship from the summer into the fall.

"So are you still up for a bite to eat tonight?" I asked. In light of what had just happened, it would be especially good to have company tonight.

But Maddy scrunched her face. "I hate to let you down, especially on a night like tonight," she said, "but I don't think I should push it."

"Understood," I said. Maybe it was for the best. I had a crazy week ahead, jammed with press for the book, and I needed to be fresh for all of it.

One of the men who'd been eye-stalking Maddy suddenly butted in with a pathetic comment about having met her once before. I backed away and started to weave my way through the crowd.

"Great remarks."

I turned. It was Carter. "Thanks," I said. "Why is it that speaking in public is so much trickier than being on TV?"

"I haven't figured that one out yet. This anchor I worked with when I was reporting in Cleveland—one of those silver-haired, old-timer guys—used to say that having an inch of pancake on his face was like a security blanket, and the minute it was wiped off, he felt totally exposed."

"Funny," I said.

"Is everything okay, Robin?"

"What do you mean?" I asked.

"You seem a little forlorn." He reached out and touched my elbow, and as he did, I felt a weird tingle in my arm. I realized that since our first handshake months ago, neither of us had ever touched the other.

"Something kind of strange happened," I said. Should I confess? I wondered. I felt the urge to tell *someone*. "When—"

"Robin, can you sign my book before I go?" A former colleague from the website was practically shoving a book between Carter and me.

"Mine, too, please," another person urged.

Carter smiled obligingly and moved off. For the next half hour, I autographed books and accepted congratulations, trying not to let what had happened mar any more of the party for me. The crowd began to thin out. After signing one last book, I went in search of my enchanting hostess.

"Bettina, tonight was so amazing," I said.

"It was good for me, too, you know," she said. She pursed her plummy lips and nodded in satisfaction. "I made a deal I wasn't even expecting. But you should go now. The guest of honor should never be the last to leave. And *please* let me know how the book does, darling."

I promised I would, though I was pretty sure that, regardless, Bettina would be checking the Amazon ranking. She had a ferocious need to ferret out all the details, especially the dirty ones, about everyone in her universe.

As someone else pulled Bettina aside to say goodbye, I spotted Maddy again, a few feet away.

"Time to get you home to bed," I said. Taking her arm, I led her from the apartment to the small vestibule outside. A group was bunched there, waiting for the elevator. One of them was Vicky Cruz, and most of the others, I realized, were part of her entourage. Vicky had probably come only because network brass had been invited, but that was okay. Her presence had added star power, and for that I was grateful.

"Your friend Bettina throws quite the party," Vicky said as we boarded the elevator. Her tone was challenging, as if she thought I'd scored more than I was entitled to.

"*Doesn't* she?" I said. "She's an incredible hostess."

I'd never been quite so close to Vicky. Though her fifty-year-old face was overly pumped with fillers, it had the perfect contours and features for TV: high cheekbones, eyes set a bit too far apart.

"How's the book doing, anyway?" she asked.

"The pub date isn't until Tuesday, so we won't know until next week."

"*Secrets*," she said, and then scrunched up her face. "Do women really *have* any? I thought we couldn't keep our mouths shut." She glanced conspiratorially at one of her female underlings, as if the other woman must be wondering the same thing.

"Oh, I think we all keep a few," I said.

Vicky shrugged. "You're the *expert* on this one, sweetie. By the way, congratulations to you and Carter on your ratings. How do you plan to take it to the next level? Because that's, of course, what our beloved president always demands."

I smiled sweetly. "I could tell you, Vicky," I said. "But then I'd have to kill you. "

I probably shouldn't have gone there, but in light of what had happened with the note, I'd no patience for her little jab. She just stared at me, saying nothing. Two female members of her team pinched their lips together, trying not to grin. A few seconds later we reached the ground floor and Vicky strode out first, the entourage scampering behind her.

"Let's find you a cab," I said to Maddy as we stepped from the cool lobby into the steamy night. I'd ordered a car for myself, but Maddy lived all the way out in Williamsburg, Brooklyn.

"That's okay, I'll just hop on the subway."

"Don't be silly," I said. I shot my hand up for a cab speeding up the avenue and then opened my purse to fish out thirty bucks for her. Just having my hand in the bag made me think of the notecard, and my stomach knotted at the memory.

"I really appreciate it, Robin," Maddy said. She slid into the cab and smiled at me through the window.

Despite the fact that we were only second cousins, we bore a passing resemblance to each other—oval-shaped face, blue eyes, our lower lip slightly plumper than the top one. I waved as she drove off.

As soon as I was in the Town Car, I collapsed against the backseat. I wondered if I should report the note. After all, there'd been an implied threat with the "you'll get yours." But whom would I tell? A party at Bettina's didn't exactly fall under the jurisdiction of the network security department. And I certainly didn't want to raise the issue with Bettina after all her generosity. Maybe the note was simply on a par with Internet trolling. Nasty, a little scary even, but ultimately nothing to be concerned about.

Back in my apartment, I eased off my shoes, tucked them carefully back in their box, and wiggled my feet into a pair of slippers. I'd eaten nothing at the party, and I was famished now. I smeared peanut butter on a few crackers and carried my snack to the small dining table in the living room, which was nestled beneath one of the lead-paned windows.

When I'd been married, my husband, Jake, and I had lived in an old loft downtown; my new place was about a quarter of the size, but I loved it. It was in a prewar building and had a small fireplace in the living room, but the closet and kitchen and bathroom had been modernized so that everything was crisp and clean.

I took a bite and began to replay the party in my mind. Though I'd known Bettina would go to town tonight, not only for my sake but also because of how it would reflect on *her*, I'd never expected anything so dazzling.

And yet, I thought glumly, the party seemed *tainted* now. Someone who'd been in that room despised me— for an imagined slight, or perhaps because I had what he or she wanted. I racked my brain, trying to remember whether anyone there had ever been hostile to me, but I drew a blank.

Finally, I stood up and tried to shake the thoughts away. I couldn't let one ugly moment color the whole evening.

I brought my laptop to the table. For the next hour, I surfed online—every place from CNN to Gawker to the UK's *Daily Mail*. Sunday night was generally worthless as far as news was concerned, yet occasionally, something crazy went down. *The Pulse* had a round-table format, derivative to a large extent of many shows on *MSNBC*, but we covered pop culture rather than politics—celebrities, buzzy trends, scandals, movies, and best-selling books. For tomorrow night we'd planned a segment on baby divorcées—stars who had married ridiculously young and then split a couple of years later. There was a chance that some celebrity marriage had blown up over the weekend, giving us an even fresher hook, but no such luck.

The segments might change anyway, as news broke tomorrow. That was part of the fun, what made daily TV so much more thrilling for me than print. I loved the scramble, the rush, the vibrations you could almost feel in the floor.

My cell phone rang, jerking me from my thoughts. I was surprised to see Carter's name on the screen. We'd developed the habit of sometimes checking in at night and doing our own private postmortem of the show, but he'd never called on a Sunday.

"Hi there," I said, answering.

"Great party," he said.

"Glad you could come and see Bettina in all her glory."

"I'm not interrupting a hot date, am I?"

"To tell you the truth, you are," I said. "His name is Skippy. Skippy Extra Crunchy. We've asked a few crackers to drop in, too."

Carter laughed. "Well, aren't we Miss Kinky Pants?"

"So what's up?" I asked. "Did you want to talk about tomorrow's show?"

"Actually, I was following up on our conversation at the party. You said something strange had happened, and then your devoted fans interrupted."

"Um—" I started to tell him, appreciative of his concern, but then thought better of it. Though I'd been ready to share at the party, it would have been a mistake. Carter didn't need to hear that someone considered me an evil little bitch who deserved to get hers.

"You know, I don't even remember now," I said. "But I do have a question. What did you think of Mina Garvin being there?"

"I gotta say, that surprised me."

"Do you know much about her personally?"

"Not a whole lot. Though a couple of people have told me that she's as hateful in person as she is in print."

Maybe Mina *was* the culprit.

"You shouldn't give that chick another thought," he added. "You've had the last laugh."

"For *now*," I said, chuckling.

"I have to tell you again, Robin. Your book is so damn smart. I love the section where you talk about how literal guys are, and how they assume, stupidly, that women are the same way. I think that was part of my problem with Jamie."

"How so?" I asked. My inquiry was more personal than I generally played it with him, but he'd opened the door earlier, so it didn't feel out of line.

"It seemed like there was something eating at her lately, but when I asked what it was, she kept saying everything was fine. Then one night she just exploded. It turned out she'd been working herself into a jealous snit."

"Did she go through your texts, stuff like that?" I asked. That's probably what I should have done with Jake, I thought. Then maybe I wouldn't have been duped for so long.

"No . . . Okay, to be perfectly honest, she's jealous of *you.*"

"You're kidding," I said. Here we go with the rumors again, I thought.

"She'd mentioned a few times that she didn't like the way I looked at you on the air, and I assumed she was just teasing. But the night we had the confrontation, we were watching a recording of the show together, and she went bat-shit about you. She threw the damn remote at my head." He laughed. "Do you think I need a restraining order?"

I laughed back. "Maybe I do, too. I know you said she wasn't a rocket scientist, but doesn't she get that it's just *TV*?"

I nibbled a cracker, waiting for his response. But he didn't say anything. Hold on, I thought. Was Carter suggesting that Jamie had a *reason* to be jealous? Clearly, he was being his flirty self. But this was further than he usually took things, and my mind went blank as I searched for the right quip to toss back.

"Well, look," Carter said finally. "I'd better let you get back to Skippy."

"Thanks for checking in. See you tomorrow."

I tossed the phone on the table and stood in the middle of the room, still wondering. Maybe Carter had stopped talking at that moment to take a swig of a beer or watch a show he'd muted on television.

There was no denying that on the air, at least, we had crazy chemistry, and it had been there from our first audition together. My agent had been told they were looking for a Nick and Nora Charles–ish connection— irreverent, flirty, sarcastic at times without ever being mean—and so that was what I tried to deliver. Carter, who'd already been hired, made it easy. Every moment of the three auditions had seemed as fun and exhilarating as good improv. I wasn't shocked when I learned I'd nailed it.

As the launch of the show approached, management decided, to my consternation, that I needed to rein it in a little. Though I was pissed, there was nothing I could do. I was the sidekick, after all, there first and foremost to introduce guests and move things along. The first weeks of shows were clunky and flat, and the reviews reflected that. I felt like I had a freaking muzzle on. And so one day, out of pure desperation, I let go with a zinger at Carter. He smiled, relishing it, and played right back. We were off and running, and no one tried to muzzle me again.

When the rumors had started about us, I'd laughed them off. Carter seemed like a player, the kind with a specific type of girl that he never deviated from—in his case, brunettes with big breasts. Jamie, whom I'd met when she dropped by after the show, had the kind of huge fake boobs that entered a room about two minutes before she did.

Oh, I'd let my imagination run free a few times, picturing what sex with Carter would be like. The up-front part would probably be fun—lots of dirty talk and clothes nearly ripped to ribbons. But in bed, he'd surely be bad-boy selfish, all about his own pleasure as he pounded away like a piston.

I set my plate in the dishwasher and then wrote a thank-you note to Bettina. It wasn't hard to sound grateful—about the party, her support, her amazing toast.

What she hadn't mentioned in her toast, when she was raving about my brilliant career, was the yawning year-and-a-half gap on my résumé—at least as far as TV was concerned. That whole time had been a nightmare for me. First Jake had dumped me for a woman he worked with. My only consolation, as I tried to deal with both his betrayal and his departure, was my work. I was the girl with the fun little show, whose picture adorned the side of bus shelters. Maybe I was clueless when it came to men, but *damn*, I was brilliant at getting my guests to open up.

Then that was gone, too. My agent was sure I'd be tapped quickly for another show, but the dual misery I felt sapped my energy, and I knew I stank at the auditions I did and the meetings I took. Four weeks later, I crashed my car while driving to Virginia for what was supposed to be a restorative trip with friends, and I spent the next weeks in bed with a broken ankle and pelvis. The requests for auditions all but dried up.

A few months later, my bones and bruises finally healed, I dragged myself out of bed. By now the only offers coming in were for me to star in infomercials. I would never be *that* desperate. I fought off my inertia long enough to write a blog for Bettina's website. It was about the female need to please. More blogs followed, and one in particular hit a nerve, sending a book editor in pursuit. I scored an advance, not huge but nice, better than I'd imagined, and I wrote the whole thing in six months, like a maniac.

Around the same time, Bettina signed me to consult for her site and help plan where it needed to go next with celebrity coverage. The calls to my agent picked up, and then, thanks to Ann, I got a lead about subbing for a show on the network. Next came the chance to audition for *The Pulse.*

As I slid the note into an envelope, my eye fell on my evening bag, which I'd dropped on the table when I returned home. I'd never thought to check if anything *else* had been left in there, something I hadn't detected earlier. I dumped the contents on the table—lipstick, blush, comb, credit card, a couple of dollar bills. Nothing else.

Then I noticed the stain. Some of the ink from the Sharpie had managed to bleed onto the pale blue lining, making a black amoeba-like mark. The sight of it disgusted me.

Still holding the bag, I stood up and walked to the entryway of my apartment and swung open the front door. There was no one in the corridor. I strode halfway down the hall to the small room for trash disposal. Inside, on one of the walls, a metal door opened to the chute that led to the trash compactor. I opened the door and hurled the bag down the chute. I could hear the diminishing sound of the bag bouncing against the metal sides.

I *hated* things with stains on them. They made me think of my stepmother. So anything with a stain had to be destroyed.

Chapter 3

I was at work before nine the next day. It was earlier than usual, but I had a conference call at ten with the publisher's PR team, and I wanted time to review my checklist first.

Due to a space shortage, my office wasn't off the newsroom, like Carter's. It was down a whole other corridor, not far from the makeup room. It would have been better, work-wise, to be near the white-hot center, where all the producers sat, and there'd been talk of moving me down there when they could carve out the space. But I liked the privacy that my office afforded me.

When the call came in, I could tell that everyone was totally jazzed about the party. I'd already seen a few items in the press, but they described others, all favorable. I thanked them for their efforts. I was pretty sure they couldn't detect the dull hangover of anxiety I had from the hate note left in my purse.

Next we reviewed the press plans for the week to come. There would be minimal TV appearances because of my own show, but tons of online coverage, about two dozen radio interviews, and a boatload of tweets and retweets. During the past month, I'd tied myself to my desk at home on weekends and ground out a bunch of guest blogs—touching on points in the book—and they'd be gradually released and posted over the coming days.

"It's clear what's starting to resonate most," said one of the team. "It's the part about women secretly not feeling that they deserve what they have. And the chapter on being ashamed about something you once did. That's hitting a nerve."

"Lots of places need photos," the junior publicist said. I could tell who she was because she made every sentence shoot up at the end. "Are you okay with us sending outtakes from the jacket photo shoot?"

"Of course," I said. I loved the shot of me in the red dress.

"Oh, by the way, I nearly forgot the best news of all," my main publicist, Claire, announced. "The book's ranking high on online retail sites. That's a very good sign."

"We can probably thank my coanchor for that," I said. "He's been nicely pimping the book on the show."

"True," Claire said. "But when I've been pitching, it's been pretty clear that you've built your own following. And people really love the show."

The convergence of the book and the show had been pure luck, but it was clearly going to drive up sales. And I would gladly take them any way I could get them.

My assistant, Keiki, was off that day, dealing with a labradoodle in surgery, so I had the office to myself. I grabbed a coffee in the kitchenette down the hall and then jumped online. I reviewed the tweets the show had generated last night and skimmed through various news sites, looking for emerging stories as well as tidbits that Carter and I could bat around in the upfront chat section. I saved a half hour of my morning to put the finishing touches on a ratings analysis I'd done. Our executive producer, Tom Golden, hadn't asked for it, but I knew he'd find interesting what I'd discovered. I wanted to read it over in hard copy before I turned it over to him.

When I briefly checked email, I noticed that someone—I couldn't tell who from the address—had nicely emailed a half-dozen photos of me from the party, probably taken with a phone. I was beaming in every shot.

That's the way I'd remember last night, I told myself, and I'd just purge the note from my memory.

At noon I headed to the newsroom. There were about twenty desks bunched there, occupied by producers, writers, and bookers. Our set, which was also used by several other shows with modifications, flowed directly from the newsroom. It was a futuristic-looking space that made me think of the bay of a Hollywood movie spaceship, hurtling toward another galaxy. I felt a rush every time I stepped on it.

My first stop was Maddy's desk, which was empty. With a twinge of guilt, I realized she might have called in sick, and I'd never followed up on how she was feeling. But one of the other interns told me that Maddy was here, just away from her desk. I took a few minutes to check in with each of the three senior producers about the rundown for the night's show, knowing that it was still subject to change.

When I strode back into my office, I found Tom sitting in the one spare chair, eyes glued to his iPhone and tapping his leg to a beat only he could hear. He was short and slim and wiry, but he tended to fill up whatever space he was in. Like most of the EPs I'd worked with, he was powered by a nervous, almost manic energy.

"Cool party," he said as I dropped into my desk chair.

"I'm glad we could entice you from Hoboken on a Sunday."

"Usually, Larry hates me going out on a Sunday night, but he's a fan of yours now, so he was happy to make an exception."

"I appreciate that."

"What price tag would you put on that apartment—ten mil, maybe?" he said, rubbing his close-cropped beard. "More?"

"Bettina's? I have no clue, Tom. I really don't."

For split second I thought of telling him what had happened last night and seeing if he'd make a guess about who the culprit was, but I quickly changed my mind. Tom, I'd learned over the past several months, liked maneuvering behind people's backs at times, and I wasn't sure if I could trust him to be discreet.

"So any big changes in the lineup?" I asked. "When I find you sitting in my office, something's usually going on."

"Yeah, we've got something I think we oughta run with today," he said.

"Great. Let me hear."

"Have you been following this cheating-politician double hitter? Hitchens, that Southern senator, is dumping his wife, and she's naming another woman. And then there's a state senator in Oregon whose wife showed up at the statehouse yesterday and left about ten Hefty trash bags of his stuff on the steps. She told the press he's banging his secretary."

"I saw the Hitchens story but not the other one."

"There's nothing new here—and nothing kinky, like Anthony Wiener, or even weird, like Sanford's Appalachian Trail bullshit—but it's a story that people never get tired of. *Why can't these dudes keep it in their pants?* Is a guy who's hardwired for politics also hardwired to cheat?"

I reminded him about our story on baby divorcées.

"We'll bump that. It'll keep."

I didn't relish segments about cheating husbands, but I'd found a way to detach myself when we covered them. "Sounds good," I said.

Tom stroked his beard, thinking for a moment. "I'm going to put Alex on this. But because we're short on time, I need you to give him a hand, okay?"

Alex was a fairly new hire, brought in to replace one of the launch producers who hadn't panned out. He was in his early thirties, I guessed, a former assistant DA who'd made the switch into TV a couple of years ago. Though he was hard to read, I liked working on stories with him. His ideas were fresh—edgy, even—despite the fact that his work was always totally buttoned up.

"Of course," I said. "But won't Charlotte want this?" She was the senior producer responsible for baby divorcées.

"She'll get over it."

I knew she'd be miffed, but that was her battle to fight with Tom.

"Who do you like for guests?"

"For starters, we need a jilted wife. I doubt we got a shot at Jenny Sanford or our dear former governor's wife, but it doesn't hurt to try. We also need a marriage expert. And most important, someone who really knows politicians, who's been on the campaign trail, for instance. You two use your own judgment, and let me know who you find."

"Okay. I'd better move."

I found Alex Lucca in the newsroom and pulled my chair up next to his desk. After making a list of potential guests, we started working at light speed. The marriage therapist was easy; we simply told the one we'd booked for baby divorcées that the topic had changed. She was a total media whore, game for anything, and wouldn't have flinched if she'd been asked to speculate on what went wrong with Adam and Eve.

We struck out, natch, with the big names like Silda Spitzer and Jenny Sanford, as well as about ten other jilted political wives, but finally, a woman in Brooklyn, whose flagrantly unfaithful husband had been in the New York State Assembly, agreed to come on.

"She looks like she's from the cast of *Real Housewives*," Alex said. "Do we want to go that skanky?"

I smiled. "Yeah, as long as we secure someone smart and classy as the third guest."

Out of the corner of my eye, I caught Charlotte staring at us. Maybe she'd put two and two together and figured out that Alex had been given the story that should have gone to her. Or maybe she just liked to look at him. He had wavy black hair and a permanent two-day scruff that contrasted strikingly with his pale white skin and hazel eyes. He wore the same basic look every day—dark pants or jeans and a super-crisp white shirt. I'd heard that some of the girls called him *GQ* behind his back, which I was sure would have annoyed the hell out of him.

Next we plowed through names for the last guest. Some of the ones we called were tied up with fall political campaigns; others didn't want to discuss the topic on the air.

"Wait, here's somebody," Alex said at last, gazing at his computer screen. "Jack Baylor. Political analyst who writes for *Politico*. And he's the author of *The Women They Marry*, all about political wives. The book's old, but I assume it's still a subject he's willing to sound off on."

"Perfect. Is he here in the city?"

"Think so. I'll try to track him down."

"Just let Tom know we've set our sights on him."

While we'd been working, I'd spotted Maddy enter the newsroom. With Alex in pursuit of Baylor, I made my way to her desk.

"You really feeling better or being a trouper?" I asked.

"Definitely better." She lowered her voice. "I just needed a good night's sleep and a lot of Midol."

"Glad to hear. I need you to give Alex a hand now. We've lined up guests for the new segment. Make sure you book their cars right away. And do a background check on the two new guests to be sure there are no loose ends."

By the time I returned to Alex's desk, he was on the phone, talking to Baylor's assistant; from the sound of the conversation, it seemed like the guy would be able to make it. I stood up, ready to head back to my office, when Charlotte walked over and planted herself in front of me.

Though she was in her late twenties, she dressed like a recent college grad and not always in a way that seemed smart to me—at least if she hoped to be on the fast track. Today she had on a short yellow sundress that seemed all about showing off her boobs. Her curly blond hair was up in a ponytail, a total surrender to the humidity.

"Is it true *Alex* is working on the replacement for baby divorcées?" she said.

"Yes. But we're not killing divorcées, just bumping it."

"That leaves me with no segment tonight," she said, clearly annoyed. "*I* should be handling the new one."

Often producers loved losing segments. Charlotte had to know that in her case, it reflected her weakness at pulling a story together quickly.

"Why don't you talk to Tom about it? I'm sure he can explain his reasoning."

"Thanks," she said coldly, and walked away.

When I'd tried early on to offer Charlotte guidance, she'd acted defensive and brushed me off.

The two o'clock rundown meeting was the first time I'd seen Carter that day. As he entered the room, about a minute after I'd arrived, he offered me a friendly smile and nod, nothing different than usual. If he had been trying to give me a romantic opening last night, he seemed to have changed his mind today. Or maybe he'd decided that his best bet was some hot make-up sex with Jamie.

People who'd been milling around took seats, and Tom started to review the plan for the night's show. The first segment was about dogs traveling in the cabin of planes—how more and more people were having their pets designated as "service dogs," supposedly necessary for emotional support but really so the dogs wouldn't have to travel in the hull of the plane. It was the kind of story that would stir a strong reaction from both pet lovers and people who didn't like sitting next to a yappy Pomeranian all the way from New York to L.A.

The cheating-politician story would be the third segment of the show. Alex announced that we were expecting confirmation from our third guest momentarily. I flashed him a smile. As Tom had said, there was nothing groundbreaking about the topic, but it would be good, juicy stuff.

It doesn't get sweeter than this, I thought as I leaned back in my chair. I was on a show I loved, with people working hard and enjoying themselves. It had taken nearly two miserable years to reach, but I'd done it. I let my eyes rove around the table. Sitting in the mix were the six people I'd invited to the party—Tom, Carter, the three senior producers, and the booker for the show. I was certain none of them had written on the notecard. I felt liked by everyone in the room, or at the very least, respected.

The show that night was like being on a bullet train: fast and exhilarating. The politician segment was stronger than I'd imagined. Baylor was terrific, both smart and insightful. And though the ex-wife *could* have been a cast member of *Real Housewives*, her hurt was raw, and you couldn't help but sympathize.

"What's your takeaway about people flying with their dogs in between their legs?" Carter asked as we wrapped the show.

"Clearly, there's abuse of the system going on," I said. "But it sounds like some people may actually need their dogs for emotional support."

"You aren't thinking about getting a dog, are you, Robin? I mean, not for plane travel but just to have. A cute little pug, maybe?"

"Come on, Carter," I said. "Don't you realize I'm much more of a black Lab kind of girl?"

"Okay, forget planes for a second. What about bed?"

"*Bed*?"

"Yeah, how do you feel about dogs in beds?"

I laughed out loud. The director gave the ten-second countdown. "It depends on what type you're talking about, but either way I'm not going to answer," I said. "Good night, everyone. We'll see you tomorrow." I was still laughing after we'd wrapped.

"Killer show," one of the crew yelled as Carter and I rose and unclipped our mics. "You guys were on fire tonight."

"Thanks," I said. "It felt really good." I turned to Carter. "Dogs in bed. I'm going to get you back for that one."

"I look forward to it," he said. He smiled and held my gaze tightly, the way he'd done at the party last night.

Ahh, I thought. So he really *is* up for some serious flirting. I could play along a little, and enjoy myself in the process, but I had no intention of taking it beyond that. I smiled back and stepped off the set. Carter wandered off in the opposite direction, and I started to look for Alex, eager to hear his feedback on our segment. Suddenly I caught the movement of something bright red off to the right, like a streaking flame. I turned my head. Vicky Cruz had just barged into the newsroom, her face covered in some kind of makeup primer and half her head full of Velcro rollers.

"Where's your producer?" she demanded, charging toward me. Her green eyes were hard with rage.

"You mean Tom?" I asked. I wondered what he'd done to make Vicky nearly foam at the mouth.

"I have no fucking clue what his name is," Vicky said. "I just want the guy in charge."

"He's probably in the control room," I said. I had no sympathy for the hissy fit she seemed ready to throw, but I also knew that with Vicky, it was smart to be diplomatic. "Is there something I can help you with?"

"How did Jack Baylor end up on this show?" she snapped.

By this point the whole newsroom had gone silent except for a monitor playing commercials before the eight o'clock show.

"You mean how did we make it happen?" I asked. "The old-fashioned way. We just called and booked him." Did she have something against Baylor? I wondered. Like she'd dated him and he'd dumped her? Well, *tough*. That wasn't our problem.

"*You* decided to book him?" Vicky's voice was nearly a snarl. Where in the world was this going: On the far side of the newsroom, behind where Vicky was standing, I saw Alex rise from his chair. He was going to take the blame, but I couldn't let him.

"Yes," I said.

Vicky took a step closer and eyed me with cold calculation. "You had no fucking right to do that," she yelled. "Don't you *dare* ever try anything like that again."

Chapter 4

I couldn't believe she was talking to me that way. I started to respond, to ask what the problem was with Baylor, when I sensed someone come up behind me. Then Carter was standing right next to me. Crap, I thought. What I didn't need at the moment was a dude playing action hero.

"I'm sorry, but I'm not getting what the issue is, Vicky," Carter said. I could tell by his tone that he was being careful, trying not to make the situation worse, but also signaling he wouldn't let Vicky flatten him like a tank.

"Baylor belongs to *my* show," she told him. "She had no fucking business calling him."

"Belongs to your show?" Carter said, clearly puzzled.

Vicky let her face sag in mock dismay at his ignorance. "Baylor's been under contract with my show for the past year," she said. "He is not *allowed* to discuss politics on another program without express permission from me or my executive producer. Of course, if you want to invite him on to talk about Justin Bieber's latest hairstyle or the size of Kim Kardashian's ass, be my guest."

"I'm sorry," I said. "I wasn't aware of any contract."

"You didn't *assume*, based on how often he's on my show, that there had to be a contract?" Vicky snapped.

"Look, Vicky," Carter said, "as Robin said, we're sorry. We're all big fans of you and your show, and we would never intentionally poach a guest of yours. You can spank me right here in front of everyone if it makes you feel any better."

Vicky let out a breath between her pouty, collagen-pumped lips. She seemed appeased. "Don't tempt me," she said after a moment. Then she turned on her heel and charged out of the newsroom.

All around me, I sensed people exhaling. I looked at Carter. "Maybe she's just having a bad hair day," I said sarcastically, though inside I was fuming. Before Carter could reply, I stalked back to my office and slammed the door.

For the next few minutes I sat there, pissed as hell by what had happened. Though I'd known Vicky had a reputation as an über-bitch, I couldn't believe she'd tried to tear my face off in front of everyone. Yes, it had been a mistake to book Baylor, but not one that justified a public reaming. And why had Carter felt the need to come to my rescue? Who did he think I was, *Bambi*? Maybe he'd been trying to demonstrate solidarity as my coanchor. But he also might have been showing off.

My one consolation about the whole episode: Vicky had looked like the *real* fool, standing there in a headful of rollers with her whole face covered in what appeared to be spackle.

I probably should have known that Baylor was a regular on Vicky's show, but I rarely watched it: too much braying and pontificating for my taste. I wondered why Maddy hadn't figured it out when she'd vetted the guests. Surely Tom would have known about Baylor. He'd been at the network for ten years. Speaking of Tom, where was *he* during the shit storm?

I massaged my temples with the tips of my fingers. Had I sustained any damage tonight? Vicky wielded huge power at the network, and I didn't want to end up on the wrong side of her. She was the type who probably kept an enemies list on her BlackBerry.

I glanced at my watch. It was after eight, but Ann frequently worked this late. I grabbed my phone and tapped her office number.

"So you're still here?" I said when she answered.

"Yeah, I'm about to jump on a conference call with the West Coast. Everything okay?"

"Not really. I stepped in some doo-doo tonight after the show."

"With Carter?"

"No. Believe it or not, with Vicky Cruz. I'd love your advice."

"This call won't take long. Why don't you come up in about ten minutes?"

Disconnecting, I looked up to see Alex standing in the doorway of my office. "Have you got time to talk about what happened?" he asked.

"Yeah, we definitely need to talk."

He dragged over the spare chair and sat down. He looked concerned but not rattled. Obviously, a few years in the DA's office had been like a course in unflappability.

"I'm really sorry about what happened tonight," he said. "I'm not going to make any excuses."

"Actually, I'd *like* to hear a few excuses," I said. "What the hell happened?"

"I try to watch Vicky's show, but I've never seen Baylor on it, and the guy said nothing to the booker about being under contract—or to me during the pre-interview. I have a feeling he assumed we knew he was a Vicky regular and had cleared it with her EP."

"And Maddy didn't discover the connection when she checked him out?"

He sighed. "Actually, she did. She admitted to me a few minutes ago that she found video on YouTube of Baylor on Vicky's show, but since it was the same network, it didn't cross her mind that there would be a problem. It's hard to fault her. At most networks, people *share* guests."

"Yeah, well, this isn't most networks," I said. "At this one there's Vicky, and then there's the rest of us. You've got to tell Maddy not to make assumptions—ever."

"I already have."

I shook my head. "I don't get why *Tom* didn't warn us. He knows everything that goes on around here."

Alex didn't say anything.

"You *told* him, right?" I said. I was going to clobber him if he hadn't.

"Of course," Alex said, bristling. "I may be fairly new at the game, but I know what the rules are. I sent him an email saying we liked Baylor, and then a follow-up after I did the pre-interview."

"And he said Baylor was okay?"

"He never responded. But that's the way it's been working at the moment. He says he's too busy right now to respond to all emails, but we should consider them read. If there's a problem, he gets in touch."

I could sense there was something Alex wasn't saying. From what I'd seen so far, he was the master of discretion, and I'd need a crowbar to extract anything else. "So does he know about Vicky's outburst?" I asked.

"He didn't seem to be around after the show. Carter said he'd look for him and fill him in."

I sighed. Alex was no more to blame than I was, but that didn't stop me from feeling exasperated. "Okay," I said, "let's move on. But we need to be careful going forward. Get your hands on a list of everybody under contract with Vicky's show, as well as anyone who shows up there on even a semiregular basis. We better stay clear of those people, too."

"Yup," he said, standing up. "Have a good night, Robin."

"You, too. And Alex?" I flashed a smile. "If I ever attempt to run around the halls in face primer, chain me to a chair, will you?"

"Promise," he said. He smiled back, but I wondered if he was annoyed that I'd questioned whether he'd followed through with Tom.

Thirty seconds after he left, I was on my way to the executive floor, one flight above.

"So tell me how you stepped in doo-doo," Ann said as I slumped into the extra chair in her office.

I described the ugly little scene in the newsroom, not leaving out any details. When I'd finished, Ann shook her head, smiling ruefully.

"The bottom line? It's not your job to know who Vicky has under contract, and besides, your using Baylor didn't harm her show in the least. You have nothing to feel bad about."

"You think I should do anything?"

"You aren't considering sending Vicky a gift basket, are you?" she asked wryly.

"Of course not. I just don't want to end up on the wrong side of her. Should I send a short note or email to smooth things over?"

Ann pressed her hands together in a steeple and, with her elbows on the desk, touched her lips to her fingers, thinking. Her nails were always perfectly manicured, and today, I noticed, they were painted gray, almost the same color as her eyes.

"This is totally under the cone, okay?" Ann said finally. "I can't stand the woman. About a year ago she insisted on hiring a personal press person. It's on her own dime, and this guy handles the auxiliary stuff that's out of my team's bailiwick, but I didn't like the way she presented it to Potts, as if my work is somehow lacking. Vicky doesn't believe in the win-win situation, and she has a gift for finding the soft underbelly of any potential enemies. If you apologize in even a small way, it's going to feel like a triumph to her. And she could use that against you."

"Got it."

"Of course, when you bump into her, be perfectly pleasant. You don't want to look like you're nursing a grudge." She leaned back in her chair, studying me. "Sounds like Carter really played the white knight tonight," she said after a moment or two.

I shrugged. "Yeah, and I could have done without it. Though maybe he meant well and didn't want to leave me hanging out to dry."

"Don't you think it was mostly about covering his own ass? I'm sure he doesn't want to end up irritating Vicky any more than you do."

"True," I said.

"Just watch your back with him, okay?"

"Is there something you aren't telling me?"

"No," she said after a beat. "But as I've advised you from the beginning, he's always going to be looking out for number one."

That was hardly a surprise. It generally came with anchorman territory.

I stood up from the chair and ran my hands through my hair. It was thick with hair spray from the show, and I felt an urge to shower and slip into a pair of jeans. Ann rose, too, and tucked a few papers into her purse.

"How was the rest of the party?" she asked.

"Oh wow, you just reminded me of something," I said, and told her about the notecard.

"How awful. Do you have any idea who could have done it?"

"None. I keep telling myself that a note like that springs from some serious rage, and I'm not aware of ever triggering anything like that in anyone."

"What about jealousy? That's what I'd guess is at play here. You know what people in this business can be like, especially other women."

She was right. I'd seen my share of cattiness and meanness directed at anyone viewed as a threat. At the morning show I'd worked at, the cohost had a real thing about one of the foreign correspondents, a gorgeous woman named Lilly. Whenever the show was about to go live to Lilly in Cairo or wherever, the anchor would watch her on the monitor and say something like, "Fix your hair, *okay*? It's all smushy on the side." She'd sound all sweet and helpful-like, but it was clearly meant to psych Lilly out.

"I know," I said. "It just always sounds so presumptuous to think that way. 'I bet she's *jealous* of me.' "

"But consider your life right now," Ann said, snapping off her desk lamp. "The show, the book. There's a lot for someone to be jealous of."

I snorted. "I guess I'll have to tweet pictures of myself from home tonight," I said. "I'll be scraping the mold off a block of cheddar cheese so I can make an omelet for dinner and eat it alone."

Ann smiled. "Yes, but you'll look awfully good doing it."

"You need a lift home?" I asked. Ann's apartment was ten blocks south of mine on the Upper East Side.

"Thanks, but I'm headed downtown for a late dinner with a friend."

"A potential suitor?" I'd sensed at times that Ann was still pining for her ex-husband and that the divorce pained her more than she let on. I kept hoping she'd meet someone.

"No, no. Purely platonic. What about you? You off now to whip up your omelet?"

"Actually, I think I'm going to swing by Tom's office and see if he's still around." As I'd been speaking to Ann, I'd decided that I wanted to make certain Tom had been looped in about Vicky's rant.

I rode the elevator one flight down with Ann and said good night as I stepped off onto my floor. I was more than ready to tear out of there, but I also knew that I'd feel better if I talked to Tom.

Though his overhead light was on, I saw as I peeked in that his desk lamp was off and his laptop was nowhere in sight. I glanced at my watch. It was eight-thirty. Clearly, he was headed to Hoboken by now.

As I trudged back to my office, my phone rang, and I dug it wearily out of my purse. It was Carter.

"Hi," I said. "I was going to call you later."

"Where are you, anyway?"

"Still at work."

"Oh. I dropped by your office on my way out, and it looked like you'd already split."

"I'm about to. I need to go home and pour myself a glass of wine."

"I'm only a block away in the car. Want to grab dinner? We can rehash what happened."

"Um, sure," I said, caught off guard. I'd just told him I didn't have plans, so he'd boxed me into a corner.

"Let's do the Lambs Club, on West Forty-fourth," he said. "I'll meet you there. Besides a postmortem, there's something else I want to discuss with you. It'll be good to do it off-site."

I did want to get his take on the Vicky smackdown, but considering the look he'd shot me after the show, I suspected he had another agenda in mind. We'd had lunch a few times in midtown but never dinner. I'd go, I decided, but I'd watch my step.

After I signed off, I stood briefly in the corridor. Far down the hall, I could hear faint laughter drifting from the hair and makeup room. It was almost time for Vicky's show to go on the air, and there were people bustling around for that, as well as for the last live show of the evening afterward. Just thinking of Vicky pissed me off.

I tossed my phone in my purse and continued toward my office. As I neared, I was surprised to see it was dark. The cleaning lady must have been in already and switched off the lights. That was probably why Carter had assumed I'd left.

I patted the wall of the anteroom with my hand until I found the light switch and flipped it on. Then I did the same with my private office. The room popped with too-bright light. I'd started to cross to my desk when my eyes were yanked left by a mess on the floor.

It was a bunch of books, lying in a heap. When I'd left my office, they'd been standing on top of the waist-high bookcase, held in place by a big rock I'd brought back years ago from a trip to the coast of Maine. The cleaning lady, I realized, must have moved the rock when she was dusting, and the books had toppled over like dominoes after she'd gone.

Leave them, I told myself. I was already running late, and I'd pick them up in the morning. But I couldn't do that. My brain had started to compute stuff and sputter it out: The rock was still on the shelf. And the three books on the floor were all copies of my book, *Seven Secrets*. The reference books on the top shelf were standing in place. I felt my stomach dip.

Instinctively, I looked behind me. There was no one around. I set my purse down and crossed the room to the pile. Hiking my dress up a couple of inches, I knelt and started to gather up the books and then gasped.

There was a jagged tear on the back of each book jacket. And each tear was right through my face.

Chapter 5

For a second I just knelt there, my heart thumping. The tear was in a slightly different part of my face on each book, almost like someone had stabbed at my picture with a nail file or scissors.

I flashed back to the message on the notecard. *You evil little bitch. You'll get yours.* Had the same person done this?

I looked up at the shelf. The metal corner was sharp. So maybe the tears had occurred accidentally. The books might have become dislodged somehow and ripped as they fell over the side, catching on the corner. I twisted my neck so I could see my wastebasket. It was empty, which meant the cleaning lady had been in. It *was* possible she'd moved the rock while dusting and set things in motion accidentally.

Or was I utterly stupid to believe that?

I glanced back at the book jackets. For the second time in twenty-four hours, thoughts of my stepmother muscled their way into my memory. I was looking at the kind of trick she'd like to play. She'd tear my things. Or stain them. And make it seem as if I was responsible. Go away, I wanted to scream. Get your face out of my brain.

I reached for the books, but as I did, I felt a tremor in my right hand. I squeezed it closed and shut my eyes. Just breathe, I told myself. I took three long, deep breaths.

Finally, the tremor ceased. I gathered up the books, wrestled off the jackets, and tossed those in the trash.

Ten minutes later, I was in the back of the Town Car. As my driver zigzagged south toward the restaurant, past high-rise office buildings pulsing with light, I kept envisioning the torn book jackets in my mind. Up until now I'd convinced myself that whoever had written the notecard was someone outside of the show's staff—the TV critic Mina Garvin, perhaps. That didn't seem to be the case.

When the driver pulled up in front of the restaurant, I instructed him to wait, saying I'd be an hour or so. I approached the maître d's stand and gave Carter's name. A couple was waiting nearby, and I could tell by their widening eyes that they recognized me. If Carter and I had thought we could enjoy a quiet dinner without being spotted, we were dead wrong. But so what? There was absolutely nothing remarkable about the two of us eating together after the show.

The maître d' led me across the restaurant. There was a huge limestone fireplace on one wall, like something out of an eighteenth-century French château, but the rest of the room was sleek and modern, with chrome standing lamps creating soft pools of light on the ceiling. I spotted Carter at a table in the corner. He looked as good across a room as he did from a foot away.

"Sorry to be late," I said, sliding onto the red leather banquette opposite him. He'd taken off his makeup, and his skin was freshly scrubbed and smooth.

"Not a problem. I ordered a bottle of red for us. I heard you say once that you're a cabernet fan." Without waiting for the waiter, Carter filled my glass and raised his own glass in salute. "Here's to having survived a Cruz Missile assault," he said.

"Hear, hear," I replied, clinking his glass.

"I hope you didn't mind my stepping in tonight," he said. "As soon as I opened my mouth, I wondered if you would have preferred to deal with the situation on your own."

Maybe he hadn't been trying to throw his weight around earlier. Or maybe he had been and was placating me now. I wasn't sure. As good as I was at bantering with Carter on the air, I didn't have a perfect read on him.

"I'm a big girl, and I can take care of myself," I said. "But I appreciate the gesture."

"I was just afraid she might head-butt you with those rollers," he said, grinning. "And I *did* have an advantage in the situation."

"You mean because you're a man?"

"Actually, I was going to say because I've been at the network for a while, and I've heard people discuss the best way to defuse her. Are you saying she has it out for women in particular?"

"That's the sense I get. From comments people have made, and just from my own brief dealings with her."

"Could be. Though as far as I know, she's an equal opportunity offender."

We took a minute to peruse the menu. Out of the corner of my eye, I caught a woman drinking in Carter with her eyes. She looked like she wanted to tear his suit off with her teeth. Who could blame her?

"Where was Tom tonight, anyway?" I asked after we'd placed our orders. "I kept waiting for him to burst out of the control room to deal with Vicky, and it just didn't happen."

"He said he had to run to the head at the end of the show."

"He knows about it now?"

"Yeah. Says he's seen Baylor on Vicky's show but had no idea the guy was under contract. I don't know . . ."

"What?" I asked.

"Tom's seemed a little preoccupied lately."

"Any idea why?"

"To tell you the truth, that's one of the things I wanted to run by you. I've wondered if he might be job hunting."

"*Job hunting?*" I said. "The show's barely off the ground."

"But he's been at the network for ten years, and he may be restless. Then there's the Potts factor. Tom was brought in by a different president, and though he's never liked dealing with suits, Potts really gets under his skin. If Tom leaves, it could be bad for the show."

He was right. It *would* be bad for the show. God, one more thing to think about. And then the torn book jackets wiggled their ugly way into my mind again.

"Wait, do you know something?" Carter asked, misjudging my expression.

"No, no," I said, trying to push the image away. "I was just considering how much I don't like that idea."

"What we need is a plan," Carter said.

Ahh, leave it to Carter. He probably had a back-pocket game plan for everything.

"Okay," I said, willing to brainstorm. "Are you talking about trying to take Tom's pulse, figure out what's going on?"

"No, because he wouldn't tell us," Carter said. "For a guy who talks a blue streak, he plays things close to the vest. I think we need to be more involved in the day-to-day of the show."

"How so?" I asked. "We already work on stories."

"But we tend to get attached to stories after they're off the ground. I think it would be smart for us to be more engaged during the front end—to sit in on the morning story-pitch meetings, for instance. If a new exec producer comes in and tries to shift the focus of the show, we'll see it immediately."

I sensed that there was more here than met the eye. Carter might be angling to score a dual host/producing role for himself down the road. At least he was viewing me as a partner. I wouldn't want him jockeying against me.

"Count me in," I said. "As long as you don't think Tom will view it as some kind of power play."

"When the moment's right, let's ask to go to the pitch meetings and see how he reacts. Then take it from there."

"Speaking of story pitching, I had an idea I wanted to share with you," I said. Carter had confided in me, and I sensed that I could trust him enough to tell him about my ratings analysis.

"Sure," he said. "Love to hear it."

"It's based on a bit of research I've done," I said. "We know that Tom is good at paying attention to how each segment rates, but sometimes he responds in a local way rather than a global one. For instance, if a segment does well, he might decide to run something similar soon afterward, but then it'll slip off his radar. I used Excel to rank all the segments we've done since the show started. There are a few trends worth looking at."

Carter tilted his head and nodded. "Interesting," he said. "What gave you the idea?"

"I spent a year working with Bettina on her website, and this is just part of what you do in that world. You're always looking for what gets the most clicks. As you'd expect, our celeb stories are at the top, but the crime segments we've put together have rated almost as well. We don't do many of those, partly because they lose out to pressing celebrity news, but I think it would make sense to have them in the mix each week."

"You gonna suggest this to Tom?"

"Yes, I'm putting a memo together. But I'd love your impression first."

"Sure. Shoot it to me and I'll take a look."

"Here's a question for you," I said. "Vicky covers crime regularly. This wouldn't be stepping on her toes, would it?"

"Well, the woman doesn't *own* crime," he said. "Plus, she likes to latch on to really big stories and stay with them for weeks."

"Right. I figured we could focus on more esoteric stuff."

"Sounds good."

Again, I wasn't a hundred percent sure what he was really thinking. It seemed he liked the idea, but then maybe he just wanted a peek at my research. I studied his face, and as I did, I realized that he was studying *me*, our thoughts tangling in midair for a moment. Should I tell him about the book jackets? *No.* I needed to sleep on what had happened, gain fresh perspective.

Our food arrived, and I took another sip of wine. I'd drunk more than a glass, but it had helped smooth my frayed nerves.

"So how've you been dealing with the no-vacation policy?" Carter asked, slicing into his steak. Since the show had debuted, we'd been discouraged from taking any time off until at least December. Neither of us had missed a night.

"It's not ideal, but I've been so excited about the show, I haven't much cared," I said. "How about you?"

"Truthfully, I miss it. We traveled a ton when I was a kid, and it's in my blood now. It was tough not to break away this summer."

I'd heard from a couple of people that Carter had come from money, which was not the typical background for male anchors. The ones I'd met were up-from-nowhere guys for whom fame was almost a better validator than money.

"I never traveled until my junior year abroad in college," I said. "We went on a lot of staycations when I was a kid."

"Not so bad if you come from an interesting place."

"And if you have someone great doing the planning. Mine were all with this fabulous single aunt of mine, and they were incredibly fun." As I said the words, I thought of my aunt Jessie in her wide-brimmed hat, laughing out loud as she drove the car. She had passed away seven years ago.

"Where were your parents?" he asked.

I'd foolishly opened the door on that one. "Unfortunately, my mother died when I was nine."

"Was she a single mom?"

I should have expected a follow-up question from Carter. He'd spent eight years as a local TV news reporter. "No, my father was in the picture. But he remarried eighteen months later, and it was easier for me to live with my aunt much of the time."

Carter had taken a sip of wine and looked at me over the brim of the wineglass. "I sense an evil stepmother in the picture," he said, setting down the glass.

Why hadn't I kept my stupid mouth shut? I let out my breath slowly. "Yes," I said. "But I'll spare you the gory details."

"I wouldn't mind hearing them," he said.

"I promise to tell you one day," I lied, "when you're in the mood to be bored to death."

They cleared our plates, and the waiter asked if we wanted coffee and dessert.

"I'm tempted," I told Carter. "I'm a terrible chocaholic. But I should head home. I have radio interviews to do in the morning for the book."

I realized that for the last hour, we'd been talking almost earnestly at times, without the nonstop repartee we typically engaged in. That was okay. It was nice not to have to exert so much energy this late at night. And Carter seemed relaxed in a way I'd never witnessed in him.

The waiter brought the check, and Carter insisted on paying. Then he walked me to the Town Car waiting on the street outside. His, he said, was directly behind mine; I noticed that his driver was staring straight ahead, pretending not to watch us. So was mine.

A crowd of tourists just out of the theater came barreling down the street; Carter grabbed my elbow and pulled me out of the way. I felt the same spark I had the other night, this time stronger, shooting all the way through me.

"Good night, Robin," Carter said after they'd moved on. "I'm glad we did this."

"Me, too. I appreciate your take on the Vicky situation."

He looked at me closely. Over his shoulder a Times Square billboard gyrated with blue, green, and white lights.

"By the way, sorry for that awkward moment on the phone last night," he said. "Jamie's no fool, as it turns out, but I shouldn't have ambushed you that way."

So this evening hadn't been just a postmortem. "I'm flattered but I'm hardly your type," I said laughing.

He smiled. "Okay, admittedly, I've dated a few first-class bimbos. But that's not what I want out of life. You're an amazing woman, Robin, and I'm really attracted to you."

"Carter," I said, scrambling a little. "I won't deny that there's chemistry between us. But I think our contracts state we'd be subjected to waterboarding if we act on it. Plus, we could end up like one of those prime-time shows that plunge in the ratings after the stars finally hook up."

He chuckled. "Maybe," was all he said. From the intense look in his eyes, I could tell it was his way of implying that the decision was mine to make.

He loosened his tie, readying himself for the ride back to his apartment, and there was a sexiness about the gesture that, without warning, sent a current of desire through my body. Part of me was inclined to grab Carter and command him to take me back to his place.

I didn't. I smiled and said good night.

In the car, my brain started to churn again, not only with thoughts about those awkward moments with Carter but also Vicky, the possibility of Tom bolting, and the damn book jackets. I did my best to banish them. I had all those radio interviews to do from home in the morning, and it was essential to be at the top of my game for them.

I leaned forward in my seat. "Just let me off on the corner of Lexington tonight," I told the driver. "In front of the deli on the east side. I'll walk from there." I had absolutely nothing in the fridge, and I needed to pick up provisions for breakfast.

"You sure you don't want me to wait?" he asked.

"No, that's okay. Thanks anyway."

I was the only customer in the deli. I grabbed milk, yogurt, and a small loaf of multigrain bread. At some point, I was going to have to get my act together on the home front, but with my workload, that was next to impossible.

As I stood at the counter paying, I realized that my legs were aching. Not only from moving around for hours in killer heels but from the stress of the day. All I wanted to do was curl up at home. Maybe I'd sneak in a bath before bed.

Carrying the small bag of groceries, I headed down my street. It was empty on the block, and the only sound I could hear was the tap-tap of my heels on the sidewalk. New York always thinned out in August, but my neighborhood was more deserted tonight than I would have expected.

Suddenly, there was noise behind me. Footsteps. A dog walker, maybe. I looked back, being cautious. But there was no one there.

I started walking faster. At the very end of the block, I could see the light spilling out from the lobby of my building, though I couldn't spot the doorman yet.

I heard the noise again, shoes scraping on pavement. I spun around. Nothing. But I felt a swell of panic. Someone was following me.

Chapter 6

Frightened, I picked up my speed, jogging as quickly as I could in my heels. Now the only sounds I could hear were the huffing of my breath and the groceries being jounced in my arm. I didn't dare slow down to check behind again.

Faster, I told myself. Go faster. I started to trip, almost belly-flopping onto the pavement, but I caught myself in the nick of time.

Finally, I staggered into the lobby. The doorman was just setting the intercom phone back in its cradle, and he looked up, startled. "Are you okay, Ms. Trainer?"

"I—I think someone was following me," I said, gasping for breath.

He touched my arm in a show of support and stepped warily from the lobby onto the sidewalk. I saw him survey the block, first one direction and then the other.

"There's nobody there now," he said, returning. "Would you like me to call 911?"

Tentatively, I shook my head. "Uh, I guess not. If the person's gone, it won't do any good."

"What did he look like?"

"I never saw him," I said, flipping my free hand over. "I just heard sounds behind me." I felt confused. Were those really footsteps I'd heard?

"Would you like me to call the precinct and report it, at least?" he said.

"Let me think about it," I said. "Maybe I just over-reacted." I thanked him for his help and took the elevator to my floor.

As soon as I was inside my apartment, I bolted the front door and put the chain on. After tossing the food into the fridge, I collapsed onto the couch. My heart was still beating hard.

What the hell was going on? Was someone *after* me? Or had the note in my purse made me so jumpy that my imagination had gone into a total tailspin? I knew I'd heard *something* tonight. I was sure of it.

I picked up a throw pillow and hugged it to my torso to calm myself. I felt lonely, I realized. Not what I would have expected. I'd had my own apartment before marrying Jake, and after my divorce, I'd readjusted quickly to the solitude that came with living alone. My mother's death—and everything that had happened in the years right afterward—had taught me not to surrender to stupid neediness.

That's not to say my divorce had been anything less than gut-wrenching. I'd loved Jake and our life together. If he'd been sitting with me, he would have listened worriedly, comforted me, and thrown in a foot rub as a bonus. We might have made love later, because for me sex was always a release. For so much of our marriage, things had been nice that way, despite the strain of our jobs—me transitioning completely from print into TV and Jake building his architecture practice.

Seven years in, everything had gone to pieces.

His affair had been in full swing for about five months when I discovered it. There may have been clues early on, but I'd missed them. I was immersed in my new show, working insane hours and obsessing over ratings that refused to be nudged upward. Yes, Jake had seemed distracted, but I'd told myself it was because of his own work commitments. He was juggling several new projects, which had forced him to work even on Saturdays.

One Saturday, knowing I'd been neglectful, I'd popped by his office carrying a gourmet pizza. She was there. The pretty coworker, in her early thirties probably. I'd caught her scrambling back to her work station, as if she'd been alerted by my footsteps in the corridor. I knew instantly that something rotten was up. She looked both terrified and gleeful about being busted.

That night Jake confessed. It had been only a fling, he said. He seemed stricken, regretful, and made frantic noises about patching things up. *I want this to work,* he'd said, flinging his arms out. But I could tell he was in a state, confusing his jumble of emotions—guilt and shame and relief over being caught—for a heightened connection to me.

He suggested counseling. Said he wanted my forgiveness and the chance to make a fresh start, with us spending more time together. I said I would consider it. But a few days later, when the numbing shock wore off, I could see clearly that forgiveness was useless. Jake had betrayed me, and in time he'd only do it again.

A buzzer rang, jerking me out of my thoughts. It was the doorman calling from downstairs.

"Ms. Trainer? One of the other tenants just came in and said she'd spotted rats scurrying around up the block. That may be what startled you earlier."

Rats. They seemed to be everywhere this summer. "Yes, maybe," I said.

"I'll talk to our exterminator. See if there's anything we can do from our end."

"Thanks so much."

Had it been only rats I'd heard? At this point I didn't know what to think.

I forced myself off the couch and into my bedroom and peeled off my hot pink dress. Everything I wore on the air had been selected by a stylist the network had paid for. She'd insisted I rely on a wardrobe of mainly slim-fitting dresses, all in what she called "bold, big-ass colors" that offset my blond hair. I couldn't deny that I liked the effect—I'd never had any genius for putting a look together—but by the time I finished undressing each night and scrubbing off my makeup, I often felt as if I'd shrugged off a costume I'd been in the entire day.

I washed my face next. Briefly, I considered a bath, but I no longer had the energy to draw it. I fell into bed and was asleep almost instantly from pure exhaustion.

I woke the next day still feeling unsettled. A hot shower helped. By the time of the first interview, I had my mojo back. I sat in my bathrobe, chatting about the book to hosts who'd read nothing more than the table of contents, but I could tell the spots went well—if I wasn't the master of the sound bite by this stage in the game, I was doing something wrong.

By the time I reached work, I was running an hour late.

"Want an iced coffee?" my assistant Keiki asked as I rushed through the anteroom where her desk was situated.

"Lovely idea, thanks," I said. "It's so muggy out today." I asked that she also pull together a report on the tweets from last night's show and send me an update on any breaking news because I hadn't had time to go online.

"Sure," she said. "I've looked at the tweets already, and I should warn you: People are pissed that you don't like pugs."

Keiki didn't subscribe to either butt-kissing or bullshitting. I had no idea if that was a particularly Hawaiian trait, but I found it totally refreshing.

"I hope they don't plan to sic the pug police on me," I said, smiling.

"By the way," Keiki said, "did you enjoy your book party?"

"Very much, thanks. I'm just sorry that I couldn't include you."

"Not a problem. Maddy filled me in about it. I heard it was awesome."

"Oh, is Maddy here already?" I asked, surprised. Because she stayed through the show each night,

Maddy didn't generally arrive until around eleven, and Keiki hadn't been in yesterday.

"No, we had a drink Sunday night after the party."

"*Sunday* night," I said, totally surprised. Maddy had claimed to be sick.

"I hope you don't mind," Keiki said. "I was dying to hear the details."

"No, of course not." But Maddy had deceived me, and I wasn't pleased.

After settling in my office, I reviewed the latest run-down for the night's show and checked in with the producers via email for a status update on all the segments. The segment Charlotte was producing—about even more aggressive stalking lately by paparazzi—seemed all over the place. I hoped Tom was going to wrestle it to the ground.

Next, I raced through emails. When my eyes started to glaze over, I paused, thought for a moment, and then typed Vicky Cruz's name into the search window. Though I'd told Carter that she might have a grudge against other females, I really knew very little about the woman.

There was a landslide of info on her: not only her CNN days, where she'd begun to develop a big following, but her stint on Chicago TV before that, as well as her early years in Albany, where she'd first made her mark as a reporter—her hair was brunette in those days—and worked her way up to local anchor.

Her ballbuster reputation seemed to have gained full-blown status at CNN; that was where she'd earned the "Cruz Missile" nickname. The comments about her fell into two categories: People who spoke on the record tended to tiptoe, using phrases like "It's a tough business, and women need to be tough to succeed," as if they feared retribution. Those who spoke anonymously didn't hold back. She was a "Queen Bee," a "five-letter word that rhymes with witch," a "total nightmare." There was even one legendary story about her making a news reporter wet her pants during a live shot. Vicky had been married and divorced three times but had kept the first husband's name. There was only one child, a 21-year-old daughter, and natch, Vicky was estranged from her.

The biggest stuff was coverage of the controversy that Vicky had been involved in about a year ago. For weeks she'd used her show to verbally attack a man initially considered a person of interest in the beating death of his daughter. Vicky had even coined a term for the guy—Punch Daddy—and used it constantly in her broadcasts. The man had suffered a near-fatal heart attack thought to be related to Vicky's endless harangue. When DNA results finally came in, they proved that the girl's boyfriend had killed her.

Since then it looked as if Vicky had tried to be on her best behavior. The most recent coverage on her consisted mostly of photos, red-carpet shots taken at movie premieres and charity events.

I'd had enough, I realized. Just as I turned away from my computer, my book publicist, Claire, called.

"Happy pub day," she said. "You in the mood for some great news? You're already sixty-five on Amazon."

I *was* in the mood for news like that. "Fantastic," I said.

"And there's been tons of engagement on your first book blog. I think we have a decent chance of a best-seller."

After signing off, I leaned back in my chair and took a minute to gloat. News like that seemed to make all the crap of the past couple of days completely tolerable.

There was a fresh email from Tom waiting when I glanced back at my computer screen. He had tossed out a suggestion for Carter and me to bat around at the top of the show.

Carter. I'd been so preoccupied, I'd let the dinner with him recede from my memory. I thought of the spark I'd felt at his touch. I still had no regrets about not acting on it.

Ten minutes later, I nearly ran smack into him as I popped into the kitchenette. He'd just filled a mug with coffee.

"Thanks again for last night," I said, scooping up fresh ice for my coffee. "I really appreciated your feedback."

His lips curled in a tiny smile, and he looked at me knowingly. He'd read my comment the right way, that I'd declared our dinner as all business and I had no interest in taking matters further.

"Glad to help," he said. "And send me that research you did. Like I said, I'd love to take a look."

"Sure."

He nodded, turned, and slipped out of the kitchen. Was there any chance that he'd be cool to me on the air because I'd rebuffed him? No way in hell, I decided. Carter would never do anything to sabotage the show.

When I returned to my office, I found Maddy sitting in an extra chair in the anteroom. She was wearing a short turquoise jacket, white pants, and gold sandals. A little beachy for work but better than the flip-flops and tank tops some interns turned up in.

"Can I talk to you for a minute?" she asked.

"I'm a little behind schedule, but I can spare a few moments," I said, ushering her into my office.

"Have you read about this new trend where girls in their twenties are traveling in huge packs these days?" she asked before she'd even sat down. "They go to bars that way and shop that way. That sort of thing."

"Girls traveled in packs even in *my* day," I said, smiling.

"Yes, but the packs are really huge now. I was thinking maybe I could do research on it and see if it would make a good segment."

"It's a fun idea, Maddy, but probably more of a *Today* show segment. I don't think it's edgy enough for us."

Maddy nodded deferentially, but I could tell the answer bugged her.

"I get what you mean," she said after a beat. "It's just— Well, I'd love to develop an idea from start to finish. All I do is work on *other* people's ideas."

"That's part of the process of learning as an intern. Don't worry, you'll get there."

"Sorry if I sounded whiny," Maddy said. "Working here has made me know that I definitely want to be a producer."

I pressed a finger to my lips, thinking. "Actually, I've got a project for you," I said. "I've been thinking that it might pay off for us to do more segments on crime. Not high-profile crimes. I'm talking about cases that aren't getting as much play yet but touch on trends and issues that should be brought to light. Why don't you start researching and see if you can find a few? Look for stories that could resonate."

"I'd love to. Thanks so much, Robin."

I dug out a hard copy of my research and gave it to Maddy for reference.

As she stood to leave, I told myself to let her deception on Sunday go, but I couldn't. I had to understand her motive. I glanced toward the anteroom to make sure Keiki was still away from her desk.

"I was surprised when Keiki mentioned that you two had drinks Sunday," I said. "I thought you felt too sick to go out."

Maddy rolled her eyes. "I did," she said, her voice lowered. "But she called me when I was in the taxi and practically begged me to share the details. It seemed so mean to say no."

"All right," I said, though I suspected she'd been happy to meet Keiki and spill to her. Maybe it had even been planned in advance.

By the time the daily meeting rolled around, I felt mostly caught up. Tom seemed distracted through much of the discussion, checking his iPhone like someone desperate for updates on a monster asteroid possibly headed toward earth. I couldn't help but think of what Carter had said. As people filed out of the room, Tom asked me to hang back.

"I hear the Queen of Mean paid you a visit last night," he said, his hands behind his head. There was an odd edge to his voice, I realized. Challenging.

"She didn't exactly pay *me* a visit," I said. "She was looking for you, and I happened to be the first one she ran into with her machete."

"Look, I'm sorry I wasn't around. But we've got to make sure we don't step on her toes again."

"I know," I said. "I've asked Alex to put together a list of who's under contract with her, as well as her regular guests, so we can steer clear of them."

"Good," he said. He picked up a stray pencil from the conference table and began flicking it back and forth. There was still that edge in his tone, as if he had an ax to grind.

I smiled, trying to lighten the mood. "I could also start watching her damn show, but please don't make me do that."

"Did you let Dave in on what happened?"

"Dave?" I said.

"Yeah, Dave Potts, our president. What other Dave is there?"

"Of course not," I said, flabbergasted that he'd think that. "Why would I want to ratchet things up? More important, Tom, I'd never go around you."

"Well, he seems to know all about it."

"It wasn't from me. I hope you know me better than that."

He dropped the pencil. "Okay," he said. "Never mind."

But as I sat later in hair and makeup, I was still stewing about it. Had Carter told Potts about Vicky's tirade? Of course not. He wouldn't want to escalate the matter, either. And then it hit me—*Vicky* was probably the tattletale.

How absolutely juvenile, I thought, to run to Potts over such a minor issue.

Back in my office, I closed the door and let my eyes fall shut, fatigued by this latest political bullshit. On-set, I sometimes drank coffee from a mug with my name on it, and as I hurried into the newsroom, I asked one of the production assistants to make it black for me tonight.

"Ready to rock and roll?" Carter asked, smiling as I slid into my seat. Good. All back to normal.

He started the up-front section by mentioning some of the tweets and emails we'd received since last night's show. "We hit a nerve with two stories in particular," he said. "Pets on planes—and cheating politicians."

"Ahh," I said. "So *both* our dog segments were winners."

"I saw that coming," Carter said, laughing.

As he started to read through some of the other tweets, I took a swig of coffee from the mug that had been left for me. The instant the liquid filled my mouth, I sensed something else in there—something brittle and crunchy. I felt like I was going to gag.

Instinctively, I swiveled to the right and lowered my head. I spat everything into my hand, letting the coffee run through my fingers. And then I saw what I'd almost swallowed. A huge cockroach was sitting in the middle of my hand.

Chapter 7

I fought the urge to retch. I flicked the bug hard from my hand and brought my other hand to my mouth, pressing tight.

"Stay on Carter," a voice commanded in my earpiece. Then: "Jesus, what's going on?"

Carter continued to talk, though I could barely focus on what he was saying. I shot a desperate glance at him and raised my index finger, trying to signal that I needed more time. Then I tore off a piece of paper from my notes and dabbed frantically at my mouth. I took another breath, filling my lungs with air. I nodded then to show Carter and the director I was all right.

"I see I've rendered Robin speechless with my ramblings," Carter said, smiling. "Let's take a break, and then we'll be back to talk about raising rich kids. Don't knock them. As we'll see, it's not always easy being a billionaire's baby."

As soon as we cut away, Carter immediately reached out and touched my arm. "You okay?" he asked.

I shook my head in disbelief. "There was a stupid cockroach in my coffee," I said. "Not a small one, either. One of those huge water bugs."

"You're kidding," Carter said.

Three seconds later, Tom and one of the production assistants came stampeding onto the set, along with Stacy, the makeup artist. Carter related what had happened.

"A *water* bug?" the PA said. "I don't think I've ever seen one on this floor."

"Well, one showed up here tonight," I said. I glanced down, and there it was—or at least half of it—lying limp on the floor, just to the right of my chair.

"Jeez," the PA said, following where my eyes had gone. "At least it was dead." He tore a handkerchief out of his jeans pocket and scooped up the bug.

"Where did this coffee come from, anyway?" I demanded.

"From the thermos I keep behind the set," he said, hitching his chin in that direction. "I poured the coffee myself. The bug must have crawled in before I brought the mug out here."

"Was I on-camera when I spat it out?" I asked.

"No," Tom said. "We were on Carter." He told the PA to open me a bottle of water.

"Here, let me touch up your mouth," Stacy said. "You're all smeary."

As Stacy worked, her hands flying, I could see the three guests for the first segment milling around on the edge of the set. Finally, I swiveled my chair forward again.

"One minute. You okay now, Robin?" the director said in my earpiece.

"Yes, thanks, Stan," I replied.

"You sure?" Carter said softly as the guests started to move in our direction.

"Yeah. Of course, you're such a pro, you would have just swallowed the freaking thing."

He chuckled. "Only because I practiced eating bugs in Boy Scouts. If you're lost in the woods, that's a survival tactic."

"Good to know I picked up a new skill today."

I did my best for the rest of the show, but I never felt fully in the groove. Once, when my thoughts wandered back to that disgusting crunchiness in my mouth, I almost gagged.

The second the show ended, I was out of there. I wanted to be home in the tub with Mozart playing.

On the car ride uptown, I noticed a text from Maddy. "Tried to catch u after show," she wrote. "So sorry about what happened. Do u need anything?"

"Thx," I texted back, touched by her concern. "I'm okay." I was lucky the incident hadn't ended up on the air, or it would have been all over the Internet.

A few minutes later, as the driver cut through Central Park headed east, another text came in, this one from Ann asking me to call her.

"Will you ever drink coffee again?" were the first words out of her mouth when I reached her.

"Wait, you *heard*? Where are you, anyway?"

"I've been downtown all afternoon at a meeting, but one of my team was in the newsroom at the time. She saw the commotion and asked what had happened."

"She wasn't with a reporter, was she?"

"No, she was with our dear friend Vicky. We're setting up a profile of her, and she was deciding on the best place for her photo. I don't think she's set foot in the newsroom in years, but that's where she wants the shot taken."

"Wait, don't tell me *Vicky* saw what happened."

"I'm sure she was too busy focusing on her own needs to notice. So other than nearly swallowing a cockroach, how are you doing?"

"I had one great piece of news today. My book's in the top hundred on Amazon."

"Really?" Ann said, sounding surprised. "I mean, I'm thrilled for you, but I thought they kept saying it was only a niche book."

I laughed. "Maybe they say that to most of their authors so they don't expect too much."

"Bravo, then. We'll have to celebrate. By the way, you didn't see Carter after the show tonight, did you? He said he wanted to talk to me, but he's not picking up on his cell."

"No, I just got the hell out of there tonight."

"He did the same thing last night. Asked me to call him, then wasn't around."

There was no way I was going to mention my dinner with Carter to Ann. She'd take it the wrong way. "Well, you know Carter. International man of mystery."

"You doing anything exciting tonight?"

"I'm going to soak in a tub and try to figure out what's wrong with my work karma this week."

"*Please.* Your karma's just fine."

"Oh yeah? For one thing, Tom's annoyed with me—he thinks I squealed to Potts about the Vicky incident."

"Robin, you need to relax a little."

In an almost Pavlovian response, I leaned back against the leather car seat. Though it wasn't dark yet, the streetlamps in the park were on, shimmering in the twilight.

"Can I ask you something?" I said. A thought had begun to stir in me over the past twenty minutes. "Do you think there's any chance that the roach in my coffee wasn't just a fluke?"

"You mean someone *put* it there?" Ann said.

"Yes. Last night after I left you, I found that someone had been in my office and messed with copies of my book. Or at least I think they did."

"Messed with them how?"

"The jackets were torn—like someone had ripped them. It might have been accidental, but after the note at the party, and now, with this bug thing . . ."

"You think someone is out to get you?"

"I don't think anyone is planning to murder me and shove my body through a wood chipper. But someone may be trying to mess with my head. Last night I thought I was being followed down my block."

"Robin, the note at the party was vicious, but I think you have to view it as a onetime thing from some hater. I can't imagine anyone here has it in for you. People respect you. Isn't it entirely possible that a cockroach fell into your coffee and drowned?"

"Someone on the crew told me that he'd never seen a bug like that on our floor."

"Robin," Ann said, "I want you to take a deep breath. You're starting to sound a little paranoid."

The words hurt.

"That's a bit harsh, isn't it?"

"It's not a criticism. I'm just looking out for you. TV can be insane. You knew that when you came back into it. You need to calm down—about Vicky and Tom and roaches, everything. Or you're going to start to burn out."

"Of course," I said. "I appreciate your concern. Have a good night."

Half an hour later, as I sat curled on my couch with a glass of wine, I still felt stung by Ann's comment. I checked my phone a few times before going to bed, wondering if she might have sent an apology. Nothing.

The next morning I woke determined to keep my mind only on my work. As I headed back from a confab in the newsroom with Alex, Claire emailed me saying that *The New York Times* had decided to run a short profile of me. Fabulous! I thought. It was ridiculous to let things get under my skin when I had so much good stuff going on. I asked the publicist to coordinate with Ann, who would need to be involved, too.

When I hurried into my office a few minutes later, Keiki announced that Ann had just left a message. Rather than phoning her back, I texted, saying I was tied up but would call later. I knew it was bratty of me, but I still felt slightly bruised. Besides, I'd begun to wonder if I'd been leaning on Ann too much lately. She'd been a good friend over the past years—and that included opening the door for me to sub at the network—but because we worked together now, I'd been turning to her more frequently for guidance. It wasn't totally fair of me, and breathing room might be warranted.

Everyone seemed to eye me when I slipped into the rundown meeting later. Obviously, the whole damn office knew about the roach.

"You recover from last night?" asked Lamar, one of the senior producers.

"I'm fine," I said, smiling. "Except if you look closely at my forehead, you'll see two antennae have started to sprout."

People laughed. Carter did, too. It was the kind of comment I knew he would have made, and it seemed to do the trick, demonstrating to my coworkers I wasn't flummoxed by the experience.

The show was strong that night. Good topics, good guests. I drank bottled water instead of coffee. Carter, I noticed, was wearing what seemed to be a new navy suit cut perfectly for his body. As he dashed from the set after the show, I wondered if he'd already found a hot little replacement for Jamie. I entertained a momentary twinge of desire—and then shook it off.

On Thursday I realized I was done sulking about Ann. I'd blown her remark out of proportion. Around mid-morning, I picked up the phone and called her office.

"So you're still speaking to me?" Ann said.

"Yes," I said. "Sorry if I acted like a bit of a drama queen."

"I'm sorry if it came out brusquely," she said. "Want to grab lunch on Saturday? It's Matthew's weekend in East Hampton."

Matthew was Ann's ex-husband, and they alternated weekends at the home they'd bought as a retreat at the end of Long Island.

"Yes, very much," I said. I'd spent so many of the past weekends developing story ideas for the show and writing up blogs for the book PR that I'd allowed myself little time to relax or play.

"If it's not too hot, we can eat outside," she suggested. "And congratulations on the *Times* piece. We're going to arrange the shoot and interview for Monday. I'll work with Keiki on it."

That's better, I thought as she hung up. The last thing I needed—or wanted—right now was any kind of awkwardness with Ann.

The morning flew by. I read through all the backup info for the night's segments and did two short phone interviews for the book. While I was wolfing down a salad at my desk, the phone rang, and I noticed Dave Potts's name on the screen. He rarely called me.

"I'll get it, Keiki," I yelled into the anteroom.

"Hi, Dave," I said.

"No, it's Jean, his assistant," the voice on the other end replied. "Mr. Potts was hoping to see you today. He doesn't want to interfere with the show, of course, so he could do it right afterward. At eight o'clock."

"Of course," I said. I could feel anger starting to stir in me. This better not be about Baylor, I thought. But that was the kind of thing Potts would talk to Tom about, not the talent.

"Great, we'll see you then," Jean said.

"Is there a particular agenda I should be aware of?" I asked. I didn't want to end up blindsided.

"I don't think so," Jean said cheerily. "He just said he wants to catch up. Congratulations on the ratings, by the way."

I thanked her and told her I'd be up right after the show. It sounded, actually, like I was being summoned for a make-nice-to-the-talent meeting. Potts didn't want his hosts getting big-headed, but he balanced that with a certain amount of stroking, just enough to deter their eyes from wandering.

A few minutes later, I hurried down to makeup. "Stacy'll be right back," Jimmy told me from the other end of the room. He was working on a correspondent for one of the other shows, wrapping her hair around a huge curling iron while chattering about a work trip to L.A. that he'd just returned from. I'd barely sat down when Vicky Cruz burst into the room. It was the first time I'd laid eyes on her since the rant.

"You'll have to excuse me, sweetheart," she said to the correspondent. "But I need Jimmy to give my hair a little juju."

"You got a big meeting or something?" Jimmy asked. For a split second I let my gaze skate down the mirror to the other end of the room. I saw the reporter's mouth tighten as she relinquished her spot temporarily to Vicky.

"Hm, hm," Vicky said. "I need some volume on top."

Jimmy gunned the hair dryer and snatched a section of Vicky's bright red hair with a brush. "*Ouch*," she said. "I said pouf it, don't yank it out."

"Sorry," he said. "I'm a little dazed still. I didn't sleep a wink on the plane last night."

"You need Ambien," Vicky declared. "It makes you sleep like a baby."

Stacy had come back into the room and fastened the nylon cape around me. I'd looked down at my notes, trying to finish prepping for the show, when I felt something tug my eyes to the mirror again. I glanced back up to catch Vicky staring at me. I held her gaze until she looked away. I was *not* going to let her get to me.

Stacy started to sponge on foundation, and I closed my eyes. A few seconds later, I heard Vicky announce, "That's *enough*, Jimmy. If it gets any higher, it'll look like there's a litter of kittens in there." Her heels pounded on the floor as she charged from the room.

"Speaking of sleep," Stacy said to me, "are you getting enough? You look awfully pale."

"Probably not," I said. "Should we switch foundation?"

"No, this shade works for you. And it looks great on your skin. Even Vicky said so."

"Vicky?" I said, and then smiled. I didn't want Stacy to sense that my guard was raised.

"Yeah, she said she loves how dewy it makes your skin look on the air and asked me to try the same brand on her. But I do think you could use a little bronzer on top of it."

How was I meant to interpret Vicky's comment? Maybe she was counting on Stacy to pass it along, a feeble attempt at making nice.

The show that night was on fire again, all except the last segment. It was a story Charlotte had produced, and it was totally lame.

"Charlotte, that shrink had zero to offer," I told her as I hurried off the set. "You couldn't tell that in the pre-interview?"

"Of course not," she said haughtily. She had on a low-cut jersey top, as if planning a pub crawl after the show. "Well, when *I* interviewed him, he didn't sound lame."

Before I could respond to her snippiness, I heard Tom say he was calling a postmortem with all the producers and interns. I was sure it had to do partly with that segment.

I rushed back to my office, blotted off the top layer of my makeup, and grabbed a notebook to take upstairs. It was the kind of brownnosy gesture that appealed to Potts. When I arrived, I saw that the outer office where the assistant sat was deserted, but I spotted Potts through the doorway, studying a piece of paper at his desk. The side of his thumb was pressed against his thick bottom lip. Sensing my presence, he glanced up. "Robin, come in," he said, lifting his beefy body from the chair. He stood just long enough for me to take a seat across from him. He had one of his two TVs on, turned low to the program that followed *The Pulse*.

"Nice show tonight," he said. "Though the last segment left me cold."

"Agree. It wasn't very strong," I said. Potts was a blowhard, and I'd learned enough about him to know that you didn't try to contradict his opinion on a show or segment. "Good topic, I think, but we needed better guests."

"People were probably too busy watching you and Carter to notice. You two are doing a great job—of course, I don't need to tell you that. You see the ratings, you hear the talk."

Good, I thought. So this *was* a be-nice-to-the talent meeting. "I like hearing it from you."

"And your book," he said. "I'll be honest—at first I was worried the timing was bad, that it would be a distraction just when you're trying to get your feet wet again, but it seems to be helping. The more buzz, the better."

I didn't appreciate the comment about the book. Hadn't he done the math and realized that it had been in the works long before I joined the network?

"Yes," I said. "And I think Ann would agree."

"One thing I've been thinking lately?" Potts said, raising a bristly gray eyebrow. "The plan was for you to play sidekick to Carter, at least in the beginning, but the time's come to up your presence on the show, let you take the lead on occasion. I'll discuss that with Tom."

"That sounds great," I said. "I have a lot more to offer." This was exactly what I'd been hoping for.

Potts hoisted himself up and toward the back of the chair and then set his elbows on the desk. He had something on his mind, I realized. Something besides compliments.

"That's not the main reason I asked you to stop by," he said. "There's another matter to discuss."

His tone was sober, stern almost, and he widened his body. That's what cobras did, I thought, right before they struck. My stomach dipped. "Okay," I said.

"Have you ever heard that old line about a college president? That his three jobs are to provide parking for the faculty, sex for the students, and athletics for the alumni? Well, you know what my two jobs are?" He flipped open a hand the size of a bear paw in a gesture that urged me to guess.

I forced a smile, wondering where the hell this was going. "I could make a stab at it," I said. "But I'd love to hear it from you."

"To be the number one cable network for talk shows—that's going to happen one day, by the way. And to keep Vicky Cruz as happy as possible."

So this *was* about Vicky. I couldn't believe it. But maybe Potts just wanted my take on the Baylor incident.

"That makes sense," I said, keeping my voice even.

"Good, because we need to discuss that. Vicky's been unhappy lately. And you've apparently done a few things to make her that way."

Chapter 8

P otts's accusation smarted, like a slap to the face. So Vicky *had* gone to him, bitching specifically about me.

"Dave, I assume you mean the fact that we booked Jack Baylor as a guest on our show," I said.

"Baylor's under contract with *The Vicky Cruz Show*," he said. "I know she's insanely territorial, but that's part of what makes her so damn good, and we have to respect that. We can't be poaching her people."

"I understand completely," I said. I felt a surge of both frustration, and anger, but I knew I had to stay in control, to *manage* this. "Unfortunately, we weren't told that Baylor was a regular on her show. We're actually setting up a system now—"

Potts waved his hand as if he'd heard all he ever needed to know on the subject. "That's not what bothers me most," he said. "You can't be consulting with her producers or coming after the kind of topics she covers on her show."

I stared blankly at him in complete confusion. What was he *talking* about? "But—I don't even know her producers," I said finally. "I mean, I know their faces, but I don't think I've ever said more than hello to any of them."

"Well, not you directly. But you sent your intern to talk to them. Pick their brains, ask for their sources. That's not right."

"My *intern*?" I said. Even as I uttered the word, I knew. Maddy. She had obviously called one of Vicky's producers about the crime stories.

"I'm terribly sorry," I said. I was scrambling now. "I did ask my intern to research possible crime segments. I—"

"Is this something Tom wanted to pursue?"

"No, I haven't had a chance to run it by him yet. I've been analyzing our ratings and noticed they spiked when we feature crime stories. But I never suggested my intern talk to Vicky's producers. She must have—"

"Look, I don't need to know all the minutiae. The point is that people can't be going behind Vicky's back or using her team. And I know we said you guys could cover crime, but for now that's gotta be Vicky's bailiwick."

"There were no plans to jump in and do it yet. I was just explor—"

"Like I said, I don't care about the details. I just need your assurance that you'll back off. Five years ago, this network brought Vicky in to goose the ratings, and luckily for us, she didn't just goose them, she jabbed them in the ass with an ice pick. We can't lose sight of that."

Part of me wanted to insist that he hear my side of the story, force him to recognize that there'd been a terrible misunderstanding. But a stronger voice told me not to press, that I'd only try his patience and make matters worse.

"Absolutely," I said.

"Look, Robin, I respect your ambition," he said, shifting in his chair. "You don't land where you are in this business without a surplus of it. You've got the talent, too. I just saw results from a survey we did—beyond the usual Q-rating stuff—and viewers really cotton to you. You're natural, accessible. But the best strategy for you is to rein in that ambition for the moment and focus on what's right in front of you. And that means the damn show, not your career.

Over time, everything's going to fall into place for you."

"Of course," I said. "The show is always first and foremost for me." I smiled, all nicey-nice. But inside I was steaming.

"Good," Potts said. He punctuated the word with a big smile and nod, as if he'd just offered me front-row seats to a Knicks game and was feeling fabulously benevolent. "Well, I've kept you long enough," he added. "I'm sure you're eager to head home."

By the time I reached my office, I couldn't even remember the last few moments with Potts, just my overwhelming desire to tear out of there. I was more than livid now. At both Vicky *and* Potts. I flung the unused notebook on my desk so hard that it skidded.

I grabbed my phone, ready to call for my car. But I stopped. I wanted to cool down first and analyze the situation.

It was hard for me to tell what I was most pissed about. I hated the fact that Potts hadn't allowed me to get a word in edgewise. He seemed to have the attention span of a goldfish. Plus, he'd painted me as some ruthless career chick, a modern-day version of Eve Harrington. Men like Potts always put you in a double bind. They demanded fire in the belly but only as long as it wasn't too hot or didn't interfere with their own blazing needs. How naive I'd been to think I was being called upstairs so he could toss a few props my way.

But none of it would have happened if Vicky hadn't ratted me out over the most minor of offenses. If she thought she could roll over me, she was dead wrong.

And then there was Maddy. I couldn't believe she'd been stupid enough to pump producers from another show for info—unless Vicky had distorted the details to Potts. And it wasn't Maddy's only transgression lately. She'd deceived me at the party and failed to correctly vet a guest the other night. I was happy to play mentor, but not if her actions bit me in the butt.

I wondered how much of a hit I'd taken tonight. Potts had praised the show, mentioned that viewers liked me, that he even wanted to expand my role. There was no way my job could be in any kind of jeopardy. But there was a blemish on my performance now, one that a guy like Potts wouldn't forget. I could just hear him punctuating what he said about me to others with a comment like "Unfortunately, she's sometimes too damn ambitious for her own good."

Though I'd warned myself to stay off Vicky's enemies' list, I was clearly on it now.

I realized I should call Richard, my agent, and fill him in. And I knew what he'd say: "Robin, why wouldn't you have alerted me in advance to the meeting?" I'd have to endure the chiding. Because I needed his counsel, needed to know if damage control had to be done.

It was 8:25. He was probably just sitting down at one of his favorite watering holes, Michael's or the Four Seasons. I punched in his cell number. When the call went to voice mail, I asked him to try to reach me as soon as he could.

I planned to call Maddy first thing in the morning, to hear her version of the story, but staring at my cell phone, I realized I didn't want to wait. I tapped her number, and she answered on the first ring.

"Hi, Robin," she said breezily.

"Are you somewhere you can talk?" I asked.

"Yes, I'm actually still at work. We had that post-mortem meeting, and I was just grabbing a latte in the cafeteria before I leave. Is something the matter?"

It would be better, I knew, to have the conversation face-to-face, but I was too incensed to wait. "Did you talk to any of Vicky Cruz's producers about the crime segments?"

There was a pause. She'd heard the anger in my voice and was probably trying to guess the cause. "You mean the ones we discussed yesterday, right?"

"Exactly."

"Um, yes. I spoke to this guy Jeremy. But I didn't tell him specifically what I was working on. I would never do that."

"That's not the point, Maddy." I said. "Tell me precisely what you said to him."

"I just asked him how to get ahold of, you know, police reports, that sort of thing."

"Was there more than one conversation?"

"Uh, no—I mean, I don't think so. No, I talked to him once, and then I think I emailed him with a couple of follow-up questions. Was I not supposed to or something?"

"No, you're *not* supposed to or something," I snapped. "You don't ever go to a producer on another show and troll for info."

"God, I'm so sorry, Robin. Just so you know, he's become a friend of mine. It was really a question from one friend to another."

"You may think of him as a friend, but he clearly views you as a member of the enemy camp. Because he informed Vicky about it. And now *I've* been told."

"Oh my God. I didn't—"

"Look, the stakes are high here, so you have to do as I tell you. If I ask you to research, then *research*. If you get an idea to try something that's not what I've told you to do, like to ask someone for help, then you need to check with me to see if it's okay. Understood? And leave the crime research alone."

"Yes. Yes, I understand."

"I know you meant well," I said, letting my voice soften. "And I want you to have more responsibility. But you can't make assumptions and then just act on them. I know Alex talked to you about this, too."

"Okay," Maddy said. "I'll check with you on everything." Over the phone, I couldn't decipher whether her tone was remorseful or sullen.

"And do not breathe a *word* to this Jeremy guy about our discussion. It will only make matters worse."

"Should I ignore him, then?"

"No, no, don't do that," I said quickly. "It's too obvious. But don't engage in any more conversations. He clearly can't be trusted."

"Okay . . . Is my internship in trouble?"

"No. But I need to know you'll be careful going forward."

I signed off and sat for a minute more, mulling over the conversation. Vicky had clearly trumped up the details to Potts. At the same time, I would have to keep a better eye on Maddy. She'd seemed to do more than an adequate job during the first couple of months, but I didn't like what I was seeing about her judgment. I felt a momentary urge to call Ann and ask for her take on the situation, but I quickly dismissed it. I couldn't keep running to her about *everything.*

There were other friends I knew I could phone, people who would listen, but since the show had been on the air, I'd been an absentee gal pal, so how could I lay all this on someone? "I know we haven't talked lately, but can I get your advice *now?* The network diva is up my grille."

I had to figure it out myself. Watch my own back. Be smart. Take control.

The phone on my desk rang, startling me. I glanced at the screen, thinking it might be Richard trying my office instead of my cell. But the screen said Edit Room.

When I answered, my hello came out tentatively. I couldn't imagine who'd be calling me from the edit room at this hour. No one said anything, but I could hear faint sounds in the background, as if the person had his attention momentarily diverted. I wondered if it might be Tom.

"Hello?" I said again. Nothing. I tossed the phone back into the cradle.

I packed up quickly for the night, desperate to flee. As I was stuffing papers into my tote bag, the phone rang again. Once again, the screen said Edit Room.

"Yes?" I said, answering it.

In the background, I could hear a weird, dull hum but nothing more.

"*Hello*," I said, this time not disguising my impatience. No one said anything. There seemed to be a problem with the connection. I glanced at my watch. Ten of nine. There was a chance it was Tom, and if so, it could be important.

With my tote bag over my shoulder, I flicked off my desk lamp and headed out to the corridor. There was no one in the immediate vicinity, though down the hall to the right, I could hear the murmur of voices coming from the makeup room. I turned left, and when I reached the T of the hallway, I made another left. Halfway down the corridor, I could see that the light in the editing room was on and the door was ajar. Reaching the entrance, I pushed it all the way open.

Except for all the monitors along the wall, the room was empty.

I had no clue what was going on, and I didn't have the patience to find out. I'd turned to leave when I heard a noise in the corridor. I pivoted all the way around. To my surprise, I saw Ann walking past the doorway. Sensing a presence, she jerked in surprise and looked quickly into the editing room.

"Oh, you made me jump," she said. "I didn't think anyone was down here."

"Were you looking for me?" I asked, though she'd come from the direction of the set rather than my office.

"No, I was down in the studio, babysitting that reporter who's doing the piece on Vicky," she said. "He's going to watch her show at nine."

"Do you have to hang around until the end?" I asked.

"No, someone on my team is going to see the guy out. I was just leaving."

"Let me give you a lift home, then."

"Perfect," Ann said, smiling.

"Oh, shoot," I said suddenly. In my hyped-up state, I'd left a folder of info I needed back in my office. "I need to dash back for something."

"I'll go with you," she said. "I always find it creepy here at this hour. It's busy enough by the set and by makeup, but it's so empty everyplace else."

As we hurried down the corridor, the only sound was the clicking of our heels on the floor, confirming her comment. Reaching our destination, I flicked on the lights in the anteroom and walked through with Ann following behind me.

I hit the light switch in my private office and plucked a folder lying on a table. Behind me, I heard Ann gasp in shock. I spun around.

"My God, what's *that*?" Ann said.

She had stepped close to my desk and was staring at the chair. I glanced where her gaze had landed. Lying in the middle of the desk chair was a doll—a blond Barbie. But it didn't have long hair, like most Barbies. The hair had been cut into a jagged shag, almost identical to mine.

I moved closer and picked up the doll. It was wearing a red dress, not unlike the one I was sporting on the back cover of my book, but shorter and sparkly across the top, typical Barbie wear.

"Look at the eyes," Ann exclaimed.

There *weren't* any eyes. They'd been poked out with something sharp. And in their place were two ragged black holes.

Chapter 9

"Where did this *come* from?" Ann asked hoarsely.

I felt my hand begin to tremble, and I dropped the Barbie back into the chair, as if it were steely hot.

"I—I don't know," I said. With the stabbed-out eyes, the doll was hideous-looking, like a prop from a slasher movie. "I was here only a minute ago, so someone must have just left it."

"This is *sick*," Ann said. As she turned to me, I saw how shaken she was. "Was there anyone around when you left?"

I hesitated, thinking. "No," I said finally. "But this is probably why someone kept calling my number from the edit room. To lure me down there so they could leave this here."

"It's clearly someone we work with—no one gets by security downstairs."

"Tom called a postmortem for the producers, so they were all here late tonight."

"We have to call Potts—and Will Oliver," she said. Oliver was the network's own security chief.

"No," I said, shaking my head.

"What do you mean, *no*? Look, I was totally wrong when I said you were acting paranoid. Obviously, someone wants to freak you out, and it has to be dealt with."

"At some point, yes. But I don't want to open a can of worms tonight—I can explain later. I need time to consider the best course of action."

"Okay, why don't we grab a drink uptown and discuss it?" she said. "Or you can come by my apartment. I'll fix us something to eat."

I pressed a hand to my temple. My head had started to pound. "You know I love your cooking, but I'm completely spent," I said. "We can talk about it at lunch on Saturday. And until then, let's keep it to ourselves."

"If you're sure that's what you want." She looked down at the doll again. "You know what's really twisted?" she said. "Whoever did this took the time to make it look just like you—the dress, the hair . . ."

"I know." Who the hell was *doing* this to me?

I thought I heard a sound in the corridor. I froze, straining to hear. But it was just the AC kicking up a notch.

"Let's go," I said. I couldn't stand being there a second longer. I looked at Ann and smiled ruefully. "Though what do we do with Bad Haircut Barbie in the meantime?"

"Why don't I keep it for now?" she volunteered. Ann tugged the silk scarf from her neck, wrapped it around the doll, and stuffed the whole thing in her purse.

In the car, neither one of us said a word about what had happened, not with the driver's ear cocked like a TV satellite dish. I could tell he knew something was up, that he could sense there was a secret throbbing beneath our silence.

As soon as I was home, I slipped off my dress and hung it carefully on a hanger, then dropped my bra and underwear in the laundry basket. I tucked my high heels side by side in one of the shoe drawers in my closet. Naked, I closed the stopper in the tub and turned on the water. When the tub was full, I slid into it.

For a moment, I just sat there, feeling the warmth penetrate my skin. Then, with both hands, I slapped the water as hard I could. It sloshed over the sides of the tub and onto the floor.

"No," I screamed. "*No.*" I smacked the water again. And again.

I'd worked so freaking hard to put all the pieces back together, but things were starting to come unglued. People were gunning for me, hoping to trip me up.

I wouldn't let them do that. And I would never allow myself to end up where I was two years ago, kicked to the curb and left to watch on the sidelines as the world rushed by without me. I wrapped my arms around my body and rocked slowly back and forth.

Finally, I dragged my arm from the water and looked at my watch, deciphering the time through the foggy glass. Ten-thirty. Why hadn't I heard from Richard?

I'd thought the bath would make me groggy, but later, I kept twisting in the sheets, too wired to sleep. From somewhere deep in my mind, words began to surface, words of comfort my mother used to say to me in a hushed voice: *Sleep, little robin, sleep.* I repeated them again and again but they did no good.

At seven the next morning, I forced myself out of bed. By the time I was in the car, I felt less frayed, but when I walked into my office thirty minutes later, a sense of dread gripped me. I could still picture the doll lying on my desk chair with the ragged holes where her eyes should have been.

For the next hour, I raced through news sites, making notes and shooting a few ideas to Tom for segments next week. I also dashed off an online interview for my book. Since Keiki was still dealing with dog issues, I was all alone in the office. Every noise made my heart jump.

On the way back from a coffee run to the kitchenette, I took a detour, ending up in the newsroom. I had a question for the booker, who was wrapping up a phone call. While I waited, I let my gaze move from cubby to cubby. I worked with these people every day, I made jokes with them and gossiped with them. Did one of them hate my guts?

I snaked through the desks until I was on the very edge of the space. From that angle, I could see down one of the corridors, the one with Vicky's office at the very end. She probably wasn't in yet, but I could sense her essence like a force field.

Later, on my way out of the newsroom, I ran into Maddy, looking lost in thought as she walked.

"Morning," I said, smiling. I wondered if she might be sulking from the reprimand, but she offered a smile back.

"Hi, Robin," she said. She leaned closer and whispered, "Just so you know, I took everything you said last night very seriously."

"Good," I said, my voice lowered, too. "And you haven't breathed a word to anyone, right?"

"No," she said. "No, never." She bit her lip. "I know you don't want me researching crimes anymore, but is there anything else I can take on?"

I had to stifle the urge to sigh. "Let me think about it, okay?"

The rundown meeting that day seemed more subdued than usual. Or was it just me? At one point I caught Carter staring at me quizzically. He was trying to read me, I realized, sensing something wasn't quite right. I held his gaze tightly, not sure what I was trying to convey.

And then I sensed someone else's eyes on me. I turned my head slightly to find Charlotte staring at me from across the table. Her cheeks were red and itchy-looking—the result of being under work stress these days? She quickly lowered her eyes to her iPad and began scrolling with fake interest through her notes.

Finally, at just after five, I heard from my agent. "Sorry, sorry," he said. He'd been in a contract negotiation.

I recapped the Potts conversation along with the backstory. As expected, Richard was annoyed with me for not informing him in advance about the meeting.

"I could have done due diligence, Robin," he said. "That way you wouldn't have been sandbagged."

"I know," I said. "But the bottom line would have been the same. Vicky has a hair up her ass about me. Should I be concerned about the meeting with Potts?"

"I wouldn't be. Your show is performing way ahead of expectations, and you're brilliant on it. I think you were simply a momentary scapegoat."

"Meaning?"

"I've heard rumors that Vicky's been taking meetings. That probably means her contract is up in the foreseeable future, and she's hoping to nab a few offers to wave in front of Potts. He may have gotten wind of that."

"So he's worried about losing her?" I asked.

"Possibly."

"Why only possibly?" The comment had surprised me.

"On the one hand, Vicky is part of the DNA of the network," Richard said. "But she's not the prize she used to be. All that stuff about Punch Daddy? It tarnished her, and her ratings have never completely rebounded."

"If her star is so tarnished, why would Potts take me to task for offending her?"

"You know Potts. He likes to keep everyone in his or her place. I wouldn't worry, Robin. But since he's developed this ridiculous notion about you being over-ambitious, I *would* be careful in that regard. Don't do anything to irritate the man."

"Got it," I said. I paused. "There's something else I need to run by you." I described what had been happening, starting with the note at the party.

"Robin, this is serious," he said, clearly shocked. "What are they doing about it?"

"I haven't told them yet."

"Wha—?"

"I will on Monday. Even though I'm a victim here, there's a chance that Potts will view it as extra drama he has to contend with. So I want there to be some cooling-down time between that pathetic conversation with him and when I drop this bomb."

Richard wasn't happy with my strategy, but he agreed to go along. After I'd signed off, I closed my eyes and tried to mentally force my shoulders to slacken. I'd never looked forward to a weekend so much.

At noon on Saturday, I took a cab to Barbuto, at Washington and West Twelfth. Ann and I had decided to eat in the Meatpacking District for a change of scenery.

The metal garage-style doors on the front of the restaurant had been rolled up, creating an outdoor space for summer, and we picked a table just off the sidewalk.

Ann was wearing perfectly pressed navy pants and a crisp blue men's-style shirt. Even on weekends, she looked dressed to take a meeting. And per usual, her naturally wavy, light brown hair had been blown into submission.

As we waited for menus, I glanced around the area. Though there were people walking along the cobble-stone street—a mix, it seemed, of New Yorkers and tourists—the city felt half-full. As one couple passed, they did a double take, clearly recognizing me though I had my hair pulled back in a super-short ponytail.

"Is that happening more and more?" Ann asked, raising an eyebrow.

"Yes," I said. Although I wouldn't have admitted it out loud, the attention gave me a rush, especially after how my week had played out.

"They're also probably wondering what you're doing in the city on a Saturday in August," Ann said.

"Next summer should be better—once the show's established, I'll be able to sneak away more. How about you? Do you wish you could be in East Hampton every weekend?"

Since knowing Ann, I'd spent a few weekends at her lovely home out there.

"Truthfully, I can't bear the thought of going anymore," she said. "We have a cleaning lady who comes in, but there's always something left over from Matthew's weekend that I unearth—like a tub of sorbet in the freezer—and I want to vomit at the sight of it."

"Do you really miss him?"

"Miss him? *No.* I can't stand the thought of him."

Her answer stunned me. Initially she'd pined for Matthew and I'd thought her reluctance to meet other men meant she was still yearning for him.

"Can you sell the house?" I asked, switching gears.

"Now's not a good time, unfortunately. We bought the place at the top of the market, and we can't afford to take a loss on it. But enough about that. Let's get to Barbie."

"Okay," I said. I'd been thinking about the doll nearly constantly since the moment I'd laid eyes on it. "Are you still concerned about me not reporting it yet?"

"No, not anymore," Ann said. "In fact, I actually feel you should continue to hold off—for a few more days."

"How come?" I said, taken aback.

"The *Times* piece. I should have realized it initially but I was so floored, I wasn't thinking straight. It's important that the article be as close to a wet kiss as possible. If you go to Will Oliver on Monday, he'll have to alert Potts and probably Tom, too, and there's a risk that the situation may leak out. We don't want the reporter getting wind of it. Then the profile becomes more about you being harassed than about your book."

"Good point," I said. I hadn't considered that.

"The reporter's talking to you on Monday, and I predict the piece will run by the end of the week— they'll want to tie in with the buzz about the book. The minute the article appears, you can hightail it to Oliver. Of course, if anything else happens before then, we'll have to reconsider."

"Makes sense." I smiled ruefully. "I'll let you know if I find a horse head in my bed or a bunny boiling on my stovetop."

Ann leaned in across the table. "You've had time to mull everything over," she said, her gray eyes intent. "Who do you think is doing this?"

"I don't know," I said after a beat. "If the Barbie and the torn book jackets are connected to the note in my purse—and I assume they are—it means we're talking about someone who was at the party. So I can eliminate the floor crew on the show, the tech people, the associate producers, the interns and assistants. Because I only invited senior producers and above."

"Do you get along with all of them?"

"For the most part, yes. There's this one producer named Charlotte whose work leaves a lot to be desired, and I've had to talk to her on a few occasions. I can tell she's not a fan of mine. She doesn't seem to like anyone else, either—unless he looks good in pants."

"Can you picture her doing this?"

"No. But you never *really* know what's going on in someone's mind. Or what they're capable of."

"How about the others?"

"Tom's seemed a little cool to me lately. Like I mentioned to you, he accused me of going around him. Yet that's hardly a reason to threaten me. As for everybody else, there's nothing really to report. If there's an issue at work, I speak my mind, but people take it in stride."

"So no one on the show seems to hold a grudge?"

"No. But the person wouldn't have to be on *our* show. There were other people from the network at the party. Some work on my floor. And all of them have access to it." I looked off, wondering if this was the moment to reveal a thought that had been percolating in my brain. Yes. "One person in particular jumps to mind," I said, glancing back at her.

"Are you thinking what I assume you're thinking?" she said, her voice hushed.

"You asked if someone had a grudge, and I can't ignore Vicky. She tore my head off in front of people and ratted me out to Potts."

"Have you seen her since the run-in that night?"

"Just in makeup. I had to sit there listening to her extol the virtues of Ambien. She didn't say anything to me directly."

"So what would her motive be?" Ann said.

I shrugged. "To throw me off my game? Or knock me off my perch? Maybe she sees me as a threat. The Queen noticing that there's someone else at court that people are starting to pay attention to."

Ann smiled. "Please don't take this the wrong way," she said. "You're doing a fantastic job—everybody thinks so—but you're still a minor player in Vicky's book. Besides, I bet she bitch-slaps about twenty people a day, and when she's done with one, she moves on to the next."

"You're probably right," I said. "But just for the record, she hasn't forgotten about me." I shared my conversation with Potts.

"Wow, that couldn't have been pleasant," she said.

"No, it wasn't. And that's partly why I didn't want to go to Potts about the doll that night—it would have felt awkward after my drubbing from him. Fortunately, the meeting wasn't *all* bad. He says he wants me more involved in the show, and he mentioned a big survey that showed viewers really like me."

"Oh, good. I heard that survey was in the works."

Our food arrived, and we took a minute to start eating.

"There's one thing I haven't even asked yet," Ann said, setting down her fork. "How are you handling all this? It must be very scary."

"I won't lie, I feel rattled," I said. "It's as if the person doesn't want to just wig me out but also undermine me professionally."

"Does it remind you at all of what happened before?"

"What do you mean?" I asked. Was she going where I thought she was?

"Well, your stepmother did creepy stuff like this, didn't she?"

Once, over a couple of glasses of wine with Ann, I'd related the broad strokes about my early years, and I'd always regretted it, not because I lacked any trust in her but because my stepmother, Janice, didn't deserve the airtime.

"That was years ago," I said. "I don't want to dwell on it." In my mind, I could see Janice's face—the piggy nose and the almost white blond hair, translucent and stiff as spun sugar. I could hear her horrible fake-sweet voice, too.

To my relief, the waiter appeared at that moment, cleared our plates and took an order for coffee.

"How about a walk along the High Line?" I asked once we'd figured out the bill. The restaurant was a couple blocks away from the stairs up to the park, which had been built on an elevated rail line once used to haul freight.

"I'd love to, but I'm due at a spin class back uptown," Ann said. "If you'd like to do the High Line, I'll walk you there."

"Yeah, I think I will," I said. "It might help me chill a little."

As we headed north on Washington Street, her phone rang. She reached in her purse for it and glanced at the screen. "Darn, a reporter," she said. "Excuse me."

She stopped a few feet away from me. I'd always accepted the fact that her work involved plenty of confidential stuff, and the firewall needed to be especially strong now that we were at the same company again. But that didn't mean I wasn't curious. I saw a grimace form on her face. She caught my gaze and held it longer than normal.

"You've asked me this before, but the answer's always the same," I overheard her say. "We don't respond to inquiries about the personal lives of people at the network. Good day." Ann dropped the phone in her purse and strode toward where I was standing, never taking her eyes off me.

"That was an interesting call," she said, sounding miffed. Her irritation splashed in my direction.

"What's the matter?" I asked.

"It's a reporter from Page Six. He wants me to confirm or deny that you're having an affair with Carter Brooks. Please tell me you haven't been playing me for a fool."

Chapter 10

"Ann," I said. "I'd never play you for a fool. You know those rumors have been going around from the beginning."

"That was the second call from this guy in five days. He claims you were seen having dinner with Carter this past week—and looking very cozy."

"I'm *not* having a fling with Carter." My words seemed to have the stilted cadence of a liar. "I did see him the other night for dinner, but it was simply to discuss the incident with Vicky."

Ann widened her eyes in exaggeration. "You don't sound very convincing," she said.

"Okay, if it seems like I'm protesting too much, it's probably because I do find the guy attractive. Despite my better judgment."

"You know, don't you, that it would be utterly crazy to get involved with him?"

"Of course. And I swear, the worst I've ever done is strip him butt-naked in my brain, despite how hard he might be to resist."

"Resist?" she said.

"He's made it clear he's open to something. But trust me, I'm smart enough not to become another notch on his belt." I smiled again. "Hey, one of the fringe benefits of friendship with you is becoming more savvy about PR—knowing where the land mines are and how to avoid them."

She smiled back, appearing mollified. "Sorry to sound agitated. I just never want to be embarrassed in front of a reporter. Besides that, this is a time for discretion. I mean, with this whole Barbie-doll incident and you in hot water with Potts, you don't want to exacerbate things."

"Wait," I said, feeling a pang of anxiety. "You think I'm in hot water with Potts?"

She shook her head. "Not exactly, but the point is, he's told you to mind your p's and q's and you need to do that. If he found out you and Carter were involved, you'd have a heap of trouble on your hands."

"What I'd love to know is who the hell's spreading the rumors," I said. Restaurant staff were notorious for calling in gossip, or it might have been Carter's driver—or mine. Charlotte popped into my brain. I had seen her catch the look between Carter and me the day before.

"Maybe it's the same person who's doing the other bad stuff," said Ann. "I'd steer completely clear of Carter except when you're at work."

After bidding goodbye to Ann, I climbed the stairs to the High Line. As I strolled, I looked off to my left at the gleaming Hudson River, its small whitecaps sliced by crisscrossing sailboats, motorboats, and ferries. The sun was hot on my skin, but I relished the sensation— I'd been cooped up inside much of the summer.

Eventually, I let my eyes fall to the old railroad tracks that ran the length of the narrow park. The landscape architects had planted the spaces between ties with tufts of grasses and wildflowers. It always stirred memories of the first summer I spent at my aunt Jessie's in the middle of New York State, when I'd been about to turn twelve. I'd wander for hours, sometimes with my bike at my side, crossing fields and dusty roads and train tracks that shot off to unknown places. I'd search for arrowheads and for wildflowers to press with my aunt. I missed my father so much that summer—sometimes I imagined him arriving heroically by train one day to scoop me up and take

me home to the Buffalo suburbs—but it was nothing compared to the relief I felt from being out of
Janice's clutches, away from her malevolent games and
machinations.

In the beginning, she'd been sugary-sweet to me,
seemingly eager to please. I was polite enough back—at
least I tried to be—but I didn't have a shred of interest in being her little best friend, and I resisted her
overtures. Soon afterward, the tricks started. The first
involved the dress she'd made for me, the Liberty-print
one that had matched hers to a T. One day my dress
was just gone, nowhere to be found, and the implica-
tion was that I'd disposed of it. Other items soon vanished—my house key, my charm bracelet, homework,
the leash for Janice's dachshund, permission slips for
camp and school. At times I even wondered if something was going wrong with my mind.

And then the stains began to appear. Smears of food
or mud or grease, all on my prettiest things. There
was an ugly tear once down the front of a brand-new
blouse. At first my father was understanding, but over
time he grew frustrated with me. Even angry at times.

And then one day I discovered the truth. I'd
begun keeping close track of my belongings, examining them before I put them in the wash or tucked
them in a drawer, and I could see that Janice had to

be responsible for what was happening. I searched her closet one Saturday when she and my father were running errands, and stashed far in the back, I found a small box with most of my missing possessions. That night, as Janice chattered away with a friend on the phone, I led my father to the closet and showed him the box. Four days later he sent me to Aunt Jessie's, promising he would remedy the situation.

At the end of that magical but melancholy summer, I returned home, ready to start school. I was sure Janice would be gone, banished. But there she was, a sly smile plastered on her face. My father, it turned out, had believed *her* version of events, that I was the true villain, planting evidence against her. She intensified her efforts, locking me in a closet every day. By the end of the year, I was living permanently with my aunt. Though my father visited sometimes, I never returned to my old home.

I was startled now when I looked east and saw the street sign for Twenty-eighth street. I'd been so engaged in my thoughts, I hadn't noticed how much ground I'd covered. I spun around, wondering if I should retrace my steps to the beginning. To my shock, the senior producer Alex Lucca was standing a few feet behind me.

"Alex," I blurted out.

Had he been *following* me? I wondered, and then realized how crazy that thought was.

"Oh, hi," he said, looking surprised. "I didn't realize it was you ahead of me. I've never seen you with your hair like that."

His hair seemed different, too, tousled in front in kind of a weekend look that went with the tight navy T-shirt and jeans he was wearing. But his expression was as inscrutable as always.

"What brings you here?" I asked. "Is your place nearby?"

"No, but I do volunteer work down this way on weekends. And I like to take a walk up here afterward." He smiled. "There's something about train tracks that always beckons me."

"What kind of volunteer work?" I asked.

"At a halfway house, helping ex-cons with their legal issues."

"Nice," I said, impressed. "Is it partly to keep your hand in the law, in case you ever want to go back?"

"I just feel sorry for some of these guys, and it's a way to assist. I'd never go back to the law professionally."

I was tempted to ask why, but he'd delivered the last line bluntly, as if it weren't open for discussion.

"And what brings *you* down here?" he asked quickly. "You live uptown, don't you?"

"Yes, but I had lunch close by. And train tracks beckon me, too."

He cocked his head back in kind of an "Ahh" expression. "Though the problem with these is that they end right *here*. I want train tracks that I can follow for hours. Of course, it would help if there were some cafés along the side where they serve a nice Italian rosé."

It was one of the first vaguely revealing things I'd heard him say, and I smiled in response. "I assume from your name that a love of Italian rosé comes naturally."

"Yes, my dad's Italian, though my mother's a hundred percent Irish."

That explained the dark hair with the pale skin.

"Fortunately," he added, grinning, "my father did most of the cooking."

I had a sudden inclination to ask if he wanted to grab a cup of coffee or even a glass of rosé. It would be good to know him better, especially in light of everything going on. I let the thought pass. I had too much to do. "Well, I should be heading home," I said. "Have a good weekend."

He nodded and lifted a hand in farewell.

On the taxi ride north, a text came in from a friend, reminding me that I was joining her and her husband tonight for dinner with an eligible male friend of theirs. I groaned out loud in the cab. I couldn't do light and breezy, not with everything weighing on me. I pleaded a work-related emergency and begged forgiveness, though I knew that would be the last time she would try to orchestrate my next great romance.

I ordered in for dinner and ate the meal alone, feeling my thoughts darken as the day did. It wasn't just the doll that was troubling me. It was what might be *next.* Was something else in store for me? As I slipped into bed, I could hear the sound of my heart beating faster.

The rest of the weekend rushed by. I spent Sunday prepping for the *Times* interview. According to Ann and my book publicist, the reporter, Rebecca Cashion, was fair but hardly a pushover.

She arrived at my office at nine the next morning, a photographer in tow. She was fiftyish, classy, with a laid-back conversation style. She took notes by hand though she was also recording the interview. I sensed that it was her way of slowing the pace down a little, making it easier for her to assess me.

The initial questions were about the book and my interest in exploring the secrets that women keep. No curveballs. Then she segued into the show. It was no surprise when she raised the question of chemistry between Carter and me. "Both of you are single, right?" she said.

"Well, I am," I said, smiling. "You'll have to let Carter answer for himself."

She raised an eyebrow. "But he's not *married*," she said.

I laughed. "Well, he wasn't when I left the set on Friday, but I haven't asked him what he did this weekend."

I'd caught her off guard with the joke, and she laughed, too. "So it wouldn't be so terrible if the two of you became an item, would it?"

I smiled again. Keep it light, I urged myself. "Well, I don't think the network would be very keen on us using the open of the show to fight over whether the toilet seat stays up or down."

"Right," Cashion said, her face neutral. She glanced at her notes and reached to turn off the tape recorder. "I think that's about it," she added. I recognized the ploy. It was used sometimes by reporters to disarm you before they lobbed one last question, one that could catch you totally off guard.

"Great."

"Oh—but I do need to clarify a few points about your career. Do you have one more minute?"

"Sure."

"You broke into TV relatively on the late side. Have you felt that you needed to make up for lost time?"

"I *am* a bit of a late bloomer in TV," I said, "but that's not as uncommon as it used to be. Many people toggle back and forth between different types of media these days."

"Was the book part of a plan to turbocharge your TV career?"

"I started the book before I returned to TV," I said, making sure not to sound defensive. "I had no clue I'd be lucky enough to land another show."

"Last question. What do you consider your biggest weakness?"

I'd banked on her asking that. "Besides chocolate?" I said, cocking my chin toward the glass jar of M&M's on my desk. "I sometimes fail to stop and smell the roses."

"Would you say you're fiercely ambitious, then?"

An alarm went off in my brain. In light of my conversation with Potts, I had to be careful how I responded. "I wouldn't characterize it quite that way. I just love my work. And sometimes a day goes by, and I realize that I've been enjoying myself so much, I forgot to break for lunch."

After she departed, I swung by Tom's office and filled him in about my conversation with Potts.

"Why would you be looking into crime stuff without checking with me?" he asked.

God, I thought, was *that* his main concern?

"I simply wanted to flesh out my ideas before showing you."

"Yeah, okay," he said, shrugging. He started rapping his knuckles lightly on his desktop, as if he had something else on his mind, but he never volunteered it. I told him I'd see him at the meeting and left. As I hurried back to my office, I thought of what Carter had said. Tom might have one foot out the door.

The *Times* reporter returned later to watch the show from just off-set. Carter had been forewarned about her presence, and he did his best to make us both look as good as possible.

With the distraction of the reporter removed, the pit was back in my stomach the next morning. Each time I stepped into the doorway of my office, I'd search the room with my eyes, wondering if another ugly surprise awaited me. I felt anxious, too, about how life might blow up after my revelation to security. Potts didn't want me drawing attention to myself, and I'd be doing just that. According to Ann, the *Times* piece was not likely to run until Thursday or Friday.

On Wednesday morning, my cell phone roused me from sleep before my alarm had a chance to. It was Ann, calling to report that the piece was in that day's edition, sooner than expected.

"I wanted to give you a heads-up before you saw it or anyone called," she told me.

"Is there a problem?" I asked. Her tone was hardly joyous.

"Not really, no. It's the kind of piece people would kill for, and the publisher will probably love it."

"*But* . . . ?"

"There's a quote in there you aren't going to like."

"From whom?"

"Unattributed. I just sent you the link."

"What's the line?"

"I want you to read it in context. Then call me back."

I'd been using my laptop in bed the night before; I snatched it from the floor, clicked on the link and began to read, racing over the words. It all seemed good—my book was "insightful and provocative," I was a rising TV star, totally charming on the air and in perfect sync with my coanchor. Jeez, I thought, what's not to like?

And then my eyes lit on the line.

"Ms. Trainer got a relatively late start in television and lost ground temporarily after her last show was canceled. But with her new show—and its strong ratings—she's making up for lost time. And there are some who say she has bigger things in sight. 'Her ambition is as naked as a porn star,' says one source at the cable network who asked not to be identified. 'Don't make the mistake of getting in her way.' "

Oh *lovely*, I thought. Now I'm Eve Harrington slash porn star.

I called Ann back. "Overall, the piece is great, but you're right, I hate that quote. Can you find out who said it?"

"You know as well as I do that they never divulge their sources."

"Who do you *think* said it?"

"I have no idea. I arranged for her to do phone interviews with Potts, Carter, and Tom Golden, but she could have gone to anyone else on her own and convinced them to speak off the record."

"Like Vicky?" I said. "It's the kind of sound bite I could hear coming out of her mouth."

"Maybe," Ann said. "But I wouldn't worry about it. The quote will probably jack up your book sales."

"I'm thinking about Potts. He practically told me I had a 'lean and hungry look,' and now this."

"If he seems put out, I'll do my best to smooth it over."

"Thanks so much, Ann," I said gratefully. "I'd appreciate your help on that."

"Now that the story's out, you need to talk to security about the doll."

"I know."

It was time. I'd made one shift in my strategy, however. Instead of going directly to Oliver, I'd decided to fill Tom in first. That way he wouldn't feel that I'd sneaked around him again.

By the time I arrived at work that morning, there were two dozen emails from people congratulating me on the piece, everyone from my book editor to college friends to former colleagues. There was one from my father, too, making me catch my breath. "Terrific story," he wrote. "Very proud of you." I shouldn't have been shocked. He did email me occasionally—from the land of let's pretend.

The day took off at light speed after that. I sent Tom an email requesting a few minutes of his time, and he replied that because we were crashing two stories, it would have to wait until after the show.

Settling into the chair to have my hair done, I could feel a sense of dread ballooning. As much as I wanted company security on the case, it worried me, too. I was about to light a brush fire without knowing how much would ultimately burn.

"You ready for me?" I called over to Stacy while Jimmy sprayed my hair.

"Yup, all set," she said.

I'd tried to focus on my notes while my hair was being styled. As I slipped into Stacy's chair, I took a good look in the mirror for the first time. Despite my walk in the sunshine on Saturday, I still looked pale as a jelly fish. "You're going to have to work your magic again," I said.

"Don't worry," she said. "I'm on it."

I closed my eyes as she dabbed at my skin with a makeup wedge. Her touch was relaxing, settling my nerves a little. But after a moment I popped open my eyes and leaned forward.

"That's the same foundation you always use, right?" I said. I was starting to experience a tingly feeling all over my face.

"Yup. Remember, I'll add bronzer later."

"It just—"

The tingling was intensifying, verging on unpleasant.

"You okay?" Stacy asked.

"No," I exclaimed, jumping up.

My face was burning like hell.

Chapter 11

No, *no*, I thought, this can't be happening.

I spun around one way and then the other, like a wildebeest with a bug boring through its ear.

"What's wrong?" Stacy exclaimed.

"I—I need tissues. My face feels like it's on fire." It was getting worse every second, as if I were walking into a furnace.

Stacy yanked a handful of tissues from a box and thrust them at me. As I swiped at my face with them, she bolted toward the big sink at the end of the room and jerked on the faucet. "Come here," she yelled.

I threw myself toward the sink.

"Don't worry about your hair," Stacy commanded. "Just get your face under the stream."

At first it stung when the water hit my skin, but after a few seconds I could feel the pain receding.

"You should wash your face, too," Stacy urged. "With something gentle." She grabbed a tube, told me to put out my hand, and squeezed a blob of cleanser onto it. As soon as I massaged it onto my face, it started to sting again. I splashed on more water and finally raised my head from the basin. Jimmy had scurried over and was hovering right next to us.

"It's turning red," Stacy exclaimed as she handed me a towel. It hurt to even touch the cloth lightly to my skin. I spun around toward the mirrored wall behind me. I caught sight of my face and gasped. It was not only red; a white coating seemed to be forming, like frost on a glass.

"Oh my gosh, are you *allergic* or something?" Jimmy said.

"You definitely used the regular foundation on me, right?" I said, ignoring him and looking at Stacy.

"Yes, of course," she said. "I've heard of people developing allergies over time, but not overnight. Look, we need to treat your face stat. And we should call a derm, too."

I followed her back to her station, where she yanked open a drawer and reached for another tube. "It's a post-peel cream, so it should help," she said. "Rub a little on while I try to reach the doctor. We've got one on call." She grabbed the wall phone and started to punch in the number.

"Wait a sec," I said as I dabbed the cream on my face. "First show me the exact foundation you used."

Stacy pointed to a familiar bottle at the front of the cluttered mix on the counter. I picked up the bottle and raised it to my nose. There was an odd odor, chemical-like. Something had been added since Stacy had last used the foundation on me. "Smell this," I told her.

She leaned a little closer to the bottle, took a whiff, and quickly pulled her head back."Yeah, that's weird," she said.

I glanced at Jimmy, who could barely contain his fascination with the scene. Stacy was a gossip, but she was in the bush leagues compared to a motormouth like him. "Jimmy, you need to give us a minute," I commanded.

"All right," he said. "But I've got a guest due."

"It's just a guy," Stacy said. "Do his hair in the greenroom."

"This makeup's been tampered with," I said as soon as Stacy and I were alone. "Have you seen anyone in here, touching this stuff?"

She frowned, looking even more worried. "No," she said. "But I only got in two hours ago. And the room is open all day. Should we call security?"

"I'll do that," I said. "But I'm going to go back to my office before anyone sees me. Let me know when you reach the doctor."

She nodded.

"Don't say anything to *anyone*, okay?" I added. "And put a gag on Jimmy."

I tore out of there, taking both the bottle and the tube of cream with me. As I flew down the hall with my head lowered, the linoleum floor seemed unfamiliar to me, as if I were racing down a corridor where I'd never been. Keiki was on the phone and didn't look up as I darted into my office.

I closed the door and sank into my desk chair. My pulse was racing even faster. I felt like someone who had just staggered out of her car after an accident on a freeway. This was different from the cockroach and the books and the Barbie. I'd been *injured*. Someone had tried to physically harm me.

Get a grip, I told myself. I couldn't come unhinged.

I called Ann first, my hand beginning to tremble as I hit her number. Her assistant conveyed she was in a meeting but due back momentarily. I explained it was urgent and asked that she get a message to Ann. Then I called Tom. "I need to see you," I blurted out. "It's an emergency."

Less than a minute later, he was knocking at the door.

"Robin, what's going on?" he exclaimed as he took in my face. "Are you okay?"

"No, I'm *not* okay," I said.

I described what had happened with the foundation. Holding the bottle in a tissue, I lifted it to his nose for him to smell.

"You don't think it just went bad?" he said. "I've heard that beauty products have an expiration date."

"No," I insisted. "Because—other stuff has happened, too."

He pulled his head back. "*What* other stuff?" he said.

"Pranks, nasty things," I said. "Someone here wants to sabotage me."

Before I could elaborate, Keiki was opening the door to let Stacy in, and a second later, Ann appeared over her shoulder, shutting the door behind her. Ann's hand flew to her mouth when she saw my face.

"The doctor said she can see you as soon as you get there," Stacy said. "The office is on the Upper East Side."

I glanced quickly at my watch. "But she needs to come *here*. The show's in less than an hour."

"I asked, but she said she wouldn't know what to bring. She can't determine how to treat you until she sees your face."

"Then I'll have to go tomorrow morning." I turned back to Tom. "Stacy can cover up the red with makeup."

"No," Tom declared, giving a hard shake of his head. "Robin, I can't let you on the air until a doctor has seen your face."

"Tom, for God's sake, it's not going to make it *worse* to be in front of a camera," I said. I was starting to feel frantic, penned in. "You can't make me skip the show." I looked quickly back at Stacy. "You've got concealer that will cover this, right?"

"Sure, there are tricks to use for redness. But I have no idea what's going on with your face, and I'd be afraid of making it worse."

She looked anxious. Was it just concern for me? Or was she remembering what she'd told me last week, a remark that was now flashing in my brain: *Vicky* had asked her what foundation I wore.

"Thanks, Stacy, we'll take it from here," Tom said bluntly. "Just text Robin the info for the doctor and copy me."

"Can someone please fill me in?" Ann urged after Stacy rushed off.

I explained quickly, stumbling over my words. I was fighting to stay calm, but I felt like the stress was engulfing me, as if someone had thrown a blanket over my head.

"This is dreadful," she exclaimed.

"Don't you *see*, Tom," I said. "Someone wants to totally undermine me. If I'm forced off the show tonight, they've won this round."

"You can't think that way, Robin," Ann said before Tom could respond. "You need to be treated by a doctor *now*. Besides, if you go on the air looking the least bit strange, it will be all over Twitter, and then the person doing this *has* won."

I consented finally, my fear fused with outrage.

"We have to let you leave for the doctor's now," Tom said, "but I need to hear about these other incidents."

"So you told him?" Ann said, looking at me.

I nodded.

"I can't believe this is the first I'm learning about this," Tom said. "But I'm not going to browbeat you. Get to the doctor's. Keiki should go with you. And Ann can bring me up to speed."

We agreed that I'd take the bottle of foundation with me and bring it back tomorrow. Tom would call security. He squeezed my arm. "We'll figure this out, Robin, I promise," he said. It was the first warm thing he'd said to me in days.

I decided against taking Keiki with me. I felt too hyped up to have anyone around. With the help of sunglasses, I managed to escape the building without anyone doing a double take. The driver who picked me up was one I'd never had, and he paid little heed to me.

As we headed toward the doctor's Park Avenue office, I kept checking my skin in the mirror of my compact. The frost seemed more pronounced. Who the hell was out to get me?

As promised, the doctor saw me immediately. She was fortysomething, earthy-looking, and I felt a sense of relief at the sight of her entering the exam room. I explained what had happened and handed her the foundation.

"My goodness," she said. She opened the bottle and took a whiff but said nothing. Then she felt for the magnifying glass that dangled on a cord around her neck and examined my face through it. "I'm pretty sure the foundation has been mixed with TCA— trichloroacetic acid."

"*Acid*?"

"Don't worry. It's used in facial peels and won't cause any lasting damage. I'm going to apply steroid cream, which will help eliminate the redness and the frosting. Your face may feel tight for a few days, but the discoloration should go away within twenty-four hours. Until then your makeup artist can use a quality concealer under the foundation."

Relieved, I let out a ragged sigh.

The doctor took a tube from the glass case along the wall and began to apply it gingerly to my face. As gentle as she was, each touch felt like a pinch.

"How would a person get their hands on this stuff?" I said when she'd finished.

"You can purchase it in small concentrations over the counter at a drugstore," she said. "But for it to cause this amount of redness, the concentration would have to be stronger. It was probably bought over the Internet."

"Is there any chance that it was added to the foundation accidentally—by the company?"

"I highly doubt it," she said. "If you haven't already, you need to report this situation immediately."

She wrote me out a prescription for steroid cream and gave me a sample to last a few days.

Back home, I texted Ann with an update and then turned on the TV. I couldn't believe that at ten minutes to seven, I was sitting in my living room and not on the set. I wondered how they would handle the up-front part of the show, where Carter and I chatted together. I decided Tom would probably shorten it and let Carter riff on his own for a bit. He was one of those TV guys who could make shopping for new socks sound exciting.

But he wasn't alone. A girl named Sherry Boggs, a reporter from one of the other network shows who sometimes did substitute hosting, was six inches to his left. Sitting in my freaking place.

"So nice to be filling in, Carter," she said, beaming. I shut off the TV and tossed the channel changer on my coffee table. I couldn't believe it. It was like I'd been *evicted*, kicked off and immediately replaced.

After pouring a glass of wine, I paced the room with it. I'm just off the show for a night, I reassured myself, I'll be back tomorrow—and security will be on the case. They'll find out who's been doing these things to me.

A minute after eight o'clock, I grabbed my phone to call Tom and then stopped. There was already a text from him. Potts, he wrote, had called a breakfast meeting at his apartment, with him, Ann, Will Oliver, and me. Good. They weren't wasting any time.

I texted Tom back, telling him that I'd see him there, that my face was on the mend, and that I'd be doing the show tomorrow night. I sat at my table and considered the meeting at Potts's. I would need to play it carefully. The guy had bullied me about toning down my act off the air, and I didn't want to look like I was a drama queen. There was no way I could raise Vicky's name as a possible suspect. In preparation, I made a few notes on a piece of paper.

The intercom buzzer rang suddenly. To my shock, the doorman announced that Carter Brooks was downstairs.

"Um, send him up," I said. I didn't want Carter seeing me now, but I needed to learn what he knew, what people had been told. I dashed to the bathroom and looked in the mirror. Though my face had begun to heal, it was still slightly pink and frosted. Before opening the door, I dimmed the lights in my living room.

"Sorry to barge in like this, but I wanted to check on you," Carter said after I welcomed him in. He was wearing his suit from the show, though the tie was off. "They gave some excuse about why you were out, but it sounded fishy."

"I'm glad you're here, actually," I said. "Come in and sit down, and I'll get you a glass of wine."

He didn't sit. As I poured the wine in the kitchen, I could hear him moving idly about the living room.

"Great place," he said distractedly when I reentered the room. He'd taken off his jacket and laid it over the back of an armchair. He seemed different to me, as if, away from work and midtown, he'd allowed the "hunky anchor" persona to fall away.

"Thanks," I said. "What excuse did they give for my absence?"

"They said you'd had a small medical emergency. But Tom looked weird and— Hold on, do you have a fever?" Even in the dim light of the room, he'd noticed the color of my face.

"I wish." I told him what had happened.

"Wow," he said when I'd finished. "And you think it was intentional?"

I nodded. "This wasn't the only incident." I explained about the books and the Barbie doll.

"Who could possibly be doing this?" he said.

"I don't know. But clearly, it's someone who hates my guts."

I looked away. Though it would be good to have Carter as an ally, I wasn't going to raise Vicky's name with him, either. When I glanced back, however, I could tell by his expression that he had already gone there.

"Whoa, wait a second—are you thinking . . . ?"

"It's hard to imagine, but yes, it's crossed my mind. I'm not making any accusations at this point."

"You've notified security, I hope."

"Yes, and there's a powwow tomorrow."

"Gosh, Robin," he said, stepping a little closer. "I just wish you'd told me all of this was going on. As corny as it sounds, we're supposed to be teammates."

"I appreciate that, Carter," I said. "At first I wasn't sure if I was imagining things or not."

He smiled sympathetically. "Robin, I've made it clear how I feel about you, but I'm not going to push you on that. What I'd like right now, though, is to be there for you—as your friend, okay?"

"Sure."

"You don't sound convinced."

"You shouldn't take it personally," I said. "I just figured out a long time ago that I have to take care of myself."

He cocked his head slightly and looked deeper into my eyes. "Are we talking evil stepmother here?"

I felt a nerve prick. "Why do you say that?"

"You told me the other night that you lived mostly with your aunt after your father remarried. So he must not have had your back."

I sighed and looked off. He was perceptive, I'd hand him that. "No, he didn't," I said. "My stepmother did things to make me look bad, and—" Much to my chagrin, I could hear my voice cracking.

"And what?" he asked softly.

"Nothing was ever the same after that."

Unexpectedly, I felt myself starting to tear up. God, don't go all blubbery in front of him, I ordered myself.

The next thing I knew, he had his arms around me, and I was leaning in to that soft blue cotton shirt.

Chapter 12

I arrived at Potts's Park Avenue apartment several minutes later than I was supposed to—intentionally. I didn't want to be the first one there and have to take him through everything on my own. My face, though improved, was pink and starting to peel, and I'd been forced to go industrial strength with concealer.

The door was answered by a housekeeper or maid in the kind of silly black and white uniform that generally turned up only in movies from the 1940s. She ushered me through the humongous living room to a humongous dining room, where the group was seated around a polished mahogany table. Tom, I noticed, was wearing a tie, something I rarely saw on him.

"You know Will Oliver, don't you?" Potts asked me after I'd said good morning.

"Yes," I replied, nodding at the security chief. He was tall, African-American, and shrewd-looking—a guy who could probably give a dead-on description of the doorman and anyone else he'd passed entering the building. I sat down at the table and accepted a cup of coffee from the maid.

Ann was perpendicular to me, and smiled warmly. It was good to have her there. I felt a sliver of guilt over the fact that I'd had another tête-à-tête with Carter and would be keeping it to myself. But nothing naughty had happened. I'd simply hugged Carter back, he'd finished his wine, and then he'd headed home.

"Robin, as you can imagine, we're terribly concerned about what's going on," Potts said. "I wanted to meet out of the office so people wouldn't be buzzing about why we were all congregating. Ann provided Will and me with details last night, but why don't you take us through everything that's happened."

He was all Mr. Nice Guy now, compared to the pompous butt-head he'd been a few nights ago. Of course he was concerned. If anything bad happened to me, it would be a blow to the network.

I described it all, even the water bug incident. When I finished, Oliver, who'd been taking notes, asked if I had the makeup with me. I handed the bottle to him in the Ziploc bag I'd stored it in.

"Okay," he said, his dark eyes sober. "We'll have this tested by a forensics firm and see if your doc's guess is right. We'll also examine footage from our security cameras. What about the note? Do you still have that?"

"I'm sorry, but I tore it up," I said. "Unfortunately, I also tossed the book jackets."

"Is it possible the rips in the book jackets happened accidentally? Perhaps that incident is unrelated."

"At the time I thought that, but in light of what else has happened, I hardly think so now." I didn't want to come across defensively, but I couldn't let them dismiss anything.

"By the way, I have the doll," Ann announced. She reached into a bag at her feet, drew out the Barbie, and slid it down the table.

"Jesus," Potts said as he took a look. "This is completely sick."

"Yes, this is very disturbing," Oliver said. He turned to me. "We're going to quickly figure out who's doing this and deal with them accordingly."

I nodded, feeling a sense of relief just from hearing those words.

"I need to ask you a few more questions, though," Oliver said. "Has anyone on the show or at the network acted at all negative toward you lately?"

How would *You had no fucking right to use one of my guests* stack up in his opinion? I wondered. Though I hadn't planned to raise Vicky's name, it was going to be hard to avoid doing so.

Fortunately, he expanded the question, so I didn't have to go there. "Think about beyond work as well," he said. "There could be an acquaintance, or even a stranger from the outside world, who resents you and has an accomplice in the building. Have you received any hostile emails or tweets?"

"Nothing I would categorize that way," I said. "As for work, things become tense on the show at times—a producer might not like being criticized for a weak segment, for instance—but that goes with the territory. Oh, and a few reviewers have had to eat their words lately," I added, making a little joke. I forced a laugh, which came out sounding like a seal bark.

Oliver glanced toward Tom and then back to me. "Tom and I had a chance to speak last night," he said. "He tells me there was an altercation recently between you and Vicky Cruz."

Good—her name was on their radar now and I hadn't placed it there. But the word "altercation" made it sound like I was partly to blame, that I was on the same level as a female Jell-O wrestler.

"Well, I wouldn't call it an altercation," I said, trying to strip any emotion out of my voice. "Vicky was upset that we'd booked one of the guests from her show, and she was very vocal about it."

Out of the corner of my eye, I'd seen Potts's sausage-y lips begin to part.

"Good God, Will, you can't possibly think that's relevant," Potts said. "That's simply a case of Vicky being Vicky. We're looking for a sociopath, here, if you ask me."

"Possibly," Oliver said. "What really concerns me is the way the actions are escalating. We've gone from pranks to bodily harm. I'm wondering if we should bring in outside security for Robin."

Potts looked ready to sputter and then caught himself. "Of course we need to protect Robin. But that will set off all kinds of alarms."

"I'm fine without that, at least for now," I said. "I just want you to catch this person."

"We will," Oliver said firmly. "Until then, I want you to lock your office door whenever you're away from your desk, and let me know if you spot anything out of the ordinary. Though we won't bring in outside security at this moment, I'm going to have our own team spend more time on the floor. It will be done discreetly."

"Yes," Potts said, shooting a look at Ann. "Discretion is key. We need to keep a lid on this." He glanced back to me. "And Robin, it's going to be difficult, but you'll have to do your best not to seem ruffled."

"Of course," I said. God forbid I look ruffled by this.

Ann raised a finger and suggested that I tell Stacy that the foundation had gone bad somehow; otherwise she'd start gossiping. Tom, who'd remained mostly silent during the meeting, nodded.

"One last point," Oliver said. "I'm going to loop in Carter on this. If the person responsible has a grudge about the show, it's possible that he could become a target, too, at some time."

I didn't divulge, of course, that Carter already knew. Carter, I was sure, would keep his mouth shut.

When we finished, Potts remained in his apartment, and Oliver went his own way. I gave Tom and Ann a lift back to the office in my car. Tom said very little on the ride, just tapped, tapped, tapped on his iPhone.

"Are you sure you're okay?" Ann asked me privately. She'd stepped off on my floor of the building, and Tom had scurried off.

"I'm hanging in there," I said.

"Your face looks better, at least."

"Thanks." I offered her a rueful smile. "And just think, when it's fully healed, I'm going to have the most refined pores in the universe."

"Remember, I'm just one floor away."

As soon as I was in my office, I called Stacy, as instructed. She'd already texted me twice about my face. I told her I was on the mend and that the foundation had become contaminated on its own. She suggested we switch to a different brand.

Next I phoned Richard to fill him in. He sounded truly alarmed and promised to call Potts immediately.

After I hung up, I popped two ibuprofen. My head was hurting, the pain bleeding from front to back. Breathe, I told myself. Just breathe.

Over the next few hours, my office phone seemed to ring constantly, making me jerk nervously each time. I let Keiki pick up and field the calls. After about the tenth one, she poked her head into my office. "There's a Mrs. Nolan on the line," she announced. "She said it's personal."

"Okay," I said, caught by surprise. It was my cousin, Maddy's mother. Though we spoke occasionally on the phone, she'd never contacted me during the workday. "Paula, hi," I said. "What's up?"

"I just thought I'd check in, say hello. I hope it's okay to call you at work."

"Sure." Though the last thing I was in the mood for was chitchat.

"Maddy is loving her internship. And we're so grateful for all you've done."

"But . . . ?" I said.

"But?" she said.

"She's loving her job, but you're calling in the middle of the day. Something's clearly up." I wondered if Maddy had filled her mother in on the screwups at work.

"Robin, you can't tell Maddy I told you this, but she's a little worried about you."

"*Worried* about me?"

"She says . . . well, that you've seemed tired lately and stressed out. I just wanted to be sure you're okay."

Was my stress really showing? I wondered if word had leaked out about the episode with the foundation.

"That's sweet of Maddy," I said, gritting my teeth. "But I'm fine. This job can be demanding at times, that's all."

"Good, I was just a little concerned."

"Like I said, I'm fine. How—how's everything with you?"

"We've been to the Finger Lakes this summer. Our old stomping grounds. Um, we saw your father up there a couple of times."

I said nothing.

"Do you ever meet with him?" she asked haltingly.

"No," I said.

"He's proud of you. And I know he'd love to be part of your life."

"Paula, I appreciate the call, but I really need to get back to work."

"Of course, of course. I'm glad you're okay."

As soon as I hung up, I swallowed a third ibuprofen. My head felt ready to explode. What I needed even less than chitchat was hearing a status report on my father. And though Maddy might mean well, I didn't appreciate her stirring the pot.

Just before noon, I headed down to the newsroom. Tom had sent an email saying there was a story he wanted to do tomorrow relating to a comment from the FCC on TV coverage of red-carpet events. It was time to check in with Alex about it. As I walked along the outside perimeter of the newsroom, I caught a few people, including Charlotte, raising their eyes toward me.

"You feeling okay?" Alex said as I pulled up a small stool. "They said you took the night off because you were sick."

It was a little more personal than he usually allowed himself to be with me. Maybe our brief chat on the High Line had made him feel more at ease.

"Yes, thanks for asking," I said. "So what's this red-carpet story about?"

He smiled. "I'll tell you, but you've gotta promise not to report me for sexual harassment. *Under*boobage. Remember how big side boobage was a while back? Apparently, this is the newest red-carpet trend. The FCC seems to be agitated about it."

Despite my foul mood, I smiled.

Alex explained that for guests, he was aiming for a celeb stylist or fashion editor and a spokesperson from the FCC. "Who else, do you think?" he asked.

"You know who would be interesting to include? An anthropologist. We can ask if underboobage is hot right now because we've seen so much outrageous décolletage lately that we're almost oblivious to it and we need a different visual to jolt our senses."

Alex laughed lightly.

"What?" I asked.

"I like the idea of adding an anthropologist, but I don't think many men end up oblivious to plunging necklines."

I laughed, too. This is better, I thought. I'm feeling *normal* now. "Point taken," I said. "So find a great guy to weigh in. Maybe an author who's written about the male-female dynamic."

"Good. I'll shoot you names by email."

I started to rise and then paused. "I bet you didn't get to deal with cool stuff like underboobage in the DA's office."

"Not true," he replied. "There were a few hookers who were in on the trend. They may have even started it."

The comment was breezy enough, but he'd taken a second to respond. The DA's office. There was something about it that didn't sit right with him.

I ate lunch at my desk, a salad from the cafeteria. As I was tossing the container in my trash basket, I heard a knock on the door frame. My body jerked nervously in surprise.

Will Oliver was standing there. "Got a minute?" he asked.

"Of course," I said, feeling my pulse kick up. "Do you have news already?"

"Not yet," he said. He eased the door closed without making a sound, like some Navy SEAL would know how to do. He motioned for me to remain seated and dragged the extra chair over to my desk. "But there's a question I need to ask you, one I didn't want to raise in front of everyone."

"Okay," I said. Something was up.

"The kind of harassment you're experiencing often occurs after a failed relationship," he said. "I need to ask if you've been involved in a romantic relationship with anyone here at work."

I probably should have expected a question like that, but I hadn't. "Absolutely not," I said.

Oliver studied me without saying anything, as if he weren't a hundred percent convinced. Well, I wasn't going to confess to a momentary rush of lust for Carter Brooks.

"Okay," he said at last, "but instinct tells me that there's something you didn't want to say in front of Dave this morning."

He was as good at his job as he looked. I hesitated.

"Robin, I need you to be honest with me," he said.

It didn't seem wise to make an accusation at this point. But if I withheld information, it might bite me in the ass later.

"Can it be between just the two of us?" I asked.

"For now, definitely."

"Several days ago, Stacy, one of the makeup artists, told me that Vicky Cruz had inquired about what foundation I used."

His eyes widened ever so slightly in surprise. "Was there a reason given?"

"She claimed she liked the way my skin looked. And that so-called altercation in the newsroom wasn't the only problem I've had with her. A couple of days later, she complained to Potts about one of my interns."

Oliver laid a long slim finger across his lips and tapped a few times. "Was she at your book party?" he asked.

"Yes. And she was on our set the night the water bug ended up in my coffee."

"All right," he said, betraying nothing. "I'll be back in touch soon. Until then, be extremely careful."

He left soundlessly, like an apparition. But his words kept echoing in my head. Later, rushing to makeup, I could feel anxiety gaining on me again, like a nasty mongrel nipping at my heels. There were two guests in the room, having their makeup done for the six o'clock show, so Stacy kept her mouth shut about what had gone down the evening before. But she gave me a sympathetic look and opened all new packages of makeup for me. I held my breath as she sponged the foundation on my face.

"Hey," Carter said as I slid into my seat on the set a little while later. He'd sent me a text earlier, just checking in. "Your face looks great now."

"Thanks. Nothing like an acid peel to pump up the collagen."

"Let's talk after the show, okay?"

"Two minutes," the director said. Then thirty seconds. Then we were live. I made myself think only about the segments, connecting with the guests, the energy I needed to summon.

The last segment was on summer concert tours, partly about the outrageous riders many singers had on their contracts. Lady Gaga, for instance, insisted on white leather couches in her dressing room; Kanye West demanded that the person chauffeuring him wear only hundred-percent-cotton clothes; and Mary J. Blige required that the toilet seat be changed before she arrived at each venue. One of our guests at the table was the entertainment reporter from another of the network's shows, a girl named Hadley who nearly slobbered over Carter, batting her double row of false eyelashes at him.

"If you were a rock star, Robin, what would you put in *your* rider?" Carter asked as we wrapped the show a few minutes later.

"Um, a private chef, I think. Truffles, too. And maybe a massage after every show. What about you?"

"I'll skip the truffles. That massage sounds good."

"That's it?" I asked, smiling.

"I'm a man of simple needs."

"Oh, I dare say we've gotten the sanitized version—for our own protection—but I'll leave it at that."

As soon as we'd stood up and unclipped our mics, I turned to Carter, but little Hadley had obviously been biding her time in the wings, and she came rushing toward him. I brushed past both of them and hurried off the set.

Half-way to my office, I stuck my hand in my purse, rummaging for my keys. As directed, I'd locked my office door and closed the outer door to the anteroom.

I rounded the corner—and then froze. Up ahead I could see that the door to the anteroom was open, and light was pouring into the hallway. I caught my breath. It's the cleaning lady, I told myself.

I moved ahead, almost tiptoeing. As I reached the doorway to the anteroom, I realized that the door to my office was open, too. My heart hurled itself against my rib cage. Someone had managed to unlock the door. I felt my gaze drawn to the floor of the anteroom, to the cheap light gray carpet.

Something dark and wet was streaked across it.

Chapter 13

I staggered backward into the corridor. A sound came from the right, and I swung in that direction. The cleaning lady. She was rolling her cart in my direction.

"Did—did you see who was here?" I blurted out.

"Here?" she asked, frowning. "You mean in the hall?"

"No, in my office," I said. I flung my arm to the left, pointing into the anteroom. I could feel my hand begin to tremble. "Someone's been in here. And there's a huge *stain* on the rug."

Her body stiffened. "I'm very sorry," she said, not meeting my eyes. "I was cleaning, and there was still coffee in a cup, and I spilled it when I picked it up."

"But where did you *go?*" I demanded. "And why did you leave my door unlocked?"

She shrugged helplessly. "I just went to the storage room to find the special cleaner." She tugged a spray bottle from a holster on her cart.

"You can't *do* that," I told her. I tried to calm myself, but by now my whole body was trembling. "I need to keep my office locked at night, do you understand? And when you unlock it to clean, you can't just step away. Please get this stain out, okay? It's—horrible-looking."

"Yes, of course," she said again, still avoiding my eyes. "I will fix it."

I sighed. "I'm sorry to speak so sharply," I said. "But—there have been some security issues."

"Of course," she said. "Do you want me to clean the stain now or come back?"

"Come back in about two minutes, okay?"

She turned and began to push her cart away. The wheels squeaked as they rolled along the linoleum floor.

I stepped back into the anteroom and flopped against the wall. I felt like I'd tugged at a strand of yarn in a sweater and the thread just kept coming, unraveling whole pieces of the sweater without my being able to stop it. I wrapped my arms around my chest and rocked back and forth. *Sleep, little robin, sleep, little robin.*

After a minute I lurched into my own office and grabbed my belongings. I felt overwhelmed with the urge to escape.

But I didn't want to go home. I couldn't stand the idea of sitting in my living room, picking at take-out food. I thought of Carter suddenly. Outside the restaurant the other night. The way his touch had made me feel.

I locked up my office, and instead of making a beeline for the elevator, I walked purposely back toward the newsroom. The green room was packed with guests for the current show, and I could hear the drone of their voices as I passed. I made another right and snaked around the outer part of the newsroom. Up ahead, the light from Carter's office spilled out into the hall. He might still be there. As I approached, he stepped, like magic, into the doorway, reaching for the light switch with a can of Diet Pepsi in his other hand.

"I thought you'd taken off already," he said, surprised.

"I was just about to," I said.

"Did something else happen?" he asked, his eyes flashing with concern. My body was still trembling, and I was sure he could see it. He backed into his office a few steps, pulling me with him, and pushed the door partly closed.

"No," I said. "Not exactly." I stared into his eyes. "Are you busy right now?"

"I was about to meet a few friends for drinks," he said, setting the soda can on his desk. "But I can be late."

"You sure?"

He smiled. "Actually," he said softly, "I could be very, *very* late."

"Thanks," I said. "I'd love to just talk for a while."

He leaned closer, and for a second, I thought he was about to kiss me. Instead, he said, "Let's get out of here and grab a drink."

Without even thinking, I closed the gap between us and kissed him hard on that full, luscious mouth. When I pulled back, he ran his fingers slowly along the side of my face.

"I happen to have a fantastic bottle of Bordeaux at my place," he said. "Why don't you cancel your car? We can take mine."

Fifteen minutes later, we were pulling up in front of his building, a prewar on Central Park West. Not what I'd expected. I'd pictured him in something sleek and modern, with walk-in closets and floor-to-ceiling windows that helped convince him that the world was his for the taking. This was the kind of old-style, tony building that law partners lived in.

The doorman nodded as we entered; I waited for his eyes to flicker but they didn't. Of course not. Carter

Brooks arriving home with a woman must be as routine in the building as a delivery from Zabar's.

"Welcome," Carter said to me as he opened the apartment door and hit the lights.

Again, unexpected. I would have bet on something bachelor pad–ish. Not Austin Powers/shag carpeting bachelor—Carter was too classy—but spare, just the cool essentials for life on the fast track. This wasn't anything like that. It was classic in design but decorated with bold contemporary stuff, slightly edgy. And then there was the view. Three windows faced Central Park, directly across the street. It was almost dark out, and the park was dotted with the shimmering lights from lampposts that lined hidden pathways.

"Wow," I said softly. "But I guess you hear that a lot."

"I lucked out," Carter said. "It used to be my parents' pied-à-terre. But they started coming to the city less and less and turned it over to me."

"Pretty nice of them."

"Yeah. I would have traded it for a few compliments about my career over the years, but WASPs have a hard time with that kind of stuff. They tend to show their love by bequeathing real estate and inviting you on bone-fishing trips in the Keys.

"Follow me," he added. "Wine's in the kitchen."

Rather than going for the overhead lights, Carter flicked a switch that turned on a hidden set of spotlights along the bottom of the cabinets, creating soft pools of white on the countertop. Were these his seduction lights? I wondered.

He slid the bottle from a wine cabinet beneath the kitchen island, uncorked it, and poured us each a glass. As I took a sip, savoring the deep, plummy taste, Carter slipped out of his suit jacket. He was wearing a fitted pale blue dress shirt, and even in the soft lighting, I could see the outlines of his taut, muscular chest.

"Something happened tonight," Carter said, tossing his jacket on a bar stool. "I want to hear about it."

"It was nothing, really. A misinterpretation on my part."

He took my right hand in his and rubbed his fingers over the knuckles. "But you were trembling," he said. "Something clearly upset you."

"I—I thought there'd been another incident. There was a huge stain on my rug. But it turned out the cleaning lady had just spilled a cup of coffee. I nearly bit the poor woman's head off."

"I'm glad you thought that having a glass of wine with me would help."

I looked into his eyes, locking on them like he liked to do to me. "No. That's not what I thought."

"No?" he said. "Tell me, then."

"I thought having sex with you would help."

I'd caught him off guard with my comment, and it was a second or two before he broke into an approving smile and set his wineglass down. He cupped my face in his hands. Then he kissed me, pressing me urgently against the edge of the island. Desire flooded through me.

There was still time to change my mind. But I didn't want to. Right then I couldn't care less what the rules were. I just needed to drive all the fear from my brain.

Carter ran both hands over my breasts, circling where my nipples were beneath the fabric, and then laid a palm against my groin, pressing. I moaned, overwhelmed with sensation. His fingers were at my mouth next, running back and forth across my lips. Then his hand was at my back, lowering my zipper.

"You aren't going to take me right here on the granite top, are you?" I asked.

He chuckled. "Oh, you're giving me far more credit than I deserve," he said. "Besides, I don't want anything restricting all the things I'd like to do to you tonight."

He led me into the bedroom, and we tugged off each other's work clothes. His body was tanned and perfectly toned. I slid my hand down his torso and began to stroke him. I still had my panties on, and Carter tore them down, caressing me between my legs with his fingers, slowly and rhythmically. So, I thought, he *wasn't* about all his own pleasure.

"You're gorgeous, Robin," he said. "Every inch of you."

He pulled the comforter off his bed, laid me down on the sheet, and slid alongside me. He fondled my breasts again, taking each in his mouth. As I squirmed in pleasure, he ran his fingers down my body and began to pleasure me between my legs. Then his tongue was there, moving in circles. I felt an orgasm start to build, and then it was exploding, making my body arc. Carter fumbled in a drawer for a condom. Finally, he was inside me, pumping slowly at first and then harder and faster until he came.

Spent, I drifted off to sleep almost instantly, and when I startled awake, I saw from the digital clock on the bedside table that it was after midnight. Next to me, Carter was breathing deeply. I pushed back the sheet that he must have laid over my body and slipped out of bed. I found my dress, flung on a chair, and wiggled into it. I needed to split. And I needed to be absolutely sure no one saw me.

"Hey," Carter muttered, stirring in bed.

"Go back to sleep," I said.

"I'm not letting you leave this late." He propped his head up on his hand. "Besides, I make excellent toast."

"Carter, there's no way in the world I'm going to walk out of your apartment in the morning dressed in what I wore on the air the night before."

"At least let me take you home."

"Not at this hour, that's just as bad. I'll sneak out and grab a cab."

First, though, I slipped into the bathroom. It was white and spalike, with a row of expensive-looking products and colognes standing at attention across the back of the marble countertop. I ran Carter's brush through my hair, subduing the bedhead effect. When I reemerged, I saw that he had climbed out of bed and thrown on a pair of sweatpants. He walked me to the door, and, before opening it, pulled me to him and kissed me on the mouth.

"Text me when you get home," he said.

"Go back to bed," I said. "I'll be fine."

He smiled. "I'm going to do my best not to have a shit-eating grin on my face during the show tomorrow night, but it'll be hard."

There was no way I'd permit myself to think that far ahead.

The lobby was empty except for the night doorman, who stepped outside to hail me a cab. He looked like the kind of guy who might not care who the vice president of the country was, let alone that I coanchored a show with one of his tenants.

The cabdriver had the AC off, so I rolled down the window and let the night air blow on me. I grinned, thinking about what I'd done. How's *that* for not seeming ruffled? I thought, recalling Potts's admonition.

As soon as I was home, I washed my face, hung my dress, and then crawled quickly into bed. I was still in a mild daze from the sex, and I wanted to float there longer, let it carry me to sleep. In a matter of seconds, I felt fatigue overtake me.

When I woke in the morning, I was hungry for the first time in days. I scrambled eggs and devoured them with two pieces of toast. It was hard not to think of Carter. The feel of his hands and his mouth. When I'd kissed him in his office, I'd been dwelling only on the present, on ridding myself of all the fear and anxiety. I hadn't wondered once about the next day and where my head would be. Now I knew. I wanted more of what we'd had last night.

I dressed for work, trying to stay with the sense of calm I'd found. But as soon as I settled into the car, dread started to build in me. How many freaking days will I have to wait, I wondered, before they find the person who was torturing me?

The moment I stepped into the anteroom to my office, my eyes went to the floor. The stain was gone, as promised, though the rug buckled slightly from having been soaked with cleaner and water. Just don't look there, I told myself. Don't look down.

The first time I saw Carter that day was at the meeting. I had my back to the door when he came in, but even before I heard his voice, I sensed his presence like a magnetic force. We locked eyes once as he sat down, but I avoided him for the rest of the meeting. I didn't want anyone intercepting a look between us.

The meeting that day seemed chaotic, with Tom distracted and often a beat behind the discussion. Some of the talk focused on a story that was quickly falling apart: Charlotte's, of course. I'd seen one of the guests she'd booked on other shows, and he was as exciting on-screen as a slab of lard.

"We need to throw him overboard and pull in someone else," I said. "It's not simply that he's uncomfortable on-camera. His answers are usually worthless."

"He's very knowledgeable," Charlotte shot back, her cheeks more flushed than usual. "He just has to be asked the right questions."

I couldn't believe the tone she took with me. "Nope, he's gotta go," Tom announced. "The guy stinks, Charlotte. Find somebody else."

She nodded, chastened, and then aimed a withering glance in my direction. I felt goose bumps race up my arms. My God, I thought, is *she* the one who's doing these things to me?

I let Carter leave the room before me, but as I emerged into the corridor, still brooding about Charlotte, he was standing there, bunched with Ann and Tom.

"Just who we were looking for," Ann said when she spotted me.

I greeted her with a smile. I sensed Carter taking me in with his eyes, but I didn't look in his direction. You're acting twelve years old, I told myself, but I didn't dare meet that glance of his in front of Tom and Ann.

"The *Daily News* is doing a story on the show, and they want to talk to the three of you," Ann said. "I need an eleven o'clock slot next week when you're all free. Can you coordinate?"

We promised we would.

"It's about time Tom got some ink on this," Carter said. "That's fantastic."

"Yes," I said, glancing at Tom rather than Carter. Tom nodded at me, but there was a quizzical look in his eyes. Was he sensing something?

"Shoot me an email today if you can," Ann said to the three of us. "I need to book this ASAP. Robin, I'd love an extra minute with you, okay?" As the men moved away, she stepped closer. "How are you doing?" she whispered. "I had dinner not far from your apartment last night, and I stopped by your building afterward. I wanted to make sure you were okay."

"Oh, I went by a friend's place for a bite. It was just, I don't know, good to take my mind off everything."

I hated lying to Ann at a time when I needed her the most. But I knew I couldn't confess about Carter.

"Nothing else has happened, has it?" Ann asked, her brow furrowed.

"No, I'm just on edge. I keep waiting for the other shoe to drop."

"I'm sure Oliver will solve this. In the meantime, I'm going to email you the name of a great masseuse who'll come to your apartment. With all the press happening for you and the show, you don't want your stress to show."

"*Does* it show?" I asked, worried.

"I hate to say this, but a little, yes. And I don't blame you. When I left your building last night, I felt totally spooked. As if someone was *watching* me."

"Wait," I said, alarmed. "*Was* there someone there?"

"No," she said, shaking her head firmly. "It was my imagination, I'm sure. But now I know how scared you must feel."

After saying goodbye, I ducked into the ladies' room down the hall. I had it to myself, and I stared into the mirror. Ann was right. Whatever good the sex last night had done for my psyche, it didn't show on my face. I looked not only pale but worn, with gray circles under my eyes, like someone who'd bitten off far more than she could chew.

I'll call the masseuse, I told myself as I let the ladies' room door swing shut behind me. More than that, I needed to keep the pressure on Oliver to *fix* this.

As I rounded the last corner, I could hear the click-clack of stilettos on linoleum. Someone was coming fast from the other direction, hugging the wall like I was. I dodged to the left, knowing we'd collide if I didn't.

I saw the red hair first. Like a fireball. It was Vicky Cruz. I reeled back.

"My, my, *someone's* in a hurry," Vicky said.

For a moment I stood there, speechless, my breath quickening.

"I guess we're *both* in a hurry," I said. It was the best I could muster.

"Well, be careful," she said, her words deliberate. She quickly twisted her head, making certain no one was behind her. When she turned back around, her green eyes were hard and filled with hate. "Because wouldn't it be terrible if you slipped and hurt yourself?"

And then she was gone, except for the sound of her heels driving into the floor.

Chapter 14

I touched a hand to the corridor wall and sucked in air.

Wouldn't it be terrible if you slipped and hurt yourself? It had seemed like a threat. The type of veiled threat that had been my stepmother's specialty. "Be *careful*, Robin," she'd say. "You wouldn't want to get a stain on that pretty new dress of yours." She'd drag out the words, the way Vicky had done. And then several days later, there *would* be a stain. Splatters of blue-black ink down the front or a huge, ugly smear of grease.

I took another deep breath. Vicky's the one, I thought. She'd practically told me so with the threatening tone and the hatred in her eyes.

"You okay, Robin?"

I glanced up. Alex was talking. He was coming down the hall with Maddy; both of them were carrying small plastic cups.

"I'm fine." I considered what Ann had warned about not letting my stress show. "It's just been a crazy day."

"They're serving frozen yogurt in the cafeteria," he said, holding his cup out. "Want me to run back and grab you one?"

"No, but thanks." That had been nice. I felt too queasy to eat anything now, though.

"By the way, did Tom find you?" Alex said. "He asked if I'd seen where you'd gone after the meeting."

"No, I'll look for him now," I said. Hopefully, Tom had an update from Oliver. Then I thought back to the uncomfortable moment in the hallway, when I'd purposefully kept my eyes off Carter. It would be just like Tom to detect any undercurrents.

I turned to go and then looked back at Maddy. "Give me a call later, will you?" I needed to follow up with her about what she'd blabbed to her mother.

I found Tom in his office with an empty sushi container on his desk. He motioned me in, and I closed the door before I took a seat.

"How you doin'?" he asked, hands behind his head.

"Okay," I said.

"I can't believe someone we know is pulling this kind of shit," he said. "Have you heard anything from Oliver?"

"No, I was hoping you had."

"Not a peep yet. There's something I wanted to mention, though. Related to you and Carter."

My breath froze in my chest. *Did* he suspect? "Yes?" I said.

"I know I've discouraged you and Carter from taking time off, but if you could use a break one night, that's understandable. Especially in your case right now."

Relieved, I exhaled. "Tom, thank you, but I don't need any time off," I replied. "As I said before, my tormenter wants me off the air, and I intend to do my best not to let that happen." As I spoke, I could see Vicky in my mind's eye, uttering her sinister comment after making sure no one could overhear.

I rose to leave, and Tom held out a hand for me to wait. "One more thing," he said. He flicked a pencil back and forth a few times. "So Potts told me you went to see him to discuss the show," he said finally.

I paused, confused. "Tom, I haven't a clue what you're talking about. I've spoken to Dave twice in the last month—at his apartment yesterday and when he told me to back off from doing the crime pieces."

"You didn't discuss becoming more involved in the segments?"

"Oh, okay," I said quickly. I had just realized what he was referring to. "It came up that time in his office. But *Potts* mentioned it, not me."

So Potts had lied to Tom, making it seem like I was the one instigating a bigger role for myself.

"Hey, no need to get defensive," Tom said.

"I'm not being defensive," I said. "I just don't like you thinking again that I went around you. That's not my style, Tom."

"Okay, fine," he said, shrugging. "Anyway, it probably *is* time to start expanding your role. But give me a few days to work this out."

"Great," I said. "I'm thrilled, of course."

I allowed myself a brief rush of satisfaction. I wondered if it was Tom who had lied, not Potts, trying to guage what my reaction would be. The bottom line: I couldn't trust either one of them.

A few minutes later, as I hurried back to my office, Keiki called out that Maddy was on the line. I pushed the door shut and picked up.

"Sorry we haven't had a chance to talk lately," I told her.

"That's all right," she said. "Alex has been giving me lots of guidance."

"Good. He's very smart, and you can learn plenty from him. On another note, I heard you talked to your mom about me."

Long pause. "I was just worried," Maddy said. "You don't seem like yourself lately. Like today, when we ran into you."

"There's a lot going on that I can't share with you, and though I appreciate your concern, I need you to be discreet. I don't want people outside of work knowing my business, even if they *are* family."

Another pause. "All right," she said, sounding disgruntled.

"Maddy, as I told you before," I said, "the stakes are high here, and you have to follow the rules."

"It's just that I can't seem to get anything right with you these days."

She was flipping the situation, making it seem like the trouble was my attitude rather than her mistakes. I said, "You can't take this personally. You have to think about whether you're up to the challenges here. It's not for the faint of heart."

"Of course," she said after a moment. I couldn't tell if she got it or was just placating me.

By the time I hung up, my shoulders were up around my ears. I grabbed my cell phone and tapped Carter's number. He'd texted me in the morning, but I hadn't replied.

"Were you ignoring me at the meeting?" he asked kiddingly.

"Just being cautious," I said.

"So can I look forward to the pleasure of your company again?"

Of course he could. That was why I'd called him. "When?" I asked.

"How about tonight? I'm supposed to be in the Hamptons this weekend, but I can wait and show at lunchtime Saturday."

I laughed. "Kind of short notice, isn't it?"

"Well, I'm sorry, I can't help myself. You've got only yourself to blame."

"All right, then," I said. I thought of the scent of his body, how it felt to have him inside me.

"I have a friend who's a big shot at the Mark Hotel. He'll gladly comp me a room tonight. Privacy guaranteed."

Carter suggested I meet him there at nine-thirty. He would arrive a few minutes ahead and text me the room number.

At home after the show, I changed into a pair of white jeans, ballet flats, and a low-cut sleeveless top I hadn't worn in ages. I stuffed a few toiletries deep into my tote bag. Instead of having the driver wait while I dressed, then drop me off at the hotel, I walked the short distance south from my apartment.

The room turned out to be a small suite, sleek and modern, decorated in shades of beige and brown.

Carter had changed into jeans, too, and a long-sleeved white linen shirt.

He pulled me to him as soon as I entered the room, and I could feel his erection through his jeans. "I hope you can wait for dinner," he said, his voice husky.

Standing in the living area, we nearly tore each other's clothes off. He was rougher this time, but I liked it. He kneaded my breasts, bit the nipples lightly. And then he spun me around. He leaned me against the table, grabbed my ass with his hands, and entered me from behind. I stretched out my arms, lost in the sensation of Carter sliding in and out, my orgasm crashing over me.

We ate dinner in bed afterward as muffled city sounds drifted up from the street below. I was ravenous. I wolfed down a steak, two glasses of wine, and a piece of warm chocolate cake with caramel ice cream. Sometime during the night, we had sex again.

In the morning, I woke to the sound of the shower running. A few minutes later, Carter emerged with a fluffy towel wrapped around him.

"Morning," he said, smiling. "Sorry to have to bail on you."

"Not a problem," I said.

"My buddy ended up giving me the room for the weekend, so stay if you want," he said, pulling a leather duffel bag from the closet. "It might be good for you to have a change of scenery after everything you've been through."

I told him I'd think about it, but I knew I wouldn't stay. I was feeling wired again. As Carter dressed, I thought of Vicky and what she'd implied: I'm going to *make* you slip and hurt yourself. She's not done with me, I thought. She's not done.

I spent the rest of the weekend trying to stay in motion—errands, tidying the apartment, my first run in weeks around the Central Park Reservoir. When I had brunch on Sunday with a friend visiting from Seattle, booked weeks before, I could barely keep my mind on the conversation.

On Monday morning, I headed down to the newsroom early. At least one of the stories we'd sketched out on Friday was not likely to hold, and I needed to see what was up. Standing there, I found my eyes lured again down the long corridor toward Vicky's office. As I stared, William Oliver suddenly emerged from the room, like someone slipping through a tear in a curtain. I caught my breath in surprise. Had he found something?

I bided my time for an hour and then took the elevator upstairs.

"Have you got a minute, Will?" I asked after knocking on his half-open door.

"By all means," he said. He motioned for me to take a seat. His office was sparsely furnished, the desk nearly empty except for the blotter, the phone, and an in-box with a single sheet of paper. Not the kind of guy who sat on his work.

"I was wondering if you had any leads yet," I said.

"I'm afraid we don't at this point," he responded. "The test on the foundation will take a few more days. And unfortunately, the surveillance videos weren't helpful."

"What do you mean?"

"There's no camera directed at the area immediately outside your office, so it's impossible to see who left the doll. We *were* able to view the makeup room traffic, but that place is like Grand Central. The talent goes in and out of there, but so do plenty of other people."

I thought for a moment, picking my words. "Something occurred with Vicky Cruz on Friday that I think you should be aware of." I described the encounter.

"Interesting," he said, his face neutral. "But the comment could have been perfectly harmless, just an expression people use."

"Her tone was threatening."

"Robin, I don't want you to get worked up unnecessarily. As soon as we have a lead, I will let you know. "

"I saw you coming out of Vicky's office earlier," I said. "I thought there might be a development."

He narrowed his eyes. "I simply found an excuse to stop by, chat and observe. As I said, I'll be in touch with you as soon as we learn something."

His tone had turned patronizing. And I didn't like what he'd just told me. Vicky was smart enough to know that someone like Oliver didn't simply drop by for a "chat."

"Since the video cameras have turned out to be a bust, what do you plan to do instead?" I asked.

"We're taking steps. But I'd like to keep those under wraps for now."

"You make it sound like I'm being pushy," I said sharply. "I hope you can see things from *my* point of view. I feel like a sitting duck around here."

"I assure you, Robin, we view this very seriously, and I guarantee we will find out who's behind it."

On Tuesday I felt even more agitated. Each day that something didn't happen made it worse. On the show that night, during the rescheduled segment about baby divorcées, I lost my train of thought completely for about five seconds. As I glanced around the table, trying desperately to figure out what had been said, I could feel myself starting to sweat. Had Carter asked *me* a question? But he wasn't looking at me; he was looking at the marriage therapist, waiting for a response. A second later, she began to rattle on about the value of "I" statements over "you" statements with your spouse. I took a breath and forced my brain to reengage.

That can't happen again, I told myself. *Ever, ever, ever.*

As soon as I was back in my office, I called Carter.

"You were in a real hurry to leave the set tonight," he said.

"I hate playing this waiting game, wondering what's in store for me next."

"Tell me how I can help."

"You can lean me over a table again and have your way with me."

He came to my apartment this time. We had sex by candlelight, the sandalwood scent filling the air. For that hour, at least, I felt bold, in control. I didn't want it to be over.

"A penny for your thoughts," Carter said afterward.

I hesitated. "I was thinking how nice your butt looks by candlelight."

"I mean what's on your mind? Come on, let me in, Robin."

"I thought that was what I'd been doing for the past hour."

"Very funny," he said, smiling. "Look, I'm just trying to help. I can tell this whole thing is wigging you out."

"What do you mean?"

"You seemed a little distracted tonight on the show."

"Oh, thanks," I said. I shoved the sheet off, thrust myself out of bed, and yanked my robe down from the back of the closet door.

"Don't take it the wrong way," Carter said. "I'm concerned for you."

"Well, it's a little hard to be at the top of your game when someone is gunning for you."

He climbed out of bed. "Are they any closer to figuring this out?" he asked.

"Not as far as I can see."

While Carter slipped on his pants, I recounted my recent run-in with Vicky.

"That does sound threatening," he said. He pulled me to him. "Look. Don't be annoyed about what I said a second ago. You've been a total trouper about this whole thing. And I promise I have your back."

"Thanks," I said, relaxing a bit.

"Tell you what," he said. "I'm going to bring you a little surprise tomorrow. I guarantee you'll like it."

"Not a Lionsgate watch, is it?" I said, teasing. I needed to change the mood. If I turned into a shrew, this would be over.

"No. Not a regift, I swear."

After he left, I paced the apartment. He'd been right. The cracks were showing, and I had to superglue them closed. Then my phone rang, making me jump. It was almost midnight.

"Sorry to call so late, darling," a woman said when I answered. Bettina.

"Is everything *okay*?" I asked.

"I wanted to give you a heads-up. My news director called me tonight and told me we're posting an item about you. Don't worry, darling, it's all very flattering. But it may ruffle feathers. It's about a survey the network did."

It had to be the one Potts had mentioned.

She promised to email me the link, and a minute later, after signing off, I read it on my laptop:

Cruzin' for a Bruisin'?

Vicky Cruz had better keep her eye on the rearview mirror. Cruz has seen her ratings go into a downward spiral since her "Punch Daddy" fiasco last year, and now, according to a top-secret network survey, *The Pulse* cohost Robin Trainer is turning out to be the network's new secret weapon. "There's all this buzz about the chemistry between Robin and Carter Brooks," says a network insider, "but Robin is the one viewers are really crazy about."

Oh, fucking brilliant, I thought. Someone in management at the network must have leaked it. It would surely infuriate Vicky. And what would Carter think? Hopefully, his ego was big enough to take it in stride.

I couldn't sleep after that. Potts had mentioned the survey to me. Would he think *I* had tattled? He couldn't. After all, he'd told me so little about it. At around four, I finally drifted off. When I woke, I felt totally ragged, my body humming with low-grade panic.

I called Ann as soon as I'd showered, but she didn't pick up. At about ten, as I stared at my computer screen in the office, she followed up. "I assume you've seen the post," she said.

"How did this get out, for God's sake?"

"I have no clue. More than a few people were given access to the survey, including Tom. You didn't say anything to anyone about it, did you?"

"Of *course* not," I said. "Do I need to do any kind of damage control?"

She didn't say anything.

"Ann?"

"I'm thinking. It should be fine. I'm waiting to see Potts about it. I'm sure he's irked, but I'll make clear there was no way it came from you."

Later, in the rundown meeting, people seemed subdued, awkward. They'd all seen the item. Were they thinking I was going all diva-like? Carter met my eyes once but quickly glanced away. I told myself he was being careful, but as we all filed out of the room, I sensed a chill coming off him.

A half hour before I was due on-set, I locked my office door and headed down to makeup for a touch-up of extra concealer for the expanding circles under my eyes. I flinched as Stacy brushed it on.

"Don't worry," she said. "I've been double-checking your makeup each day."

When she was done, I flew back to my office. I felt drained, desperate for a few minutes alone to jump-start my energy. I opened the door to the anteroom and froze. In the black wire basket on the door to my private office, where packages were sometimes left for me, was an object wrapped in a white napkin. I stepped closer, wary. With one finger, I lifted the edge of the napkin. There was a huge chocolate brownie nestled inside. Written on the napkin in pen: "I thought this would make you smile. C."

Okay, I thought, relieved. Carter had said last night that he had some kind of treat for me. This meant he wasn't annoyed—though it had been stupid to leave the note out in the open this way. I carried the brownie into my office and devoured half of it, careful not to smear my lipstick. The caffeine and sugar seemed to kick in almost instantly.

"Cutting it a little close today," one of the crew said when I rushed onto the set five minutes later.

"Sorry," I said. "It's your fault," I whispered to Carter as I took my seat.

"What do you mean?" he asked. His tone was challenging and his eyes cool. I didn't get it.

"The brownie you left," I said. "I was so busy savoring it, I lost track of the time."

"I didn't leave you a brownie," he said, and looked away.

Chapter 15

Everything in the room seemed to soften, go mushy, as if there weren't any outlines anymore.

"Are you just teasing?" I asked him. "Because you—you said you were going to bring a surprise." My tone sounded plaintive, almost desperate, and I knew I had to buck up. Our mics were on. People could hear.

"Nope, wasn't me," he said. "Maybe your buddy Dave Potts left it."

He was rifling through a stack of notes in front of him, not bothering to meet my eyes. It was because of the item that morning. I'd been called the secret of the show's success, not him.

But who had left the brownie? I could feel panic flooding me, making my arms and legs limp. C., I thought. Who was C.? Charlotte? There was no way she would have done anything sweet like that. Stacy? No, no, what was I thinking? Her name started with an S. I felt loopy suddenly, listless.

"One minute," the director said in my earpiece.

I needed water. I reached beneath the table for one of the bottles kept there. My hand touched the cap, but I knocked the bottle over, and I could hear it roll away. I looked down, searching for it.

"Thirty seconds . . . Robin, what are you doing?"

I started to answer, but then Carter was talking to the camera. Fragments about the fall TV lineup and the number of new shows about serial killers. We were live. I stared at him, clueless. When he turned and asked me a question, I didn't understand what he'd spoken. Just say *something*, I thought.

"I bet—I bet you love serial killer shows, Carter," I said.

"Oh, really? Why do you say that, Robin?"

"I mean, you're a guy, right?" My words sounded slurry, and I urged myself to slow down. "And jeez, guys, they love that stuff. All the blood and everything. Gore, gore . . . gore. Blood everywhere. What is it with guys and gore, anyway?"

"Not *all* guys are like that, are they?" he said. "Some of us even like schmaltzy stuff occasionally."

"Nah, you just *say* that, you know. Tryin' to seem sensi— I don't know. Maybe some do. I knew a guy who shwore, I mean *swore*, he loved *Little Mermaid*."

"Jesus," someone said in my ear. "Cut to Carter. Carter, just *fill*. We are going to a commercial in thirty seconds."

I touched my hand to my head and closed my eyes. I couldn't think anymore. Then someone was by my side, taking me by the arm and leading me off the set. I stumbled. My arms and legs felt as floppy as rubber bands. What was happening? Was I dying?

"Find Will—Will Oliver," I begged. "*Please*." I sank to the floor, my eyelids too heavy to lift open anymore.

After that, I was aware only of being laid down on a cushiony surface and then being lifted and jostled. The sound of car horns. Dreams about houses that had no doors. Then light nudging me awake.

When I opened my eyes, I saw that I was in bed, high off the floor in a pale blue room. A dull light seeped through venetian blinds. I tried to move my arms but couldn't. For a terrifying moment I thought I was strapped in a straitjacket. But then I discovered my arms were just wedged between the sheets. I wrestled them free.

"Hello," I called out. My voice was hoarse. I tried again, but no one answered, though I could hear noises outside the room, hospital ones—echoing footsteps, the squeaking and rolling sound of a trolley. I twisted around and found a call button and pressed it once, then again. And again. A few moments later, a nurse appeared. She was about forty, Latina, dressed in blue pants and a smock top.

"How are you doing this morning?" she asked, smiling kindly.

"I don't know," I said. My brain felt like a giant marshmallow. "I just . . . What day is it?"

"It's Thursday, about nine a.m. You came to the ER here at St. Luke's just before eight last night. Why don't I arrange for you to have breakfast now? Some tea and a little food should help."

As the nurse raised the back of the bed, I flung other questions at her. She told me that the doctor would be in shortly to discuss my condition and determine when I could be released.

I remembered a few snatches. Sitting next to Carter on the set. Trying uselessly to talk. Stumbling off the set. I'd been *drugged*, I realized.

"By the way, there's someone waiting in the lounge to talk to you," she said. "A Mr. Oliver. Are you up for that?"

"Yes, please," I said. "I need to see him *now.*"

"Why don't you use the bathroom first?" she suggested. "And then I'll bring him in. Just so you know, people have called to check on you. Your friend Ann more than once."

I wobbled as she escorted me toward the bathroom. I couldn't believe my face in the mirror. My eyes were puffy, almost slits, and there was makeup smudged all over the lids. I used a paper towel to scrub off what I could. Two minutes after I'd returned to bed, Oliver entered the room. He nodded somberly and lowered himself onto the fake leather guest chair. "You've had quite a night," he said. "We were all very worried."

"Do they know yet what I was given—what made me pass out?"

"It appears you were under the influence of some kind of a tranquilizer or sleeping medication, though more than a normal dosage. The tox results should be in later today."

I felt my eyes brim with tears, as much from anger as anything else. I pressed a fist to my lips and then pulled it away. "It must have been in the brownie," I said.

"Mr. Brooks mentioned a brownie. He said you told him you'd eaten it right before going on the air."

So Oliver had already debriefed people on the set.

"Yes," I said. "Someone left it for me in the basket on my office door. There—there was a note. Otherwise I never would have eaten it."

I realized how stupid I sounded. Like Alice in Wonderland, gobbling cake and mushrooms because the messages told her to.

"What did the note say?" Oliver asked.

"Just that the person thought the brownie would make me smile. It—it was signed C. So I assumed it was from Carter."

Oliver had drawn a notebook from his suit jacket pocket and jotted a few words down. He seemed so calm, *too* calm, as if we were discussing the theft of a stapler from my office rather than a threat to my life.

For the first time, I focused on what I must have looked like last night on the air. To anyone watching, I had probably seemed plastered or stoned. The thought mortified me.

"Has the network issued a statement?" I asked.

"They put out a release this morning saying you may have had a reaction to medication. Do you still have the note?"

"What? Uh, no—it was on a napkin. And I threw it away after I ate the brownie. Wait—I think the cleaning lady had already been in, so the napkin would be in the trash can in my assistant's area."

"Okay, let me have an associate check immediately." He sent a text. As he slid the phone back into his suit jacket, he studied me intently.

"Ms. Trainer, are you involved with Carter Brooks?"

I tried to form a look of utter stupefaction.

"I told you the other day that I wasn't," I said firmly.

"But someone may think you are. And jealousy could very well be behind the attacks on you."

I shook my head.

"They might have simply counted on the fact that Carter and I are friends and that I wouldn't be surprised to find a treat from him. Ultimately, what does their motivation matter? You've got to *do* something about this. I ate only half the brownie. What would have happened to me if I'd eaten the whole thing?"

"We've already broadened the investigation significantly, and I've decided to pull in the New York City police."

I leaned back against the pillow. I could feel a quiet fury building in me.

"Are you going to share my suspicions about Vicky?" I asked. "Or do you still think I'm letting my imagination get the better of me?"

Oliver narrowed his eyes.

"Do you have any more reason to believe she's responsible?" he asked.

"Nothing concrete, no. But there's a pattern. All the incidents have occurred after she may have needlessly felt threatened by me. The note was at a huge party in my honor, the torn books right after she claimed I poached her guest, the Barbie doll after she thought I was tapping her producers."

"And was there a trigger this week?" he asked.

I scoffed. "You bet. There was an item online saying I was the rising star of the network. I am sure that seriously chapped her ass."

"All this information is very helpful," he said, blank-faced.

After Oliver took his leave, a wave of fatigue walloped me. But I couldn't fall back to sleep. I needed to make calls, to get on top of the mess.

I had no clue where my purse was. While I picked at the breakfast, too nauseated to really eat, I called Keiki from the bedside phone and arranged for her to locate my handbag and my iPhone and bring them to me.

Then I tried Ann. She didn't pick up at her office or on her cell phone. Where *was* she? I needed her help now more than ever.

No luck reaching Tom, either, though I left a message with his assistant. I explained that I was hoping to leave the hospital today and would be back to work tomorrow. I *had* to get back to work. I knew the rumors must be flying, rumors that I'd been smashed or stoned, and I had to prove there was nothing wrong with me. At the same time, the thought of returning there terrified me.

I called Richard, my agent, next. He had tried my cell phone numerous times, he said, and failing to reach me was headed to the hospital. I asked him to hold off and pick me up when I was released. Six hours later, just before I left, the tox report came back. According to my doctor, I'd been given zolpidem, aka Ambien, a higher than normal dose. With a jolt, I remembered Vicky in the makeup room recommending Ambien to Jimmy, one of the hairstylists.

If there were press people outside the hospital, I never saw them; at Richard's suggestion, we sneaked out via the emergency room entrance. It was a strategy I could tell he'd used before, probably with some A-list client who'd OD'ed or been in a bar brawl. Keiki had brought my belongings, and Ann had texted, saying she was dealing with press and promised to call at four.

Richard and I didn't dare talk in the car he'd ordered. Once we were ensconced in my apartment, he made tea and then brought it to the living room. I took a sip but couldn't taste it. "What's the fallout been?" I asked. "Be honest with me."

"Pretty much what you'd expect. Lots of coverage about whether you were drunk or taking drugs. The release from the network went out this morning, and when you're back on the air, it will all blow over. Look what happened with Diane Sawyer. They claimed she looked tipsy that election night, and now everyone's forgotten."

"But *she's* Diane Sawyer," I said, gripping my head. "Please work with Ann on the press, will you?"

"Of course. But frankly, Robin, what I'm worried about is your safety. It's time they hired private security for you."

"I know. If I'd eaten the entire brownie, I could have been in real trouble."

"It may be misinterpretation on my part, but they seem to be dragging their heels on finding the culprit. You're closer to this than I am. Are they afraid of the potential fallout?"

"Yes," I said, "but it's even more complicated than you realize." I took a breath and told him my suspicions about Vicky.

Richard had put on his reading glasses when he was making the tea, and he peered over them in shock. "Good grief," he said. "This is staggering."

"I know, and I'm sure Oliver prefers to think it can't possibly be true."

"Robin, I know your instincts are excellent, but let me play devil's advocate. Why would a woman in Vicky's position behave so crazily? Admittedly, her star is tarnished these days, but she's still more or less at the top of her game."

I took another sip of tea. I felt queasy and fuzzy. "I know it's far-fetched. It would have to be out of a weird kind of jealousy."

He pursed his lips together, clearly trying to digest it all. I struggled up from the couch and walked back and forth in the living room, trying to pump oxygen to my brain. "Maybe I'm wrong," I said, shaking my head. "Maybe it's someone who hasn't even occurred to me. Because *whoever* is doing this is acting irrationally, without any real justification."

Richard was a guy who never seemed to sweat things, but right now his face was pinched with worry. "Okay," he said, bringing his hands down on his knees with a slap. "I'm going to attempt to meet with Oliver this evening. I'm going to demand round-the-clock private security and more people assisting Oliver."

"Please make sure they know I'm planning to be back tomorrow night. And Richard? Thanks for all your support on this."

After he'd gone, the apartment was utterly silent. I felt stuck in a strange vacuum, disconnected from the universe, but I knew if I went on the Internet, I might stumble on vile comments about myself, and I wasn't mentally prepared to see them.

I checked my email. There were hundreds, it seemed. Some were from the book publishing team and my literary agent. They were concerned, probably freaking in part on their own behalf, worried about what this would do to book sales. I responded, assuring them that everything was fine and that I'd follow up with them in a day or two. There were a couple of emails from people at the show, including one from Alex that stated simply, "Hope you are on the mend." One, too, from my ex, Jake, saying his thoughts were with me. Go to hell, I thought.

Nothing at all from Carter. You couldn't say I hadn't been warned. And yet I felt a pang of sadness.

At four, Ann called, as promised. By this point I felt desperate to talk to her.

"I'm so sorry I couldn't swing by the hospital," she said. "But I knew you'd rather have me in the trenches on your behalf. I've been doing nonstop damage control."

I groaned. "Has the press release helped?" I asked.

"It was good to send it out right away. But I'm not going to pretend the situation is anything other than wretched. YouTube has changed everything. You went viral."

I'd assumed all that, had told myself that it must be wretched, but hearing her say the words—her voice as grim as a freshly dug grave—made my stomach twist painfully. "What can I *do?*" I pleaded. "Ann, you've got to help me."

"We're going to try to fix this. I promise you."

"*Try?*" I said. "What do you mean *try?*"

"We *will* fix it. But Robin, first and foremost, you need to stay calm. If you appear frantic, it's only going to fuel the rumors."

I felt like a child being reprimanded. "I would hope I could let my guard down with *you*," I said.

"I know. But for the next few days, as we sort our way through this, I'd prefer if you let me be a hundred percent PR director with you. That's what you need from me now."

It made sense. "Understood," I said. "So what's the plan?"

"Right now I'm mostly fielding calls, reiterating what's in the release. I've kept my comments vague."

I told her that the brownie had contained zolpidem.

"Let's not go out with that. People will wonder why you were taking it in the middle of the day. It's better to make it sound like a reaction."

"Doesn't being vague lead to more bizarre speculation? Shouldn't we announce that someone *did* this to me?"

"I don't think you want that out there. In this case, the less said, the better, at least until you're back on the air."

"Well, that will be tomorrow night," I said.

I was wrong. Tom called after the show to ask how I was. The first I'd heard from him, but I let that go.

"Better," I told him. "Anxious to be back tomorrow."

"Um, yeah. We want you here, too. But both Potts and Oliver think it's best to hold off until Monday."

I couldn't believe the words coming out of his mouth. "*What*?" I exclaimed. "No, I can't accept that, Tom."

"Robin, it's for the best. Plus it gives you the weekend to fully recover."

"I don't need any more recovery time. Someone is trying to sabotage me, and we're allowing that person to triumph. Is *that* for the best, Tom? Is it?"

"Your personal safety is at stake."

"What about my darn reputation? That's in tatters at the moment."

"Robin, I understand how you must be feeling, but this is what Will Oliver is advising."

"Tom—" I was nearly yelling.

"Robin, I know it's hard, but I need you to get a grip. Please."

Oh, that's rich, I thought. You make *me* feel like the crazy person in this whole freaking mess.

After I hung up, I plopped on the couch again and rocked back and forth, trying to calm down.

The weekend was miserable. Ann had a wedding out of town, and I spent both days alone. I studied the notes for Monday's show and worked up the nerve to surf the Internet, doing my best to avoid anything about me. I scrubbed my kitchen floor and cleaned out a closet. Both nights I crashed early in a weird haze, as if traces of the drug were still snaking through my brain.

Sunday at five, Richard phoned. "Great news," he announced. "Potts's assistant called and said he and Oliver have something to report and want to meet with us first thing tomorrow."

"Thank God," I said. I felt euphoric, as if I'd just been given a pass out of hell. "Did they share any details?"

None, Richard said. But five minutes after I hung up, Ann called. Once I told her the news, she admitted she'd just heard it from Potts directly.

"Do you know anything?" I pleaded.

"I'm being kept mostly in the dark," she said. "But they've apparently determined who's behind everything."

"Vicky?"

A pause.

"No, I don't think so," she said finally.

"What do you mean?"

"I couldn't get the name out of Potts, but he said it's someone who never would have crossed our minds."

Chapter 16

Ann's words nearly floored me.

"But—but maybe it just never crossed *his* mind," I said.

"Remember, though? Vicky's name came up that day at Potts's apartment, so she was on his radar, whether he liked the idea or not. No, it's somebody different."

"So I was wrong," I said.

"Don't focus on that," Ann told me. "Focus on the fact that you're finally going to feel safe again. That's all that matters."

After signing off, I lay back on the couch, trying to absorb the news. If Vicky wasn't the person behind all the mayhem, then it was likely someone who worked on my own show, someone I saw every single day. Earlier in the week, in Oliver's office, I'd briefly considered if

I should raise Charlotte's name because of how prickly she'd been acting. Was it her?

Another name suddenly rammed against the inside of my brain. *Maddy.* She'd been upset with me recently, on more than one occasion. It couldn't be her, though. She was my second cousin.

Whoever it was, the news would be shattering.

Richard called back right before I went to bed to give the location for the meeting. I'd assumed it would be at Potts's apartment again and that I'd head to my office from there. Instead, it was scheduled for a conference room on the executive floor. Richard and I arranged to meet in the building lobby so we could arrive together.

I told him what I'd learned from Ann.

"Frankly, I'm relieved it's not Vicky," he said. "The lower the profile of the person, the less likely it is for the story to go wide and blow back on your career."

"At least I'll be back on the air tomorrow night," I said.

"Ideally, yes. But depending on what happens tomorrow, they may suggest a different timetable, and we need to be prepared for that."

"What are you *talking* about?" I knew I sounded abrupt, but my patience was shot.

"Someone's going to end up fired over this," Richard said. "There may even be an arrest. And if that happens, the network may prefer a buffer period between then and when you return to the air, so you aren't mired in the mess."

"I'm not a delicate flower. I can handle it. I just need to be back, before the rumors get any worse."

"Let's try to hear them out, Robin. If they suggest anything we aren't expecting, I'll say we want the day to think it over. That way you and I can discuss matters privately. The key thing is for us to seem cool and collected."

"You're right," I said. "And I'm sorry to sound rattled. I just feel so tense from everything that's happened. And from wondering what name I'm going to hear tomorrow."

"That's understandable. But try to rest now."

I took a long hot bath, hoping it would make me sleepy, but I ended up tossing and turning for hours in bed. When I was finally asleep, I dreamed that in the morning I took the subway instead of the car to work, and the train stalled in the tunnel between stations. Minutes passed and then more minutes, and I knew I was going to be horribly late. I tried to pry open the doors and escape from the train. A man watched me, speechless. He was a stranger at first, but then he morphed into my father. When I woke, my cotton camisole was soaked with sweat.

As planned, I met Richard in the lobby. He seemed oddly preoccupied, and as we waited at the front desk for his security pass, he kept monitoring his BlackBerry.

"Is there an issue with another client that you're trying to deal with?" I asked, not disguising my irritation.

"No, no," he said. "I'm sorry. Just a minor headache I had to handle."

"Richard, I need every ounce of your attention right now."

"Of course," he said. "And you have it. Let's go up."

As we headed toward the elevator bank, I caught sight of Charlotte stepping into another car, her blond curls piled on her head. She looked back in my direction, and I could have sworn I saw a sly smile form on her face, as if she could read at a glance how distressed I felt and was gloating about it. If she *was* the one, she clearly had no idea she was about to be busted.

The receptionist was expecting us. We were shown to a conference room at the far end of the hall, one I hadn't even known existed.

The receptionist asked if we'd like coffee. Richard accepted the offer, but my stomach balked at the thought. When she returned two minutes later to deliver Richard's drink, she told us that Mr. Potts would be down momentarily.

But it wasn't momentarily. We sat in the room alone for at least twenty minutes. The wall that abutted the corridor was floor-to-ceiling glass, and it felt as if I'd been trapped in a terrarium. What was taking so fucking long? I glanced up at one point to see Richard staring at the glass wall.

"What is it?" I asked. His pinched expression unsettled me even more.

"I've just seen Ross Carey go by for a second time. He's the in-house attorney. My bet is that he's coming to this meeting, too."

"That's not so odd, is it?" I said. I'd dealt with Carey once or twice during my contract negotiation. "There are legal ramifications for putting a coworker in the hospital."

"Yeeeees," he said, dragging the word out as if he couldn't commit to it. "Of course." Then he turned to me, lowered his head, and whispered, "There's something else, something I need to forewarn you about."

My body tensed. "What?" I asked.

"The reason I seemed distracted in the lobby is that someone with inside info sent me an email saying that the meeting might turn ugly—but didn't elaborate. I didn't want to alarm you, and as far as I know, this person could be dead wrong. But now that I see Carey, I've got a bad feeling."

"Ugly *how*?" I asked.

"I'm not sure. Originally, when you thought Vicky Cruz was behind this, I was afraid Potts wouldn't want to throw her under the bus. She's his major cash cow, after all. I figured she might be forced to admit what she did and promise to stay clear of you under threat of being canned and the story leaked. But since it's not her, I don't know what to expect."

"Maybe Ann misinterpreted what Potts said," I told him.

"Whatever the situation, you need to stay calm today, Robin. Promise me—"

The conference room door swung open, and Oliver, Potts, and Carey entered single-file, their faces forbidding. They looked like spokesmen from the C.D.C., about to announce a resurgence in bubonic plague.

"Gentlemen," Richard said, rising and shaking each man's hand. I simply nodded. Oliver made eye contact with me, and so did Carey. Potts didn't bother. Stay focused, I told myself. Don't start overreacting.

"Thank you for coming in," Potts said. "We have important information to share today."

"Good," Richard said. "I've been terribly concerned about Robin's situation, as I know all of you have."

"Let me turn it over to Will Oliver," Potts said. "He's done a thorough investigation, and his efforts have paid off. We've finally learned who's behind these—events."

Simultaneously, Richard and I shifted attention to Oliver.

"As I explained to Ms. Trainer previously, we had no luck when we viewed the tapes from the security cameras. Then we took the investigation a step further. We began examining people's work emails and their Internet usage. As Mr. Carey can attest, that's all within our rights."

"Of course," Richard said. "That's a smart move. And I assume that's how you discovered the truth."

"Yes, it is." Oliver turned to me, his gaze boring into me. "Ms. Trainer, did you do a search about Ms. Cruz on your office computer?"

Why was he asking that? I had done a search about Vicky the day after she'd dressed me down in the newsroom.

"Um—yes, actually, I did." A faint pounding had begun in my head. "Why is that relevant?"

"The timing is interesting. It was shortly after an argument between the two of you."

I couldn't tell where the hell this was going. Maybe Vicky *was* the guilty one, and he was trying to suggest I was partly to blame so they could make a case for keeping her. I tried to catch Richard's eye, hoping he would give me a sign, any sign, but he was staring at Oliver, perplexed.

"First let me point out," I said, "that it wasn't an argument. Ms. Cruz came to the newsroom and admonished us for poaching a regular guest of hers. I happened to be the first one she encountered. And yes, I did do a bit of research afterward. I wanted to learn about her in case there was ever another incident. When people are angry, it's good to figure out the best way to diffuse it."

"You were quite upset about the way she treated you, weren't you?"

Had Tom told them that? Or Carter? "I was a little annoyed, if that's what you mean. Why wouldn't I be?"

"Then she went to Mr. Potts with several other complaints."

"What are you getting at?" I asked.

"Yes, Mr. Oliver, *please*," Richard interjected. "Is there a point here? We need to know what's going on."

Oliver dragged his gaze back to mine and held it. "All right, then," he said. "We received the test results back on the makeup, and TCA was definitely added to it. Ms. Trainer, according to our findings, you also used your computer to search for information on trichloroacetic acid."

"I—I don't believe I did," I said. The pounding in my head was intensifying, like the muffled sound of a party raging from the floor just above my head. *Had I, though?* "The whole thing was very upsetting, so maybe I did—without remembering."

"Except your search was done two days before the acid was used on your face. You also searched the official site on Barbie dolls—three days before the Barbie was left on your chair."

"*No,*" I said. "That's not true at all. I never did anything like that."

"What in the world are you suggesting?" Richard demanded.

"We believe Ms. Trainer actually staged all these incidents herself, including taking the zolpidem."

I felt like I was in an airplane being torn apart at the seams. I glanced at Richard and then toward Potts. I willed my voice not to rise. "Dave, you can't believe this," I said. I was nearly gasping for air as I spoke. "It's absurd. What could my motive possibly be?"

"According to Will, you've suggested from the beginning that Vicky Cruz was responsible. It appears Vicky made you mad as hell, and you obviously wanted to even the score. I assume you also fancied the attention that being a victim could bring if this went pub—"

The lawyer touched his arm. "I think it's best not to speculate about motivation."

"But Will *asked* if I had any suspicions, and I shared them only as part of the investigation," I said. "There were comments from Vicky that made me think it *could* be her."

"How do you explain the searches from your office?" Will asked.

"The person obviously sneaked in there. I used to keep my office open, and my assistant has been in and out lately. I—I bet there was nothing about zolpidem on my computer, was there? Because I'd started locking my door by the time the brownie was left."

Carey, Potts, and Oliver stared at me completely stone-faced.

"I'm right, aren't I?" I said. "No one could plant anything from that point on."

"As for the zolpidem," Oliver said, ignoring my comment, "there was no way Ms. Cruz could be responsible. She took the shuttle to D.C. that morning and did her show live from there that night."

My mind raced, searching frantically. "If it *is* Vicky, then—then she probably has an accomplice," I said. "Or maybe someone else entirely is tormenting me. Did you analyze the handwriting on the napkin? You said you'd try to find it."

Oliver shook his head. "We looked through your trash. The wastebasket was still full, but there was no napkin in it."

I turned to Richard, desperate, but he appeared completely bewildered. I'd never seen him like that.

"Wait," I exclaimed. My memory had snagged on something. "*Stacy.* Vicky asked her about what makeup I used. Did you talk to her yet?"

"Yes," Oliver said. "And she doesn't recall Vicky ever saying anything of that kind to her."

I shook my head.

"*I* get it," I told them. "Stacy's afraid if she says anything, Vicky will have her canned." I threw my hands in the air. "What about Vicky mentioning Ambien? Jimmy must remember that."

"Robin, let's leave that for a moment," Richard said. He looked directly at Potts. "Dave, there clearly needs to be further investigation. It seems that there's been some horrible misunderstanding. I suggest that we all take a deep breath, put Robin back on the air to quell the gossip, and then dig deeper here."

"Dick, I respect you. You know that," Potts said. "But we've already taken a breath and dug deep. And Robin's not going back on the air. We're terminating her immediately in violation of the morality clause in her contract. We will pay out part of her contract, which we can discuss separately. And for her sake as well as ours, we will do our best to keep this ugly business under wraps."

I fought the urge to wail in disbelief.

Richard patted the air with his hands, as if trying to calm an angry mob. "Gentlemen, please," he said. "Allow us at least to bring in an outside investigator. We're not trying to witch-hunt Vicky Cruz. We just want to find out what's really going on."

Potts shook his head.

"Dave," I said, my voice pleading. "Think about it for a moment. The only thing I wanted for the past two years was to get back on the air. Why in the world would I sabotage my performance by taking a sleeping pill before a show or putting acid on my face?"

Potts shot a glance at Oliver, who spoke next.

"We don't know why, Ms. Trainer," he said. "But there's history of this type of incident happening in your life, isn't there? As a girl, didn't you accuse someone of harming you, and then it turned out you had done it yourself?"

"What?" I exclaimed. "Who *told* you that?" The pounding in my head was so hard that I could barely hear, and my hands were shaking. There had never been any public record of what had happened with Janice.

"We're not at liberty to say," Oliver said.

"That's a complete and total lie," I said. "My step-mother was guilty. I never harmed—"

"Robin, I think it's best that we leave," Richard interrupted. "Gentlemen, Ms. Trainer will be enlist-ing the services of an attorney." He cupped my elbow, urging me up. But I couldn't leave, not yet. I looked across the table at Potts.

"Dave," I said. "You have to give me a chance to prove that none of this is true. Think about it. Think about *me*. Have you ever known me to do one unethi-cal, untrustworthy thing?"

He stared at me, his eyes piercing. I sensed a finger squeezing against a trigger.

"Well, for one thing," he said, "you've been having a secret affair with your cohost. I wouldn't call that the most trustworthy move in the world."

Chapter 17

I looked at him, dumbfounded. How had he found out?

"All right, I admit, that's true," I said desperately. "But it's irrelevant to what we're discussing. I didn't do those things to myself."

"I think we've said all there is to say," Potts said.

I leaned forward, frantic. I had to reason with him. Before I could speak again, Richard tightened his grip. "Robin, let's go," he said.

As I stood, I realized my legs were floppy, in danger of folding up under me. I grabbed the table briefly for support.

This can't be true, this can't be true, I thought as Richard led me away. The next thing I knew, I was in the elevator, shooting downward, and then in the vast marble lobby, with people rushing by us in a blur. I realized Richard was talking to me. "What?" I asked dumbly.

"Robin, can you call a car? We need to get out of here."

I fumbled in my purse for my phone. My hand was still trembling, and as I stared at the screen, unsure what to do, the phone jerked back and forth.

"Actually, why don't we grab a cab," he said. "Considering how they've acted, they've probably already closed your account with the car service."

Out on the sidewalk, I waited numbly as Richard stepped off the curb. My stomach had started to churn, and I gulped a few breaths in defense. A woman did a double-take at the sight of me.

After flagging down a taxi, Richard practically hoisted me inside. The stupid cab TV was playing, and I punched several times at the off square until it went silent.

"Robin, I know it's hard, but you have to try to calm yourself. Let's stop by my office, and we'll figure out our next steps."

"No," I said, shaking my head. "I need to go home. I feel ill."

"All right." He gave the driver my address and then directed his attention back to me. "If you don't mind, I'd like to jump on the phone now. I have to find you a lawyer."

"Aren't *you* a lawyer?" I asked.

"I'm not the kind you need at present," he said.

I turned my head and stared out the window, seeing only a blur of motion. Everything was gone now. *Everything.* Even if the full story didn't leak out, people would assume I was guilty of *something*—of being a cokehead or embezzler. Someone had squealed about Carter and me. And someone, someone who knew me well, had blabbed about Janice, dragging that nightmare story into my job. The only people at work who knew were Ann, Maddy, and Carter.

My stomach was roiling, and I pushed my hand against my mouth, trying to fight the nausea. Next to me, Richard droned on the phone, but I could barely make out what he was saying.

As soon as we were in my apartment, I raced to the bathroom, ran a washcloth under icy water, and dabbed at my face with it. There had to be a way to *fix* this. Richard would help me, I told myself. So would Ann.

"Okay," Richard said when I stepped back into the living room. "I've left messages for Steve Katz at his office and his cell. He's an employment attorney—the best there is."

"The main thing he's going to have to do is convince Oliver to continue the investigation," I said quickly.

234 • EYES ON YOU

"And share information. Someone clearly sneaked into my office and did those searches. If I knew the times, it might provide a clue."

Richard nodded and announced he was returning to his office, promising to be in touch when he heard from Katz.

"Is it true about you and Carter Brooks?" he asked at the door, his tone somber.

"Yes. But a lapse in judgment hardly makes me a psychopath. And my contract doesn't actually forbid fraternizing with coworkers."

"I know. But it gave Potts a clear advantage today."

As soon as Richard was gone, I called Ann. I reached only her voice mail, so I left a message, saying it was beyond urgent.

For the next hour, I mostly roamed between rooms in my apartment. Two calls came in, one from my book publicist and one from Jake, my ex, but I ignored them. I left a message for Keiki, asking her to messenger over my belongings, and I sent an email to Tom on his Gmail account. Surely he'd be able to see the absurdity of the accusations and would be willing to urge Potts to look further.

There were moments when I felt flooded with determination and others when it seemed as if the floor were about to cave in, and any second I'd find myself gripping jagged edges of concrete. I couldn't help but think about money. I'd been making a sweet salary for the past few months, but it wasn't as if I had huge resources to fall back on.

My phone rang again. I felt a surge of relief when I saw that it was Ann.

"My God, Robin, what's going on?" she asked.

"What have they told you?"

"For now, just that you've been let go. But Potts wants to meet in a few minutes about the press release."

"They think *I'm* responsible, that I did all those horrible things to myself."

"How could they possibly believe that?"

"Ann, you've got to talk sense into Potts," I begged. "Help him realize the truth, please. "

"I'll do whatever necessary, you know that. When can I see you?"

"Any time. I've nowhere in the world to go at the moment."

"Why don't I duck out early and come by your place around six? By then I will have heard more and can better assess the situation."

"All right. What's the release going to say?"

"He suggested announcing that you've resigned to pursue other interests, but I told him we absolutely had to clear it with you."

"That makes it sound like I'm going into fucking drug rehab."

"Stay strong. There's surely a way out of this."

"Wait—" I yelled out as she was about to sign off. "There's something I need to ask you. You didn't say anything to anyone about my stepmother, did you?"

"Of course not. How could you think that?"

"Sorry, I—I'll see you later."

Who had told Potts? Carter? Or had Maddy gossiped, and it had worked its way back to him?

At about five, the employment lawyer phoned, with Richard conferenced in to the call. I went through the entire situation with him. As I spoke, I kept waiting for him to break in, express his outrage on my behalf, but except for a few questions, he listened in maddening silence. I might as well have been describing a problem I had exchanging a pair of pants at Bloomingdale's.

"So what's the first step?" I said, having raced through all the salient facts.

"You need to get your hands on the so-called evidence," he said. "That's the only way you can begin to refute their charges."

"But how do I do that?"

"One approach to is to sue in civil court for unjust termination. Since it's a legal process, it would give you the opportunity to discover and learn all the evidence against you."

"I have to *sue* them? Isn't that horribly expensive?" What was I supposed to do? Launch a Kickstarter campaign for the cash?

"It is," he said grimly. "And no lawyer will take it on a contingency basis. Another option is to commence an investigation of your own. But with no subpoena power or the power to compel testimony, it would be difficult. Coworkers will be reluctant to cooperate for fear of losing their jobs or their standing."

"So then I *should* sue?" I asked, frustrated. "Is that what you're saying?"

He sighed. "Not necessarily. Ms. Trainer, I'm going to be blunt here. Even if you wanted to spend the money, once you sue, the genie is out of the bottle, and it's impossible to put it back in."

"Wait, are you saying there's no other recourse? That I should just suck it up and watch my career be crushed like a grape?"

There was only silence.

"*Hello?*"

"Yes, I'm here. Ms. Trainer, these situations are vey difficult. As unfair as it seems, it's within their rights to fire you if they feel they have cause. Sometimes the best course of action, the best thing a good lawyer can advise, is to do *nothing*. Richard tells me that they plan to keep the reason for your termination under wraps. And offer compensation. That may actually be better for your career than having the situation explode into the open."

"Who do you think would possibly hire me with a big fat cloud of suspicion over my head? The ratings have been great, so people will assume I was fired because I did something ghastly."

"Robin, let's take this one step at a time," Richard interjected, though I had no freaking clue what he meant by that.

"Why don't you give yourself a day or two to think it over," Katz said. "We can speak again midweek."

"Should I get another lawyer?" I asked Richard after Katz had signed off. "I can't just stand by and let them roll over me."

I heard him sigh. "Sit tight for now. Let me investigate the matter further."

I tossed the phone down. I began to pace again, raking my hands through my hair. It was clear I was going to have to work from the inside, using Ann to help make my case.

I glanced at my watch. 5:33. I texted Ann and asked if she'd meet me in Central Park. I was feeling like a caged animal inside my apartment.

"Sure," she wrote back. "Where?"

I suggested the entrance at Fifth Avenue and Seventy-ninth Street, just south of the Metropolitan Museum.

I stuffed my hair under a baseball cap, threw on a pair of sunglasses, and set out. Ann arrived at the spot two minutes after I did. We hugged tightly in greeting.

"Why don't we walk a bit and find a more private place," she suggested.

She had a point. The area was clogged with dog walkers, mommies, nannies, and kids. We headed into the park, uphill past a lawn strewn with Frisbee players and late-day sun worshippers. Farther west, along a shaded path by the turtle pond, we agreed wordlessly on an empty bench. Sitting down, I tugged the sunglasses from my face. "Have you heard the full story by now?" I asked.

"Yes," she said, her expression pained. "Potts filled me in."

"Can you *believe* it? I feel like I'm in some absurdist play."

"I want to talk to you about everything. First I need to know if you're okay with me sending out the release, the one claiming you're leaving to pursue other interests."

I looked off, my mind a jumble. "I haven't even had a chance to think about that yet."

"I understand. If we don't issue it quickly though, the rumor mill will be out of control."

"Um, okay. I trust your judgment. But the rumors will be out of control no matter what the release says."

She nodded and rested her hands in her lap. "Have you talked to anyone about what's going on?" she asked.

"You mean in the press?"

"No, no, I know you'd never do that. I mean for advice, for guidance."

"My agent. And a lawyer, which was next to useless. He says I could sue, but it might damage my career even more. He thinks I should just move on. I can't do that, though. I can't just let my career become some epic failure."

"Have you talked to anyone else?"

"You mean another lawyer? I'm thinking about it."

"I meant someone who's more of a counselor, who could help you with all the stress you must be feeling right now."

"It would be useless to wallow in my misery."

"Robin, this is a lot to wrestle with. Especially with what you went through when you were younger."

"I need to *do* something, Ann. And right now it seems my only course of action may be working on the inside with people like you, and maybe Tom, to help make my case. Tell me what Potts had to say."

She glanced away, as if she found it too hard to look at me as she uttered the words. "It was what you told me earlier today. That he and Oliver believe you did all of those things yourself."

"Ann, I need to make a confession before we discuss my situation any further."

On my walk to the park, I'd made the decision to come clean to her about Carter. I couldn't depend on Ann to help me if I weren't honest with her.

"That's what I'm here for," she said softly.

"I had a brief fling with Carter over the past week or so. I swore to myself that I wouldn't go there—and I know I assured you I wouldn't—but I felt so distraught, I ended up turning to him. I'm sorry not to have been straight with you."

She smiled wanly. "I know."

"Are you furious at me?"

"No, of course not," she said. "It was your choice, Robin. But you see, don't you, how it's added to this terrible mess?"

"You're right," I said ruefully. "I know what guys like Carter are all about, but I let myself feel a connection to him. I actually thought he cared."

I looked off toward the pond. There were several boys standing on the large flat rock at the edge, tossing torn slices of bread to the turtles. I would have done anything to change places with them at that moment.

"Right now I have to focus on the bigger problem," I said, turning back to Ann. "I can't believe that meeting today, the way Potts wouldn't even let me defend myself. They seemed caught up in the idea of me wanting to take down Vicky. I'd raised Vicky's name with Oliver, but only after he pressured me about whether I had any reason to suspect anyone. It was as if they decided I was obsessed with the woman."

"I think Carter might have said something to Potts about that," Ann said. "That you kept focusing on her."

Her words felt like a wrecking ball swinging into my chest. "I can't believe he'd do that," I said. "I wasn't expecting true romance with Carter, but why would he undermine me like that?"

"My guess? It's Carter covering his ass. Most likely Oliver questioned him, maybe Potts, too, and they must have let on that they were privy to your relationship with him. He's smart enough to know they wouldn't be happy about it, so he compensated by being super-cooperative, throwing them a bone about you."

"That validated the view that I was gunning for Vicky."

"It certainly helped."

I covered my face with my hands, trying to summon strength.

"Can I ask you a question?" Ann said. Her voice was barely audible over the rustle of the tree leaves above us. "About the night we found the Barbie doll?"

"Of course," I said. "Has something occurred to you?"

"There's just one point I've wondered about . . . When I ran into you that evening, you were on your way out of the building. You had your tote bag with you. And then you remembered you needed to go back to your office."

"Right," I said. "I'd left a file back there, something I needed to review that night." I wondered what she was leading to. Was she trying to figure out the timing for when my tormenter had left the doll?

"In hindsight, I realized you never *did* take a file with you," she said.

I looked at her, puzzled, trying to grasp her point. "I was completely stressed and forgot it," I said. "What are you suggesting? That I'd seen the Barbie already, but I lured you back to my office so you could get the full impact and recognize that I wasn't paranoid?"

She didn't respond.

"Is that what you think?"

"I didn't say that, Robin. It was just something I always wondered about."

I wagged my head, beyond frustrated. "You know what's really scary about this whole thing?" I said. "It's how diabolically clever the person is. She—and I'm saying 'she' for now, because I still think it could be Vicky—wasn't content with hurting me. She wanted everyone in the world to doubt me, like you're doing. And she's not the least bit afraid. For God's sake, she stole into my office when I wasn't there and used my computer. That takes *guts*."

Ann didn't utter a word, just looked ahead anxiously.

"Ann? What is it?"

"Robin," she said, turning to me. "There's a detail that Oliver didn't bring up in the meeting with you. He felt enough had been laid on the table and there was no point in elaborating."

"Tell me," I demanded. My heart felt frozen in my chest.

"The searches on your computer? Each one occurred when Keiki was in the anteroom doing email or surfing the Web. So the truth is, no one could have sneaked into your office and done them."

Chapter 18

"That's not possible," I exclaimed. "Unless—unless Keiki is in league with the person. But I can't imagine that."

Ann looked away again, and when she returned her gaze to me, her expression was stricken. "They—they also found that the computer searches were done during periods when you were ordinarily in your office. In a couple of cases, you had sent emails only a few minutes before."

I started to bristle. "Ann, I'm not sure what your point is, exactly. As I said before, the person who's after me is extremely clever. She—or *he*, if you want—obviously waited for me to leave, sneaked into my office while Keiki was gone for a second, and then got busy in there after she came back. If the inner door were shut, Keiki would assume it was me."

My mind was racing, still trying to make sense of her revelation. "Or—or maybe the person told Keiki they needed to wait for me. Tom did that sometimes. So did the producers. Keiki wouldn't have been aware the person was on my desktop computer."

"Right," she said, but the word came out tentatively.

"Hold on a second. Are you seriously *doubting* me, Ann?"

"I didn't say that."

"But you're thinking it," I said, feeling the blood rush to my face. "You're wondering if I *did* stage all those things, aren't you?"

"Not intentionally, Robin. But—but you told me that when you crashed your car in Virginia, you'd felt out of it. And I'm just wondering if there's any chance that with all the stress you've been under, the whole awful business from your past caught up with you. And you acted in a kind of fugue state."

"Fugue state?"

"Yes. Without ever realizing it."

I couldn't believe what she was saying. She was my friend, and she was buying *their* story.

"Go to hell, Ann," I said, leaping up from the bench.

Without thinking, I started to run north along the path. From behind me, I heard her call my name, but I kept going. Through the trees, I could see the glass wall at the back of the Metropolitan Museum and people running and biking along the park drive. Just past the obelisk, a footpath appeared in the grass, cutting through to the drive. I bolted down the path toward the road. As I started to lunge across, something rammed into my right side.

The force knocked the wind out of me and lifted me off my feet. I came down hard on the pavement, hands first, and skidded across it. I could feel skin tear from my palms.

A woman on Rollerblades had toppled me. I looked up to see her ass pumping up ahead on the road. "Are you okay?" a man called out, just to the right of me.

"I—I guess so," I said. I couldn't catch my breath. I struggled to a sitting position and looked down at my trembling hands. They were scratched and oozing blood.

A young couple helped me to my feet. As I glanced up, I spotted recognition in their eyes and then puzzlement. Was the word out? I wondered. That I'd been fired in disgrace? I muttered a thank-you and started to jog again, desperate to be back in my apartment.

Finally, I reached my block. As I neared my building, I saw the doorman step out onto the sidewalk, away from the entrance, and wave as if trying to flag me down. What was going on? Then a man jumped out of nowhere and thrust a silver recorder in my face.

"Robin, why are you leaving the show?" he shouted. "Were you fired?"

I shoved his hand away. "No comment," I said, and rushed into the building.

The doorman followed quickly behind me. "I'm so sorry, Ms. Trainer," he said. "I was trying to warn you. There was another one around here earlier."

"Uh, okay, thanks," I said, hurrying past him. "Can you try to get rid of him? Say—say I'm not coming out."

It just keeps getting worse, I thought as I slumped against the elevator wall. By the time I reached my floor, my whole body had begun to tremble, like a toy top on a table. I held the key pinched tightly between my fingers to unlock the apartment door.

Inside, I sank onto the couch, tears welling in my eyes. *Fugue state.* I couldn't believe Ann had suggested such a thing. Was she also hinting that I'd been in a fugue state as a little girl and that I'd faked my torment by Janice?

I struggled up from the couch and slunk into the bathroom. My palms were scratched and raw, as if I'd run a grater across the skin. I dabbed at them with a wet tissue. After rummaging through a drawer, I found a tube of Neosporin, smeared it on, and wrapped each hand messily with gauze.

When I finished, I texted Keiki on her cell phone. I *had* to talk to her.

The intercom buzzer rang, making me jerk in surprise.

"He's back," the doorman said when I picked up.

"Who?" I said. For a brief, stupid moment, I thought he meant Carter, that he'd come by to see me unexpectedly, like he had that other night.

"That second reporter. I just wanted you to know there's two of them now."

Fifteen minutes later, he called again to report that there were more. A swarm, he said, including TV camera crews. Go away, I wanted to scream. *Go the hell away.*

I pressed my hands to my head. They wouldn't go away, that much I knew. They would encamp in front of my building until they scored the shot they wanted, the one of me looking bedraggled and undone. I couldn't stay here. I couldn't let them swoop down and peck me to death. In the kitchen, I poured a glass of wine and drank half of it in two gulps.

My phone rang. Bettina's name appeared on the screen. Answer it, I told myself. Because maybe she could help.

"Darling, what in the world is going on?" she asked. "Has Dave Potts lost his mind?"

"There's been a massive misunderstanding," I said. "I—I've got to find a way to fix it."

"Why don't you come see me? Or I could stop by wherever you are."

"No. You can't come here. There's press outside my building. I don't know what to do—I can't stay here."

I could almost hear her brain working, hatching a scheme.

"I have an idea," she said. "Why don't you stay in my guesthouse in Westport until the worst is over. They'll never find you there. I'll try to get up in a day or so, and we can have lunch and talk this out."

"I don't have a car. How—"

"Take the train. My housekeeper, Nancy, will pick you up. And I keep a car out there for the help. You can use that."

I'd just have to be careful around Bettina. I knew she cared for me, but she'd also be thinking of her website, which was surely covering the news that I'd been axed.

"All right," I said. "I'll go out tomorrow."

"Text me what train you'll be on, and I'll have Nancy meet you."

I needed to eat something, but the thought of a meal made me want to heave. I toasted a piece of bread and poured another glass of wine, slopping some of it onto the kitchen counter. I was reeling still from my encounter with Ann. She didn't believe me at the moment when I needed her most. The friendship, forged over endless conversations about work and love and loss, was done.

At seven, an email came in from Richard, saying that Potts and Carey wanted to talk to him in the next day or two about my compensation package, and he was going to use the call to try to reason with them.

"There's some real weirdness about the times they claim the computer searches were conducted," I wrote back. "We *must* see the evidence."

I sent Tom another email, asking him to please call. Why didn't he have the fucking decency to reach out to me?

At last, Keiki phoned. "Oh, Robin, I'm so sorry," she said.

"Thanks, that means a lot," I said. *Could* she be in league with the person? I wondered.

"No one's told me anything, just that you aren't coming back."

"At this point I can't explain what happened, but I will someday, okay?"

"I'll send your stuff over, like you asked," she said. I realized that her voice was choked with tears. "Some jerks were in here moving things around, but I don't think they took anything other than your computer."

"Keiki, I need to ask you an important question. Over the past few weeks, do you recall anyone stopping by to see me and then waiting in my office?"

There was a long pause as she thought. She *had* to remember.

"Not that I recollect," she said eventually. "I've seen Tom wait in there, but it's been awhile."

Damn. "All right. If something occurs to you, will you let me know? And it's probably best not to tell anyone we spoke."

"Okay. Look, I know this seems silly to ask—I mean, with everything you're going through—but what do you think is going to happen to me? Am I going to lose my job? I've got all these vet bills to pay."

"Speak to Tom as soon as possible," I said. "Tell him you love the show and want to stay. And he knows how highly I regard you."

Keiki couldn't have been in on the incidents, I thought after I signed off. With me ousted, her own job was in jeopardy. But then how had the person searched on my computer?

I packed an overnight bag and grabbed my phone again. There was something I needed to do, and it necessitated a call to my ex-husband. I tapped his number quickly, not giving myself a chance to change my mind.

"It's Robin," I said when he answered. "Do you have a minute?"

"Of course," he said. "I've left you a few messages. What's going on with your job?"

"I—I can't talk about that now. But I need to pick up one of my boxes. Is it possible for me to come by at eight tomorrow morning and do that?"

The loft we'd shared had extra storage space in the basement, and when we'd divorced, Jake had agreed to let me keep a few boxes there.

"Sure," he said. "Do you want me to go down tonight and bring it up?"

"Yes, if you wouldn't mind."

"Whatever you need."

I told him it was the box with "Oneonta" written on it—the town in New York state where my aunt Jessie had lived.

When I left the building the next morning, my head throbbing from too much wine, I wore sunglasses again and a scarf around my head, but I didn't need them. The press hadn't dragged their asses out of bed yet.

"Duane Street," I told the driver. Saying those two words was like uttering a language I'd spoken in another lifetime. As we barreled south on the FDR Drive, I sank into the backseat. It was drizzling out and streams of water raced sideways along the windows.

I'd last seen Jake about six months ago when we'd met at a midtown coffee shop to sign papers related to an old investment. The get-together had been clunky but cordial, and I'd been relieved by how, over time, I'd managed to distance myself emotionally when I was with him, as if we were talking through one of those Plexiglas barriers they use in prison visits.

But when he opened the door that morning, I felt my heart catch. His brown hair was shorter, and there were streaks of gray at the temples. He was growing older without me, something I'd never envisioned.

Jake touched my elbow in greeting. I saw him glance down at the piece of gauze I still had around one of my hands.

"Hey," he said. "I've been so worried about you."

"Thanks," I said, shifting away. "Did you find the box all right?"

"Yes, I've got it. Robin, what's going on? The Internet is on fire with all this hysterical gossip."

"I can't really discuss it at the moment," I said.

He motioned for me to enter and led me toward the kitchen table, where I could see the old box sitting forlornly. I tried not to look around the loft, but I could sense new things in various spaces, filling spots left empty by the few paintings and furnishings I'd departed with. I felt an ache begin to build inside me.

When I reached the table, I tugged open the top panels of the brown cardboard box. Inside were the possessions I'd brought from Jessie's after she died—photos, the quilt she'd sewn for my bed, the wooden flower press she'd bought me. I searched until I found what I was looking for: a manila envelope, soft as cloth from age.

"How about a cup of coffee?" Jake said.

"Actually, I need to catch a train in a few minutes," I said. I stuffed the envelope into my overnight bag and glanced at my watch. "Would you mind putting the box back? I'd appreciate it."

"Robin, please talk to me."

"Jake, thank you for your concern, but like I said, I'm not really able to go into it."

"I'd like to be there for you right now."

I bit my tongue, saying nothing.

"Will you let me do that? Be there for you?"

I cocked my head. "That just seems a little *strange*," I said, "coming from the person who didn't want to be married to me anymore."

"I made a huge mistake, Robin, but that didn't mean I wanted out of the marriage. You were the one who decided to go down that road. It's like you couldn't even entertain the idea of forgiving me."

"What choice did I have, Jake?" I said, my voice rising. "Do you think marriages ever really get back on track after someone's had an affair? I would have just kept wondering if you were going to abandon me again—and the next time for good."

"I didn't abandon you."

"No? What do you call it, then?"

"I felt walled out by you—I mean, you were never home during the years you did your show. So I let some stupid girl turn my head momentarily. But that's not abandoning you. I'm not your father, Robin."

I felt a flash of anger, like a firecracker going off in my head. "To *some* extent that's true, Jake," I said. "Because he's in a league of his own." I closed the flaps on the box. "I'll arrange to pick up these boxes as soon as possible. I shouldn't make you keep them any longer."

I hurried across the loft, flung open the door, and nearly flew down the stairs.

Because of the rain, hailing a cab was a freaking nightmare, and I just made the 9:35 train. I found a seat alone and stared out the window for most of the trip, trying to avoid eye contact with other passengers. As promised, the housekeeper, Nancy, was waiting for me on the platform. She greeted me cheerily, as if I'd arrived for a day of antiquing.

The drive to Bettina's took under ten minutes. There was a long driveway lined with trees, and then the house emerged, gray-shingled and rambling, though not the kind of huge mansion you could expect to find in Westport. Bettina once confided to me that she'd bought the place with her first few millions and liked it too much to ever upgrade. Besides, she now had big-ass houses in Aspen and West Palm Beach.

Nancy parked directly in front of the house and led me by foot around to the back. It was clear from the ground that the rain had bypassed this area. The guest-house was behind and to the right of the main house, alongside a gorgeous black-bottomed pool. Nancy unlocked the door, and we stepped inside a room with whitewashed wood beams and a stone fireplace. At some other point in my life, I would have relished being there.

"I stocked a few things in the fridge," Nancy said. "I wish I had time to make you lunch today, but I need to be with my sister. It's her chemo afternoon."

"I'm so sorry about your sister," I said. "Don't worry about me, I'll be fine. Bettina said there was a car I could use, and I'll just drive into town if I need anything."

Nancy wrinkled her nose. "Oh dear, she didn't mention that. I'm using the car this afternoon to take my sister. You're welcome to it tomorrow."

"That's okay," I said, though I couldn't help mind. I'd thought there would be a car, and now I felt trapped. I dropped my duffel bag to the floor.

"Enjoy the pool and the grounds," Nancy said. "Ms. Lane said she would be up in a day or two."

After she left I helped myself to a container of chicken salad in the fridge but ate no more than a few bites. I wandered into the other room, flopped onto the bed, and stared up at the whitewashed beams. Finally, I slept. When I woke, I forced myself up and stumbled toward the bathroom.

I washed my face with a cool cloth. Then I dug the manila envelope from my duffel bag and set it on the table. The envelope had been addressed to my aunt Jessie during the first year I'd lived with her. The return address had been made with a rubber stamp: Martha Brenner, CSW, 149 Sherman Avenue, Oneonta, New York.

I'd found it among my aunt's things when she died of cancer seven years ago, but I'd never looked inside. I'd told myself none of it mattered anymore. But I had to look now.

Chapter 19

I picked up the envelope and carried it out to the umbrella-topped table on the deck. The only sign of life outside were the automatic lawn sprinklers between the pool and Bettina's house, their spray catching the bright afternoon light as they spun around.

Though the envelope had been unsealed long ago, the flap was secured with two prongs of a rusted metal clasp. I squeezed them together and tugged the flap up over them. Inside the envelope my fingertips found a thin piece of paper, which I slid slowly out.

It was what I'd assumed would be inside—the report from the social worker that Jessie had sent me to after I'd returned to stay with her for good. She had claimed it would be a chance for me to talk to someone about what I'd experienced.

"I can talk to *you*," I'd pleaded. I hadn't been able to, though. I could sense it would be a relief to share, but I couldn't form words to describe my psychic pain, the terrible hours spent cooped up in the closet, my father's betrayal of me. Over time, Mrs. Brenner pried it all from me.

I realized now that Jessie probably had been anxious to learn the whole story herself. Despite her love for me, she must have had doubts, especially considering the factors at play: a dead mother; a newly smitten father; a stepmother smug about the prize she'd snagged and not pleased with the idea of sharing. It would have been easy for Jessie to imagine me acting out. In little ways at first, nothing atrocious, but then one event leading inexorably to another, with no chance of me ever going back. There had been so many moments that year, particularly as I lay in my bed in Oneonta—not the pink canopy I'd slept in at my old house but the narrow headboard-less one in Jessie's tiny guest room—when I'd wondered if I really *was* the evil one.

I picked up the paper and began to read.

Robin was referred to me at the age of 12, suffering from extreme stress. Her symptoms included headaches, tremors, and a self-soothing rocking motion. It was obvious she was an intelligent and thoughtful girl, but she was very withdrawn at this time. Her mother had died about two years before and her father had remarried fairly soon afterward.

Though initially Robin was uncommunicative, by the fifth session she began to open up about her experiences over the past year. Not long after her stepmother, Janice, moved in, she began to hide or stain Robin's belongings. It appears she did this primarily to incriminate Robin in her father's eyes—so that he'd withdraw from her.

Robin found proof of her stepmother's actions and alerted her father. She was sent to live with her aunt for the summer. During that time, her stepmother convinced the father that Robin had planted this evidence.

The situation accelerated once Robin returned home. Her father made it clear that he didn't believe her but he was hopeful Robin could learn from her mistakes. Robin was needy of her father's love and approval since her mother's death and this lack of belief in her was extremely difficult. The stepmother began locking Robin in the closet while her father was at work, knowing that if Robin reported it, the father wouldn't believe her.

It was in late November that the first symptoms of severe stress began to appear in Robin— headaches and tremors, mostly. She developed the rocking motion to help her cope.

I let the paper drop to the table. When I'd had tremors lately, they had felt familiar to me, but I'd forgotten I had also suffered from terrible headaches back then. I'd lost track, too, that the rocking motion that comforted me had started in the closet. I'd vaguely thought it had begun with my mother's death. I began to read again:

Whatever trauma Robin is experiencing now is complicated by the fact that she is still grieving over the loss of her mother.

There has been concern that Robin may have actually been responsible for the behavior and faked evidence as a way of acting out against the stepmother.

I have found no reason to suspect this. I do not believe Robin is capable of this kind of conceit. That said, Robin has been through considerable trauma, and she has psychological wounds to show for it. I recommend continued sessions for an indefinite period of time.

In so many ways, I realized, Janice and Vicky were alike. I hadn't been a real threat to either of them, but they had perceived me that way—as the interloper who could undo all that they'd claimed for themselves. And their plan had been the same: Convince people I was half-crazy, that I'd dreamed up an elaborate and dangerous scheme to portray myself as a victim.

I stood up from the table, stripped off my clothes, and plunged into the pool, exhilarated by the feel of the water on my naked body. I'd been so committed to work this summer that I hadn't been out of town any weekends, hadn't been swimming a single time. I swam lap after lap, caught up in the rhythm of my arms and legs slicing through the cool water. After finally climbing out, I wrapped myself in a beach towel and stood on the deck, thinking hard. Years ago, I had proved my innocence to Jessie and Mrs. Brenner. Once again, I would have to find a way to exonerate myself. In this case, it meant figuring out who'd had the motive, means, and opportunity to harm me.

As I'd realized earlier, I would have little chance attacking the situation from the outside. It would be like trying to ram a fortress with a straw. So I needed to work from the inside, and that meant recruiting an ally. Ann was out, but there might be someone else.

Over the past few days, I'd felt too overwhelmed to read emails or return calls, but I'd glanced occasionally at the screen of my iPhone and knew that a few people from work had reached out. Clutching the towel around me, I traipsed into the house and dug my phone from my purse.

I started scrolling down, bypassing emails from friends and reporters, as well as panicky ones from the book publishing team.

Maddy had emailed more than once. She was anxious to see me, she said, and had gone by my apartment looking for me. I emailed back, explaining that we couldn't meet because I was staying at Bettina's house in Westport, and I asked her to call me. I knew it wouldn't be smart to take her into my confidence, but she might have info I could use. Plus, talking to her would help me gauge whether she could possibly be behind what had happened. And there was one specific thing I needed to know from her.

There was nothing from Carter, of course. For the first time in days, I thought of the two of us in bed, the reckless pleasure and release I'd experienced on each occasion. There was no kidding myself. I felt more than a twinge of loss and regret.

To my surprise, there was an email from Alex Lucca. Three, in fact. He needed to talk to me, he said. It was important. Why so eager? I wondered.

When I called him, I reached voice mail, but fifteen minutes later, he phoned back. I could hear car horns honking in the background. He'd clearly gone down to the street in order to speak to me privately.

"How are you doing?" he said.

"I'm not great," I said. "But I appreciate your concern."

"I wanted to find out how you were, but I also have information that might be worthwhile."

I felt a jolt of adrenalin. "Okay," I said quietly. "I'm all ears."

"I don't think it's smart to talk on the phone. Can we meet in person?"

"I'm staying outside the city right now."

"How far away are you? I have a car. I could drive to you after the show this evening."

"I'm up in Westport, Connecticut. You wouldn't want to come all the way out here tonight."

"I don't mind. Robin, I really think you need to hear this."

I couldn't turn this down. I found the exact address on the mailing label of a magazine lying on the coffee table, and I gave it to him, knowing it would take at least an hour to drive here following the show.

After hanging up, I warned myself not to become excited, but I couldn't help feeling a surge of hope. There was one person on the inside who at least claimed he wanted to help. And that was a tiny start.

At around six, I finished the chicken salad I'd found in the fridge, eating it outside on the deck. The early-evening sky was streaked with pinks and reds, and the air began to fill with the rhythmic call of katydids. As I stood in the yard, I realized something funny. Despite the mess my life was in, for the first time in days, I actually felt safe, out of reach of my tormenter.

After dinner, I cleaned up the kitchen and tried leafing through magazines, but all I could think about was Alex and when he would be here. I walked back outside and stood for a while on the deck. The light, which had seemed to linger so long, finally faded and the air was cool. Outdoor security lights popped on, but the interior of Bettina's house was totally dark. I had assumed that Nancy was a live-in housekeeper, yet there was no sign of her. It meant that I would be all alone on the property tonight.

Back inside I turned on lamps, dug a sweater from my duffel bag, and slipped it on. At nine-thirty, I heard wheels on gravel and then the sound of a car door slamming. I watched from the doorway as Alex—I could tell by the tall, slim shape—emerged from around the corner of the main house and made his way in my direction.

I stepped outside and crossed the dark lawn to greet him. He was still in that work uniform of his—the white dress shirt paired with jeans—though he'd rolled up the sleeves. His hair was mussed a little, as if he'd driven with the window down. It was a relief to set eyes on him, but I warned myself to keep my guard up. I hardly knew him.

"I appreciate you coming, Alex," I said as he reached me. "Was the drive okay?"

"Yes, fine. It's good to see you, Robin."

Inside, I asked if he'd like something to drink, and he accepted a beer. I poured myself a glass of sparkling water.

"I feel terrible about all you've been going through," he said as we took seats at the small dining table.

"How much do you know?" I asked. I realized that it was odd to be sitting with him in a guesthouse of a Westport estate, like one of those improbable things that happen in dreams.

"More than most people, I think," he said.

"Why is that?" I asked, feeling a prick of concern.

"Other than Tom, no one around work has been told anything, though people are speculating like crazy. There are rumors that you had an affair—with Dave Potts or Carter or whoever. That you're addicted to painkillers. All sorts of crap. But by a fluke, I ended up hearing what really happened."

I stared at him, expectant.

"Tom confided the story to his partner, and he ended up blabbing to a lawyer pal who, coincidentally, is a friend of mine. So much for the cone of silence."

"What exactly did she say?" I asked, wondering if Alex knew less than he was letting on and was fishing.

He ran through a capsulized version of my story, with all the basic points correct, including the fact that I'd considered Vicky as a possible suspect.

"I can't believe they think you're responsible," he said at the end. "It's preposterous."

"Why are you so sure I'm not?" I asked.

"I spent four years in the DA's office, and I'm pretty good at spotting liars, narcissists, and sociopaths." He smiled. "You seem to own a lot of shoes, but that's the only obsession I've picked up on."

I smiled back. "I appreciate that endorsement."

His expression clouded. "Do you really think it's Vicky Cruz?"

I threw up my hands. "I don't know what to think anymore," I said. "There *is* circumstantial evidence pointing to her."

I told him about the remarks Vicky had made regarding Ambien and the makeup I used, as well as the hostility she'd directed at me in the corridor.

"Could she see you as a threat?"

"That's what I wondered initially, but maybe I over-reacted. Over the past few days, I've been trying to entertain other options. Different people at work."

"It can't be a very long list."

"I never set out to be adored by everyone, but most people appear to respect me. The only one who's seemed to have her knickers in a twist lately is Charlotte."

"I've noticed that," he said. "And she's been the one doing the most whispering and snickering about you. Says she saw you in the lobby yesterday morning and that you looked white as a ghost."

So I'd interpreted her expression correctly. "She clearly blames me, not herself, for her job woes. The question is whether she'd act on her pent-up animosity." I paused. "I feel awful saying this, but briefly, I wondered about Maddy. She seems to have developed a chip on her shoulder about me as well."

Alex scrunched his mouth. "I've worked with her closely lately, and she seems to hold you in awfully high regard."

It had helped to articulate my ruminations, but Alex had promised information, and that was what I was most eager for. He seemed to read my thoughts.

"Let *me* share now," he said. "Like I mentioned on the phone, I have a piece of information. And it's about Vicky."

Instinctively, I caught my breath.

"You know the night you found the bug in your drink?" he said. "I'm not sure if you were aware of this, but Vicky Cruz had come up to the newsroom around then."

"Yes, I knew that."

"At one point I came around the corner to that little area with the table just behind the set. Your coffee mug is always there, the one with your name on it, and a thermos they keep the coffee in. As I rounded the corner, I discovered Vicky just standing there.

"It seemed an odd place to find her," he added, narrowing his eyes at the memory. "Even odder was that a guilty look crossed her face when she saw me, as if I'd caught her at something. Just a micro expression, but it was definitely there. And then she was calling me sweetheart and asking if I knew whether there was any bottled water around our set."

"What you're saying is she might have dropped the bug in my coffee?"

"Possibly. I have no proof at all, but after I realized what had happened, I flashed back on her at the table. At the time, though, I didn't feel justified making any kind of insinuation. There was no evidence."

"Are you willing to go to Potts and Oliver with it now?"

"Absolutely. But I wanted to talk to you about it first. I'd like to make a suggestion, too. What I'm conveying is very circumstantial, so it might be best to present this in conjunction with anything else you have that could prove your innocence. Do you have a lawyer helping you put a defense together?"

"Not yet," I said. "And the so-called evidence against me is pretty damning."

I shared what Potts had revealed about the searches on my computer, how they'd been orchestrated while Keiki was at her desk, so it would have been tough for someone to have sneaked in. Alex listened pensively, his hazel eyes flickering.

"You know," he said. "There's a way someone can search from your computer remotely, so that it looks like you've done it yourself. They send you a phishing email with an attachment, and that in turn attaches what's called a botnet to your computer. It sits there unnoticed and allows the other person to download information."

"Why wouldn't Oliver have looked into that?" I said, flabbergasted.

"That kind of investigation has to be done by an outside forensics company, and from what I know, it's pricey. Once security became convinced you were behind everything, they probably didn't want to spend the money."

"That's appalling."

"I know. Can you recall any emails with attachments that were sent to your office computer lately? One you weren't expecting?"

"Not off the top of my head," I said, smiling woefully. I felt deflated. After Alex's call, I'd let myself become hopeful, but all I had was Vicky's proximity to my coffee mug. Once again, Alex seemed to read my thoughts.

"I want to help you, Robin. There's got to be a way to clear you."

"I'm not going to reject your offer. But where do we even start?"

"Over the next day or two, go back in your mind and see if you can remember receiving any unexpected emails with attachments. I also want you to list everyone you know at the network and any recollection you have of someone acting miffed at you, no matter how silly it seemed."

"Will do."

"That said, I think we should turn the spotlight on Vicky. She's the first person you suspected, so let's start with her and work our way from there."

"If she's done torturing me, how do we catch her at anything?"

"By checking out her past."

"Her past?"

"Yes. If there's one lesson I learned in the DA's office, it's that people who do bad things have generally done the same kind of thing before. Maybe not identical but close enough. I also want to find out how tech-oriented Vicky is. That could explain if she knew how to send a botnet."

"One point you should be aware of?" I said. "The brownie was left for me when Vicky was in D.C. So if she *was* after me, she didn't operate alone."

"Good to know."

I reached out and touched Alex's arm. "There's a chance, Alex, that you could put your own job in jeopardy by snooping around on my behalf."

He smiled warmly and ran a hand through his dark, wavy hair.

"It wouldn't be the end of the world not to cover underboobage anymore," he said. He glanced at his watch. "I better hit the road."

I walked him to his car. The night sky was practically white with stars, but there was no moon this evening, and Bettina's house was a dark, hulking shape.

"Have you watched the show the last few nights?" Alex asked.

"No, it would kill me to see it," I told him.

"If it's any consolation, it's a disaster. They've named Hadley as the temporary fill-in, but she couldn't do it tonight, so they tapped that chick Erin from the morning show *This Just In*. Carter ended up calling in sick tonight. Apparently, he despises her."

I didn't want to hear any more.

"Drive safely," I told him as he slid into the car. I felt more than grateful for his visit.

"Yup. Give me a few days to start my research, and then I'll be back in touch."

As he drove off, I hurried back toward the guesthouse. Inside, I slammed the door tight and pushed the bolt in place. It was late, but I wanted to mentally review what Alex and I had discussed. I set a kettle of water on the stove for tea.

When the teakettle whistled, I offed the flame, letting the room go silent again, and filled a mug with water. As I went to set the kettle back on the burner, I heard a noise outside the house. A snap.

I held my breath.

Another snap. It was like the sound of someone's boot coming down on a twig and breaking it in two.

Chapter 20

I froze, the teakettle still in my hand. Had Alex returned? Or was it Nancy, finally back? I hadn't heard a car.

My eyes flew to the door. I waited for a knock, but it didn't come.

"Nancy?" I called out. My voice was like a mouse squeak. I spun toward the back of the house. On some level, I'd sensed that the sound had come from behind me.

Quietly, I set the kettle down and listened hard. Nothing. Except the katydids. I'm just jittery being alone, I told myself. It was the wind, or the house creaking. I let out my breath.

I dropped a tea bag into the mug, dunking it a few times. But my body was on guard, straining to hear. Stop, I told myself. Who would be out there, anyway?

And then I heard it again. Not a twig this time. It was the rustle of bushes out back, as if someone were brushing past. Fear shot through me. I looked toward the back wall of the room again, at the row of three windows. The drapes were all drawn. I'd done that earlier, before Alex arrived. As I stood there watching, the fuzzy silhouette of a person appeared briefly on the curtain and just as quickly vanished.

My legs seemed to melt from underneath me. I glanced back at the door again; yes, I'd bolted it. But with terror mounting, I remembered: I'd opened the back door earlier—the one off my bedroom. And I hadn't locked it.

I launched myself away from the counter, pushing off with my hand, and nearly hurled my body into the bedroom. I'd left one light on in there, the one on the bedside table, and I could see the back door. It was closed. Yet I could sense a presence on the other side.

I lunged toward it. The bolt was like the one on the other door. I fumbled with it clumsily, but finally I shoved it into the slot.

I hurried back into the great room. Phone, I commanded myself. I upended my purse until my iPhone bounced in its rubber case onto the coffee table. I snatched it and tapped 911.

"What is your emergency?" the operator said.

"Um—" I ran back for the magazine with the label, blurted out the address, and told her there was a prowler.

"Is the house secure?"

"The doors are locked. I don't know about the windows."

"I'm dispatching the police. I need you to stay on the line with me until they arrive."

"Just tell them to hurry," I begged. "*Please.*"

Outside I heard another sound, a scrape of shoe on pavement. On the pool deck.

"The person's still *here*," I whispered hoarsely.

"The police are close. Continue to stay on the line."

There were no sounds after that. Just my heart pounding in my ears. Finally, I heard the police car, its siren screaming in the night.

"The police—they're here," I said to the operator. "Tell them I'm in the guesthouse. With the lights on."

A minute later, there was a sharp knocking and a voice calling, "Police."

I unbolted the door and opened it a few inches with the chain on. Two cops were standing there, an older woman and a younger guy, both with their guns drawn. I undid the chain and flung open the door.

"I'm okay," I said. "Just scared."

"You reported a prowler?" the woman said, holstering her gun. She was about forty, with black hair peeking out from under her cap. Her name tag said Orsini.

"Yes, I saw the person's silhouette in the window."

The two cops exchanged a look.

"What?" I asked.

"There was a car taking off just as we approached," Orsini said.

"You saw it come out of the driveway?" I asked. I hadn't heard a vehicle.

"It appeared to be parked along the road, just by the start of the driveway," she said. "Dark, could have been a luxury vehicle. We dispatched another patrol car to try to find it, but it's going to be tough without a license plate number. What about the main house, is anyone up there?"

I explained, stumbling over the words, that I was a houseguest, Bettina was in the city, and the house-keeper apparently didn't live in.

"Does anyone else know you're staying here?"

"A work colleague. He was here earlier—we had a few things to go over. But he left almost thirty minutes ago."

"Maybe he came back," the young cop said.

"He wouldn't sneak around that way," I said.

"We'll take a look around and be back in a minute," Orsini said.

While they were outside, I snatched my laptop out of my tote bag and checked the train schedule. The last train was leaving for Manhattan in two minutes. Shit, I thought. *I can't stay here.* Should I hire a cab to drive me all the way back there? But then I'd be facing the press again.

I looked up as the door swung open.

"The ground's dry, so unfortunately, there aren't any footprints," Orsini said as the two reentered the house. "There's no one around now."

"I don't feel safe here," I said. "But I don't have any way to get back to the city."

"We just came on our shift, so we'll keep an eye on the place tonight," she said, her face sympathetic. "I don't think the person will be back. We had our lights flashing, and I'm sure he saw us coming."

"He?" I said. "You could see the driver was a male?"

"No," she said. "That was just a manner of speaking."

They checked the windows and the rear door before they left. As soon as I'd let them out, I threw the bolt and dragged the dining table in front of the main door. Then I scrambled into the bedroom and shoved a bureau against the door in there.

It's almost funny, I thought. My life goes to hell, and now *this.* The top I was wearing was damp, and I peeled it off, replacing it with another from my duffel bag.

One option I had was to spend the rest of the night in a hotel, taking a cab there. But not only would it be pricey, I also might be recognized, resulting in the press being tipped off. I mulled over what the cops had said. There was little chance of the prowler returning, knowing that the police had been alerted. I decided to tough it out and stay.

But there was no way I was going to bed. I dragged a pillow and a blanket to the couch and set my phone on the coffee table, along with one of the fireplace pokers.

Should I call Bettina? I wondered. She would need to be informed. But it was after midnight, and I didn't want to wake her knowing there was little she could do.

My brain was muddled from fear, but I tried to make myself think about what the cops had asked: *Who knows you're here?* Bettina, of course. The housekeeper, Nancy. And *Maddy*, I remembered. I'd confided that I was staying at Bettina's. She might have let the information slip, and it would have been easy enough for someone to track down the actual address.

There was another comment from the cops that echoed in my head: *Maybe he came back.*

Would Alex have returned? The sounds had occurred a few minutes after he'd driven off. Enough time for him to park the car along the side of the road and traipse back in the darkness. His car was a dark Audi. A luxury car.

But it made no sense. Why would he want to spy on me?

For the rest of the night, I sat bolt upright on the couch, my head jerking constantly as my eyes chased any little sound. I was like a bird on a wire.

At first light, I moved the pillow against the armrest and let my head flop on it. My whole body ached—from fatigue, from stress, from being buffeted all night by fear. I closed my eyes and dropped into sleep like a performer falling toward a circus net.

When I woke, the sun was streaming through the sides of the curtains, and someone was pounding on the door.

"Ms. Trainer, are you in there?" It sounded like Nancy.

I hauled myself across the room, shoved the table over, and swung open the door.

"Is everything all right?" she asked, startled by the sight of the table.

"Unfortunately, no," I said. "There was a prowler last night. I had to contact the police."

Her hand flew to her mouth. "A prowler?" she exclaimed. "Dear mother of God. Did he get in here?"

"No, and I don't think the main house, either, but you'll need to check. Do you not live on the property?"

"I do," she said. "But my sister was feeling poorly, and I spent the night with her."

"We need to inform Bettina immediately. And though I appreciate the offer to stay here, I don't think I could handle another night. I'd like to take a train back to the city in the next hour or two."

"Oh, but Ms. Lane is arriving this morning," she said anxiously. "The cook has come in and is going to make lunch for both of you. I can take you to the train afterward."

"Um, all right," I said. If the chance to speak to Bettina was happening today, I couldn't forgo it.

After Nancy left, I staggered into the shower. As I was toweling off, Bettina called to check on me. She said she would be there at one and would debrief me then.

I did my best to pull myself together. I blew out my hair and pulled on a light cashmere sweater over a pair of white jeans. I applied a little makeup, but my face was drawn and haggard, hardly something a few swipes of bronzer could rescue.

I made coffee and phoned the police station. The two cops who'd answered the call were now off duty, but according to the officer who answered, no car had been located.

Mug in hand, I wandered outside and made my way around to the back of the house to the spot where I'd seen the prowler standing. There were a few feet of lawn that gave way to woods, a mix of fir trees and deciduous. I searched the ground with my eyes, realizing how unlikely it would be for me to find any kind of clue, like a button or cigarette butt. Indeed there was nothing, just random piles of twigs and pine needles.

I examined the windows next. On one of the great room windows, there was a gap between the frame and the cream-colored curtains inside. I leaned forward and peered in. The person could have caught a glimpse of me easily.

Maybe it had been a Peeping Tom. Or a burglar. But it all seemed too coincidental. Could it have been someone from the press, I wondered for the first time, perhaps even a reporter from Bettina's own website?

I hurried back inside and pulled out my laptop. Before heading up to lunch, I wanted to research botnets. I found several articles and learned that they worked just as Alex had described. All someone needed to do was send an email with an attachment, counting on the receiver to open it.

I no longer had access to emails that had been sent to my office computer, so I had only my memory to rely on. I thought back day by day, but it was fruitless.

Anyone at the network could have forwarded me an attachment that seemed work-related—a schedule, for instance, or a company announcement—and it wouldn't have struck me as odd.

Frustrated, I gave up for the time being and dug a notebook and pen from my purse. I jotted down the phrase "Who's doing this to me?" I racked my brain, trying to think of anyone whose name had not bubbled up yet. I remembered a production assistant who'd been weirdly hostile to both Carter and me during the launch of *Pulse*. But I'd heard since that he'd moved back to L.A.

At five of one, I hiked over to the main house. Nancy and another woman were shuffling around the long brick terrace at the rear, and as I approached, I saw that one of the umbrella tables had been set for lunch.

"Please sit down and let me bring you a beverage," Nancy said. "Ms. Lane will be out in just a moment."

I took a seat as instructed and watched as Nancy filled my glass from a crystal pitcher filled with ice water, sliced lemons, and twigs of rosemary.

"Would you care for a glass of wine?" she asked.

I said no, thank you. I wanted my wits about me at lunch. From the time I'd agreed to come here, I'd been thinking of how I should handle Bettina. Though I needed whatever help I could wrangle from her, I also had to be careful. She ran a huge website, and one of their missions was reporting on the foibles of people just like me.

"Robin!"

It was Bettina's voice, coming from behind me, and I rose to greet her. She was dressed in a crisp white pantsuit accented with a chunky gold necklace, and her pale pink lipstick was luminescent, playing off her jewelry. Instead of a double air kiss, I was offered a hug. A little brittle, but probably the very best Bettina had to give.

"This must all be dreadful for you," she said, taking a seat. "The prowler, the mess at the network . . . Nancy, some rosé, please. Will you have wine, darling? I'm indulging in a glass."

"Not right this second, thank you."

Nancy and her helper slipped away. Perhaps the request for rosé had been code for "Leave us alone right now."

"I want to hear everything," Bettina said. "But tell me about last night first. I've called the security company, and they're coming by as soon as we're finished with lunch."

I explained the little I knew. The footsteps; the silhouette; the car the police had seen pulling away.

"How terrifying. It's clearly time for me to hire a guard for nights. Other people have them out here."

I glanced down at the table and turned the pale blue linen napkin over in my hands. "I'm not a hundred percent sure you need one," I said, looking back up. "Because I think the prowler had something to do with me."

She must have entertained that possibility but gave nothing away with her expression. "A reporter, perhaps?" she asked.

"Maybe. Or someone spying on me, trying to see what I was up to. I need to ask you, did you tell anyone I was here?"

She dabbed with her long slim fingers at something invisible in one corner of her mouth. "Not anyone in editorial," she said. "I did mention it to a member of my executive team. I told him I was worried about you and that I'd invited you to stay with me."

That annoyed me, but I didn't let on.

Nancy returned then, poured a glass of wine for Bettina, and plunged the bottle into a silver bucket filled with ice. The other woman set down bowls of cold soup, fragrant with cucumbers.

As soon as they were gone, Bettina leaned forward. "Talk to me now—about work. I want to help you, Robin."

I sampled the soup, buying a few extra moments to think. "First tell me what you've learned," I said.

She shrugged a padded shoulder. "Not very much. That PR friend of yours has kept a tight lid on this. I heard that you acted unethically. And then tried to blame a colleague."

Inside I flinched at the words but I held her eyes, keeping my emotions in check. "I want your help, Bettina," I said. "But I need assurance that everything I tell you is off the record."

"You have my word, darling."

"For weeks, someone at work has tried to sabotage me," I said. I told her about the note at her party, the acid in my makeup, the brownie laced with zolpidem, and how in the end it was made to appear as if I was responsible.

She leaned back in her chair, absorbing it all. A breeze blew across the table, rustling the yellow petals of the flowers in the vase.

"This is appalling, Robin," she said at last. "I'm so terribly sorry."

I sensed there was more, something she wasn't saying. Her face tightened with worry.

"What is it, Bettina?" I urged.

"Your saboteur," she said. "I think I know who it is."

Chapter 21

I waited, stunned by her comment. She may have heard rumors, but how could she know what the truth was?

Bettina took a long sip of rosé, tugged the bottle from the silver bucket and splashed more wine into her glass. "What I'm going to share with you is top-secret," she said. "You asked for my confidence a minute ago, and I need to be sure I have yours."

"You have my word."

"Are you aware of a man named Tony Judd?"

I shook my head.

"He's made a fortune on the digital front, and he wants a fresh project now—one that's glitzy and glamorous. You don't recall him?"

"Would I have met him when I worked for you?"

"Not necessarily. But he was at your book party that night, darling. I invited him myself."

She'd tried to say it casually enough, but I felt something stir in me, the way a memory—or a warning—detaches from part of your brain and begins to surface.

"I may have been introduced to him," I said. "But it doesn't ring a bell."

"Well, he asked me to assist in his efforts, and I've been working with him, trying to find just the right thing. He's decided to buy your network."

The last line practically blew me off my chair. I hadn't heard a single rumor about any kind of takeover.

"Needless to say," she added, "that's making a few people, particularly Dave Potts, extremely unhappy."

Of course it would. If the network were sold, Potts's job would have next-to-zero shelf life, which might explain why he'd acted more gruff than usual lately. And if the network were rebranded, almost everyone would be impacted.

I couldn't see how that connected to the attacks against me, though. "When is this supposed to happen?"

"It's in the early stages, but it's picking up speed. So far we've contained the information, but it won't be long before news leaks out."

"Who's my saboteur, and what does the sale have to do with any of it?"

Bettina took another long sip of wine. "It's a guess," she said. "And for now it must stay completely between the two of us. I'm wondering if Potts is the guilty party."

"*Potts*?" I exclaimed.

"Deep down, David is a *nasty* man. I wouldn't put it past him to want to wreak havoc with you."

"But for what purpose?" I said.

"With you gone, your show will be in a tailspin. He may think that could discourage Judd as a buyer and thwart the sale. Or he's exacting revenge on the network, making sure we end up with damaged goods."

"We?"

"I'm an investor, darling. But just a small one."

That, I realized, was why she was so keenly interested in aiding me. She wanted to know exactly what was going down and what the ramifications could be for her and her partners. She might be using me, but still, I needed her. If she was right, we were in the same fight, which meant there was a chance she would want to save my ass.

"Tell me what you think I should do," I said.

Again the dabbing at her mouth. "I have to mull it over, darling. Let me figure out the best way to attack this. I'm going to make a few calls, and then I'll follow up with you."

Two hours later, I was in the back of Bettina's black Mercedes, headed toward the city. She'd told me to take advantage of her car and driver since she would be working out of her Westport house for the next day or two while she dealt with the security situation. Over the poached salmon, she'd pressed me for any theories I might have about the episodes, but I claimed to be clueless. There was no way I was going to raise Vicky's name with her. I didn't know how far I could trust Bettina.

She had also urged me to stay another night, saying I could use a bedroom in the main house, but she hadn't seemed surprised when I'd declined.

Before I packed up, I'd phoned my doorman. The vultures had dispersed, searching for scraps elsewhere. *Vultures.* Without thinking, I'd used that word to describe people who were basically in my line of work.

I was mystified I hadn't heard back from Maddy, so I emailed her a second time, alerting her that I'd be back in the city that night and would appreciate it if she could call or, even better, stop by my apartment. As I ducked into the car, she texted me, saying she would come by after the show.

I let my body sag back against the seat. Despite the shower I'd taken earlier, I felt grubby. I was also tired, my eyelids begging to close. I couldn't sleep now. I had to think about the bomb Bettina had tossed on the table at lunch.

Maybe it wasn't so far-fetched to believe in Potts blowing up my career for his own needs. In the back of my mind, I could hear remarks made about him after I'd been hired: "He can be a real a-hole." "Don't cross him, because he's vindictive as hell."

If it were true, he would do everything in his power to block my access to my work computer so an outside firm could examine it.

Despite Potts's possible motive, my thoughts were tugged back to Vicky. What if she were working in conjunction with Potts? One way or the other, I wasn't going to discourage Bettina from assisting me. It was another hand reaching down into the rubble, and I would grab it.

I chuckled to myself as a thought shot to the front of my brain: That was why Bettina had thrown the book party for me. It had been a sneaky little tactic for placing Judd in a room with Potts and all the major players from the network. He'd be able to size people up firsthand.

On my fingers, I counted backward. The party had been only three weeks ago, but it seemed an eternity.

I'd been so smug during the early part of the night, reveling in the return of my good fortune and certain I'd never lose it again. *Ha!* I doubted I'd ever look at the photos again, the ones of me beaming at the camera in my sexy black dress and fuck-you shoes.

Photos. I gasped in surprise, and the driver, curious, glanced into the rearview mirror. There'd been lots from that night, but I thought specifically of one batch emailed to me right after the party, with a return address I hadn't recognized. That could have been the attachment that had allowed a botnet to sit on my computer. I clenched my fist in triumph.

I had to let Alex know. And I had to find a way to share with him the relevant aspects of Bettina's theory without violating my pledge of secrecy about the sale. I texted him, announcing I had news.

There was only light traffic on the route to Manhattan, and we made the journey in just over an hour. After last night, all I wanted was to be back in my own space. But as soon as I crossed the threshold into my apartment, I felt a fresh sense of unease. My living room was utterly silent, yet there was an eerie sense of something lingering, as if, moments before I'd arrived, people had been sitting in the room and tiptoed away, closing the door with a hush. This was where my great new life had been happening, but it was all over now.

Don't go there, I told myself. I would have to find a way to start again yet another time. I realized then that I hadn't heard from Richard.

"I was just about to get in touch," he said after I phoned him. "Though unfortunately, I have nothing good to report. They're going to take a few more days to present the financial package. And they're refusing to discuss the dismissal further."

"I may have figured out how the Internet searches were conducted from my office," I said. "Someone on the inside is assisting me."

"Robin, I've been giving this a great deal of thought, especially after our conversation with Steve Katz. I really think we should let sleeping dogs lie."

"You aren't suggesting I do nothing, are you?" I said.

"If you continue to press them and make demands, there may not be a payout."

"I'm looking for more than payout, Richard. I want to be vindicated."

"There's just so much evidence against you. Let's be smart about this."

"I *am* being smart. And you need to consider whether you want to be on my team or not. I'm sorry, but I have to sign off now."

Maybe I'd been rash, speaking to him that way. But I wasn't going to let him bulldoze me into acquiescing.

Maddy arrived exactly at nine. Her hair was in a gleaming blond twist, and her clothes were all career girl—a sleeveless pink dress that she'd paired with black patent heels. Funnily, the type of outfit I'd worn every day to work.

"Omigod, Robin," she said hugging me. "I'm so relieved to see you. Are you okay?"

"I'm better, thanks," I said, ushering her away from the doorway so we couldn't be overheard.

"I'm sorry I didn't call you yesterday. Carter was off, so they had two substitutes, and it was all such a hot mess, I never had a chance."

"That's okay, you're here now. I've opened white wine in the living room. Why don't we go in there and sit down?"

As she perched on the end of a couch cushion, I poured her a glass of wine and then a small one for myself. "Do you know anything at all about my situation?" I asked.

"People are talking about it—I mean, everybody is whispering—but they're not saying anything to the interns. I guess they think we're going to post it on Instagram or something. Are you going to another network? Is that why you left?"

God, that was a laugh. "Not at the moment, no. Tell me, has anyone in management asked you questions about me?"

"You mean like Tom?" she said. "No."

"What about a man named William Oliver? Did he try to talk to you?"

She wrinkled her nose. "No, I've never heard of him."

"I need to ask you this, Maddy. Did you say anything to anyone about what happened years ago with my father?"

"Of course not," she said, laying a hand on her chest. "I'd never do that. It's a private family matter."

Was that the truth? She seemed anxious, though it might have been from just being there with me. I'd gotten fired for a reason she didn't know, and regardless of her concern for me, she was now collaborating with the enemy.

"That's good. You—you haven't felt any repercussions at work, have you?" I asked. "I mean, because you're related to me?"

"No, nothing like that. I'm not sure most people know we're related. Though Charlotte asked me if I'd heard from you, like she knows about our connection."

"Charlotte?" I said, alarmed. "What did she say, exactly?"

"She just asked if I knew what had happened to you and whether you'd landed on your feet."

"Oh, really?" I said. That was the second reference to her nosiness in twenty-four hours. "Don't tell her anything. Her concern isn't genuine."

"Okay. But is there anything I can do to help, Robin?"

"Actually, there *is* something," I said. "I don't want you to put your work situation in any jeopardy, but I'd like you to keep your ears open for me. If you hear something you think I might need to know, will you call me?"

"Of course."

"Enough about me. School must be starting soon, right? Have you figured out what hours you'll work once your courses begin?"

"Yes, I'm sorting that out. It's been such a fun summer, I kind of hate the idea of going back to classes."

"Are you seeing anyone special these days?" I realized I had never asked her that question.

"There's someone I like," she said. "Right now we're just friends, but it's pretty clear he's interested, too." She drained the last bit of wine from her glass. "Well, I should go. I have to spend time on campus tomorrow morning before work."

I walked her to the door and hugged her goodbye.

"Oh, one last thing," I said. "And I won't be mad if the answer is yes; I just need to know. Did you tell anyone at work that I was in Westport last night?"

She pressed her lips together tightly and flicked her eyes to the left for a moment.

"I'm so sorry, Robin, but I told Keiki," she said, looking back to me. "It slipped out. She was packing up your office, getting ready to send your stuff to you, and I told her you might not be at your apartment, that you were at Bettina's house. But she was the only one."

"That's okay," I said.

As I was closing the door behind her, I heard my phone ringing from my purse. It was Alex. And I could see on the screen that I had missed an earlier call from him.

"You've got news?" he said after I answered.

"Yes, plenty." I relayed the information about the prowler.

"That's terrifying," he said. "Do you think it's connected to everything else?"

"Yes, but that's my instinct talking. I have no proof."

He sighed in frustration. "I felt a little weird as I was pulling away last night. It seemed so desolate, and I didn't love the idea of you being alone there. I should have tried to convince you to leave."

"I wouldn't have left then, so don't beat yourself up about it. And I had lunch with Bettina, which was good. Seeing her reminded me of my book party, and that prompted a thought on how the botnet may have ended up on my computer."

I told him about the party photos from the mysterious sender.

"That could definitely be it," he said. "When you're ready to go to management, you can have them search the address the photos came from. It's probably a temporary address, but it's a start."

"There's something else, but I can only give the bare outlines," I said. "I learned that there might be a reason Potts would want me out of there, and he could be the one orchestrating this whole thing."

"Why destroy his new hit show?"

"I can't go into the reason. But it needs to be factored in."

"Gotcha. In the meantime, I've been making calls. It's going to be a bit slow going, because I don't want to raise any red flags."

"I'll be patient," I said. "I can't thank you enough for this."

That night, despite how exhausted I was, sleep proved elusive. As I lay there, I replayed my conversation with Maddy. She'd let it *slip* to Keiki that I was at Bettina's. That wasn't the first time she'd shared info she shouldn't have. Was she just twenty-one and careless, or was there more going on?

The next day I left my apartment only once, to stretch my legs in the neighborhood, wearing my baseball cap and sunglasses. I ordered food over the phone and had it delivered.

Later I spent time online doing research on Vicky. I read far more about her than I had that day in my office, but I found nothing truly incriminating. She was a bitch who liked to kick ass and take names but there was no sign she'd ever gone beyond that.

I also forced myself to finally connect by email with Claire, the book publicist.

"It's so good to finally hear from you," she wrote back, clearly uncomfortable with me being M.I.A. "We would love to have a sit-down conversation with you at your earliest convenience to discuss how to proceed with our plan in light of these new circumstances. The good news is that sales are up and there's been a huge demand for interviews in the past two days."

Of course. The woman who'd written about secrets now had a big, fat one of her own. I wrote back, advising Claire to continue rolling out the guest blogs, but not to count on me for interviews at this time. I ignored the meeting request.

I thought I'd hear from Alex, but by late Thursday, there was still no word; nor from Bettina. I'd felt optimistic from the scraps I'd been thrown, and it was in danger of dissolving. I scrubbed my kitchen, trying to control my agitation.

On Friday night, just after eight, Alex called. "I think I may have hit pay dirt," he said.

"Tell me," I said.

"Remember what I said to you in Westport? How someone who does a bad thing has probably done the same thing in the past, that it never just comes out of nowhere?"

"Yes," I said, my heart beating fast.

"If Vicky *was* the one who did those things to you, you're not the first woman she tried to destroy."

Chapter 22

Yes, I thought. Finally. "Who else?" I asked. "And where?"

"Up in Albany," he said. "A reporter. Or rather, a former reporter. Her name's Sharon Hayes, and she's a real estate agent these days. After her stint twenty years ago, she never worked in TV again."

"What did Vicky do to her?"

"I'm not sure of all the details. I talked to Sharon briefly on the phone, and she said that Vicky not only targeted her but made it look like she was the one responsible. It led to Sharon being fired. She doesn't want to say anything more until she meets us in person."

I let out a long breath. "How did you find all this out?"

He snorted. "I called friends, and friends of friends, at Vicky's former workplaces, saying I was exploring my next step professionally and wanted to pick their brains. Then I shifted the conversation around to a little gossip."

"That must have been tough," I said. "You seem like the least gossipy person I've met."

"Somehow I managed." I sensed him smiling. "I started with the Chicago station. When I told this producer on staff that I knew Vicky Cruz once worked there, he jumped at the chance to bash her. Said she was pure evil, the type who ran over everyone in her quest for the six and eleven anchor jobs. Then I went on to Albany, one of her first jobs, and the person I talked to there coughed up Sharon's name."

"What's the next step?" I warned myself not to get giddy, but I couldn't tamp it down.

"She's willing to meet tomorrow. I thought we could drive up to Albany together, if that works for you."

"Of course," I said. After feeling paralyzed, I was now on a train that was moving fast.

"A word of warning, though," Alex said. His tone sounded suddenly playful. "She wants to meet at International House of Pancakes. Are you going to be okay going into one of those?"

I laughed, the first time I'd done so in days. "If she tells me what I need to know, I'll eat a double stack of flapjacks with whipped cream."

"I'll believe that when I see it. She wants to meet at four, so why don't we leave the city around noon? It should only take about three hours to drive there but I want to allow extra time."

"Should I come to you?"

"No, I'll swing by and pick you up."

"Okay. But wait, what about your volunteer work?"

"Huh?"

"Your work at the halfway house on Saturdays. Is it a problem to miss it?"

"Oh—it's a slow time right now. I wasn't planning on going in."

"I'll see you tomorrow, then. Thank you, Alex. I feel completely grateful about all of this."

He picked me up right on time, dressed in his casual weekend look. I'd opted for black pants and a simple short-sleeved blouse. I needed to make a connection with this woman, and it wouldn't help to strut through the door of IHOP in head-to-toe Michael Kors.

"How about listening to some Neko Case?" Alex asked as we pulled away from my building.

"Sure," I said, surprised. "I love her." I fastened my seat belt and stretched out my legs. For the first time in days, I felt emboldened, in charge of my destiny.

"And I picked us up a couple of sandwiches," Alex said, cocking his head toward the backseat. "Help yourself."

"Perfect. I've been so hyped up about today, I hadn't even factored in lunch."

"I don't blame you. This is important, and we have to play it right."

"How exactly did you find Sharon?"

"Through a guy named Nate, a friend's uncle who had been the promotion director for the station while Vicky was there. He's retired now, so I felt I could pump him without being cagey. He left the station for another one in the area a year into Vicky's stint, but it was enough time to get a bead on her. As you'd expect, she was a real fireball. People were impressed, he said, but also intimidated. Vicky took no prisoners. You didn't dare cross her. And before long, there were rumors that she played dirty."

"Dirty how?"

"He said she'd steal message slips off people's desks, looking for story tips to hijack, that sort of thing. Management let the stuff slide; they were intimidated by her, too, but they recognized her value. Before long, she was subbing as an anchor. I pressed Nate whether there had ever been specific problems with another woman, and that's when he told me about Sharon.

"She'd grown up in the area and had been covering sports for about three years before Vicky arrived. Nice girl, he said. She wasn't aiming for the big time, but she had a lot of natural charisma, and viewers liked her."

"I found a couple of old clips of hers on YouTube last night," I said. "She was a natural at sports."

"I checked them out, too. As you know, sports isn't generally a track to anchoring, but she ended up pinch-hitting one weekend, and she was good at it. She often worked a sixth day in the week just for a chance to anchor."

"Ah, so a rivalry was born the minute Vicky walked in the door of the station."

"In Nate's opinion, Sharon was never the ferocious type, like Vicky. He said she underestimated herself, and when Vicky was tapped to anchor, Sharon tended to think, She's good, she's better than me, and I just need to work harder. About six months after he left, Nate heard that Sharon had been let go. According to the grapevine, she'd accused Vicky of harassment. That's what we need her to share with us."

Please, I begged silently, let it be close enough that there's a clear connection to my situation. This was the biggest thing I had. "How do you want to play the interview?" I asked. "I've talked to my share of bratty celebrities, but you know the best way to deal with a witness."

"We need to avoid coming on too strong. Even though she's volunteered to talk, she could pull back if we pounce. I think it's key for you to try to bond with her. The overriding message should be: 'What can we do to make sure this doesn't happen again to someone else?' "

"Got it." I settled back into the seat and tried to will the ride to go faster. I just wanted to be there and find out what had happened to Sharon Hayes.

We reached Albany forty-five minutes before we needed to. Alex suggested we grab coffee from a small café about a mile from the IHOP. It had been sunny when we left New York, but the sky was overcast now, and when I stepped from the car, the air was cool.

"So much for the dog days of summer in Albany," I said.

"August is tricky up here. You can end up with scorching days, but you also start to get that first hint of fall."

"Have you spent much time in this area?"

He smiled. "Summer camp in the Adirondacks. Farther north, but we always drove by here on our way up from the city."

"I thought you were from the Philly area," I said, realizing I had never asked.

"I went to Penn undergrad, but I grew up on the Upper West Side. My father taught at Columbia."

The café was just a quarter full; the only customers seemed to be nearby office workers taking a break.

We ordered and found a small Formica-topped table. I took a sip of coffee and then set the mug down, staring into the blackness.

"You look worried," Alex said.

"I am, a little. Right now this is my only lead. Except for those photos someone emailed me. And they could simply be from a person whose address I didn't recognize."

"Wait—I was so caught up talking to you about Sharon Hayes, I forgot to mention this. It turns out Vicky *is* a bit of a techie."

"You're kidding. How did you find out?"

"Maddy, of all people."

What the hell was she up to now? "She's not snooping around, is she?"

"No, no. Not as far as I'm aware, anyway. As I mentioned, she's been coming to me for help lately, trying not to repeat her mistakes. There was the Baylor fuckup, and she admitted that when you'd given her a research assignment, she asked for help from a producer on Vicky's team."

"True," I said, frowning. I'd told Maddy not to talk to anyone about it.

"Since she'd opened the door about Vicky's producer, I asked if the guy liked his job. She told me he'd never revealed much other than the fact that no one should ever underestimate Vicky. He said that she was fluent in Spanish and French but never let on—better for eavesdropping—and that she was a whiz with technology."

"So she could have known how to attach the botnet."

"For sure. She may not have needed any accomplices."

I thought for a second. "That doesn't explain the brownie. Vicky was in D.C. that day, so if she *is* behind everything, a cohort must have put it there."

"Then we need to find out who on her team accompanied her to D.C. and who stayed behind." He glanced at his watch. "We should split. We want to be the first to arrive."

Though breakfast hours were long over, the smells of bacon grease and syrup greeted us as we opened the door to the IHOP. We were ahead of Sharon, so we took a booth and waited. I sat with my back to the door, and Alex, across from me, kept watch. I was anxious, but I knew I couldn't let it show.

At two minutes to four, I saw Alex's body shift expectantly. "I think this is her," he said under his breath. He lifted his hand in a wave and slid out of the booth to introduce himself.

As soon as Sharon approached, I could see why he'd recognized her from her old video clips. She'd put on weight but not a lot, and her hair was still long and blond. The almost luscious prettiness she'd possessed in her twenties was gone, though. She'd been in the sun too much, and her skin showed it. And that sparkly quality she'd had on the air, the phenomenon that happens when you think of yourself as the luckiest girl in the world, was gone as well.

Alex gestured for Sharon to sit where he'd been, and he scooted in next to me. He introduced us, and we shook hands across the booth. She looked as nervous as I felt.

"Thanks so much for meeting with us," Alex said.

"You drove an awful long way to see me," she said.

Her tone was defensive. Great, I thought. Don't tell me we're going to need a pickax to extricate anything from her.

"There's a lot at stake," Alex said. "Like I mentioned on the phone, it appears that Vicky has sabotaged Robin's job."

The waitress swung by at that moment. None of us ordered anything other than coffee.

"First I need to know what you want to do with the information," Sharon said.

"Right now we'd just love to hear your story and compare notes," Alex said. "Hopefully, we can use it to help Robin reclaim her job."

Sharon lowered her head so that she was staring straight down at the table. Was she having second thoughts? Had she lured us up here for nothing?

"Sharon, we so need your help," I said as gently as I could. "My career may be beyond full repair, but at least we can make sure Vicky doesn't do this to anyone else."

She kept studying the table, her eyes flicking over the surface.

"Please, Sharon," I pleaded. "I know it must be hard, but—"

Alex pressed his shoe against mine, warning me not to push too hard. At the same moment, Sharon looked up.

"It's not that," she said. "It's just such a relief. Vicky Cruz ruined my career, and for twenty years, the only people who believed me were my mom and a few pals from the station. I feel vindicated."

I wanted to yelp with gratitude.

"Can you tell us what happened then?" Alex urged.

"When Vicky was hired, I immediately thought we were going to be good buds," Sharon said. "The other women at the station were all married, and it was nice to have another single gal around. We started going bar-hopping occasionally after work. I even fixed her up with my friend Neil."

She shook her head in dismay at the memory. "But before long, I got this weird vibe from her. She seemed kind of sneaky, and she started verbally bashing other people at the station to me. Then Neil stopped seeing her and told me that it was partly because Vicky had bombarded him with questions about me, even mocked me to him. I started making excuses not to grab drinks with her, though I tried to be friendly toward her at work, just to maintain the peace.

"One week I was asked to anchor the Saturday-night news when the regular female anchor was going to be off—that was something I did from time to time—but I woke up that morning with a terrible tummy virus and I told the news director I'd have to bail. Vicky found out and volunteered to take my place. I had to admit, she was super at it, probably better than me, but my boss was really loyal. Though they did let Vicky sub sometimes after that, they kept using me, too. I sensed that really bugged her. Before long, she stopped talking to me. And right after that is when the real trouble started."

The waitress slid the coffee in front of us. I was surprised to see Sharon's cup shake as she lifted it to her lips.

"Take your time," I told her. "We have all night if you want."

"It was awful," she said. "She—she started stalking me."

"Stalking?" I exclaimed. I'd been waiting for words of recognition, but this wasn't one.

"Yup. It started with hang-ups at night and on the weekend. Next I got these horrible letters and stuff in the mail. The notes called me a slut and a whore. And then she began watching the townhouse I lived in."

"How did you know it was her doing this?" Alex asked.

"At first I didn't. I could just see a figure in the shadows. I called the cops once, but they couldn't find anyone. I told Neil about the letters, and he said that similar ones had been sent to a new girl he was dating and he was pretty certain Vicky had found out about the relationship. That's what made me begin to see the truth."

"Were the notes handwritten?" I asked.

"No. They'd been typed on a computer."

"Any chance Neil could have sent them?" Alex asked.

She shook her head vehemently. "Not on your life. We'd been buddies for years. Besides, one night I found the nerve to sneak outside when I saw the figure there. It was a woman, and I watched her jump into a car. It was Vicky's car. I recognized the press plates she had."

"Did anything happen while you were at work?" I asked, desperate for more than what Sharon was providing us. The transgressions against me seemed different from what Sharon had experienced.

Her eyes welled with tears. "Work was where the worst thing happened. I went to management and let them know what was going on. I showed them the letters and told them I'd seen Vicky outside my home. They seemed really worried at first and said they would look into the situation right away. But . . ." She bit her lip, fighting back tears. "But then they found that all the letters to me had been typed on my desktop computer. They accused me of framing Vicky and let me go. "

"Did you try to fight it?" Alex asked.

"Yeah, but I couldn't afford a lawyer for long."

"That Friday you fell sick and couldn't anchor the next day," I said, after a few seconds of thought. "Is there a chance Vicky tampered with your food?"

Sharon straightened up. "Oh, gosh," she said. "I never once thought of that. She might have. My desk was right out in the center of the newsroom, and I always had an open can of Diet Coke."

"Did she ever do anything to make you look bad on the air?" I asked.

Sharon shrugged. "Not directly," she said. "I did most of my stories on location, just as she did. But I was worried about the stalking, and I'm sure it showed a little in my face."

Alex sprang the big question next. Would she be willing to come to New York, at our expense, and share her story with management at the network?

"Yes," she said. "I mean, I don't love the idea of having Vicky know I'm resurrecting this. But what can she do to me at this point? I'm a *Realtor.*"

Alex thanked Sharon, said we would be in touch shortly, and stressed that discretion was critical. As he paid the bill, Sharon announced she intended to stay at the restaurant a while longer and have a bite to eat. She felt too worked up to leave at the moment.

"Talk to me," Alex said after we were back in the car. "Are you bothered that there's not a clear overlap?"

"Yeah. The stories are just different enough that it might seem to Potts that Sharon and I are simply two Vicky haters. Women who, twenty years apart, wanted to make it appear like she was after us."

"But it could be enough to start a dialogue again. And convince Oliver to search for a botnet."

"Wait," I blurted out, my mind racing. "Give me a second."

I flung open the car door and tore back into the restaurant. Sharon looked startled as I slid into the seat across from her again.

"You said *stuff*," I said, breathless from running. "That Vicky sent letters and *stuff*. What else did she send you?"

Sharon looked off, thinking. "There was a smashed-up lipstick in one," she said. "The exact shade I wore. And—oh gosh, this was horrible. There was a Barbie. And the eyes had been stabbed out with a knife."

Chapter 23

"A Barbie doll," I said. I had to say the words myself so they'd fully sink in.

"Yes." Sharon curled her lips in disgust. "It was a blond one, just like me."

"And it was in your mailbox?"

"Uh-huh. I had one of those with a lid, and she'd dropped it in."

"You don't still have it, do you?"

"No. I'm sorry. But I have a photo of it. Will that help?"

"Yes," I said, squeezing her hands. "That will help."

After saying goodbye once again, I darted back to the car. It was raining lightly now, drops of water plopping onto the pavement of the parking lot. In the car, I blurted out what I'd learned.

"Fantastic," Alex said. "You've got more than enough to take to Potts now."

"I need a lawyer. Someone to speak on my behalf and introduce Sharon."

He rubbed his hand across the scruff on his chin. "I know someone who'd be great," he said. "A friend of mine from law school works for her." He went on to describe the attorney's success on big white-collar cases.

"She sounds like just what I need."

Alex fired up the engine and maneuvered out of the parking lot. The rain was coming down harder, pounding on the roof of the car.

As soon as we were back on the thruway, we discussed how events should unfold. Once Potts and Carey agreed to a meeting, I would arrange for Sharon to travel to Manhattan. Alex asked if I had any fears, based on her demeanor, that Sharon might develop cold feet about cooperating. It was a possibility, I said, but I was betting otherwise. This was her chance to be exonerated.

"I wonder if I should have her stay at my place to keep tabs on her," I said. "But that could also be a little awkward."

"Agreed. Are there any small hotels near you, ones that aren't so public?"

"You know, a friend of mine from Seattle just rented an apartment here for a week, one she found over the Internet. I'll look into that. It would be close but private."

"Sounds good. The sooner we move on this, the better." He glanced quickly toward me, just a quarter turn of the head so his eyes weren't off the road long. "Once they figure out the truth and oust Vicky, you'll want to be back on the show, right?"

"Yes, of course," I said. I'd waited a beat to answer, but I wasn't sure why.

"You hesitated," Alex said.

"It's going to be uncomfortable at first, I'm sure. Unlike you, most people didn't reach out to me, though I suppose I can hardly blame them. I was fired under a black cloud. But what bothers me most is that one person there betrayed me, and I don't know who it was."

"Betrayed you how?"

To explain, I would have to tell Alex about Janice. That was okay. He'd more than stuck his neck out for me and had led me to Sharon. He deserved to know everything.

"Gosh, Robin, it must have been awful to go through all that," he said after I'd shared the story. "Do you think Vicky knew about your history and tried to pull similar stuff?"

"At first I saw that as a possibility, but now, especially after talking to Sharon, I think it was coincidental. Those were just the vicious tricks in Vicky's arsenal. But I told a few friends at the network about my past, and someone tipped off Potts. It helped undermine my credibility."

"Could he have found out another way? Was there any press about what happened to you as a girl?"

"There was a small item a few months after I returned from the first summer at my aunt Jessie's. I didn't know until I was home that Janice had convinced my father I was behind everything. I guess he thought that being banished for the summer would have taught me a lesson and that we could all make a go of it again, be the sweet happy family of his dreams. As soon as school started, Janice began locking me in a closet when I returned home each day, and she'd only let me out a few minutes before my father was due back from work. Said it was for her protection. She knew I wouldn't dare tell him because it would seem like I was fabricating things again. One day I ran away, and there was a search for me. That ended up in the papers."

"Will Oliver might have found it and explored things further."

"I almost hope so. That would be easier to accept."

Alex glanced at me again. "I can't believe what you've been through these past weeks," he said. "It must have triggered a lot of scary memories."

"Yes. It's as if the old and new got tangled up somehow. I've felt at times as if I'm coming unglued. There was even a moment when I wondered if I *had* done those things at work without knowing I had. I worried about that as a little girl, too."

"Is Janice still with your father?"

"I believe so. I have a couple of relatives from Buffalo whom I still talk to—Maddy's mother, for one—but they know not to bring her up to me. And my father never mentions her."

"You talk to him?"

"Now and then. In the years since I lived with my aunt, I've seen him on only a dozen occasions, and the last time was probably five years ago. He emails me sometimes. And once in a blue moon, we speak on the phone. What's really sad is that for years I waited for him to tell me he'd figured out the truth and to ask for my forgiveness. I would have given it. But I saw that it was never going to happen. He'll go to his grave believing Janice."

Abruptly, I felt drained from sharing so much, and I rested my head against the seat.

"Take a catnap if you want," he said.

"No way. You need a copilot in conditions like these."

"Don't worry. I've had enough caffeine to keep me alert till Miami."

I didn't sleep. I stared out the window, thinking about Sharon, trying not to let my faint hopes magnify into something they didn't deserve to be. As we drove through the foothills of the Catskill Mountains, I saw a huge buck standing undecided on the side of the highway. *Don't cross*, I wanted to yell.

Finally, the rain let up, becoming a drizzle. Alex turned down the window wipers so that they made their hypnotic swish every few seconds. Because of the weather, night seemed to come early. Even in the dark, Alex's light skin was luminescent.

"You know . . ." I said. The sound of my voice made him jerk in surprise.

"I thought you'd fallen asleep," he said.

"No, just thinking. We've spent so much time talking about me and my situation in the past few days, but I've asked you practically nothing about yourself."

He leaned his head back and smiled, staring ahead at the gleaming wet highway. "There's not much exciting to report," he said. "I landed in TV pretty late, so I've been trying to make up for lost time and not let myself be distracted."

"How old are you, anyway?" I said, smiling. "I'm not interviewing you for a job, so you can't sue me for asking."

"Thirty-three. I'm the oldest senior producer on the show."

"I had to play the catch-up game, too, since I'd come from the outside like you did. Would you want an EP job at some point?"

"Definitely, though I'd prefer politics or news in the future. Don't take this the wrong way: Topics like pets on planes and badly behaving rock stars leave me cold."

"Even underboobage?"

"Okay, that's probably an exception."

"What made you want to switch into TV?"

"I majored in journalism in college, but I took the law boards as a lark. When my parents saw how well I'd done—a total fluke—they put a lot of pressure on me to go. I have to admit, I had a bit of Jack McCoy syndrome."

"Meaning?"

"Justice for all, that kind of thing."

"You didn't like it in the end?"

Though the inside of the car was dim, I could see his expression cloud.

"No," he said flatly. "Definitely not the right fit. But I picked up a few decent skills, so it wasn't a complete waste of time."

Though I sensed there was more to the story, I decided not to push. I didn't want to alienate him, and I, more than anyone, knew about the desire to keep the past private.

Alex dropped me off just after seven-thirty. For a moment I wondered if he was going to suggest that we grab dinner, but I didn't give him an opening. I felt exhausted from the long ride and churned up from hearing Sharon's story. Besides, a guy who looked like him surely had a girlfriend waiting on a Saturday night. I thanked him profusely, and he promised to text me contact info for the lawyer, which he did about an hour later.

Her name was Lisa Follett, and I spoke with her briefly by phone the next day, the quick response facilitated by Alex's friend in the firm. Follett agreed to meet with me early Monday afternoon.

For the first time in days, I dressed the way I used to for the show. It was almost painful to put on one of my TV outfits, which just three weeks ago had seemed to be the bold emblem of my new success. I also felt vaguely ridiculous, like one of those married guys who's been fired from his job but, too much of a wuss to confess to his wife, leaves the house every morning dressed in a suit and tie. But I wanted to impress Lisa Follett, convince her I wasn't a nut job. What I needed most was for her to say that Sharon's story was strong enough to open a door for me with Potts and Carey.

Her office was all the way downtown in Battery Park Plaza. Even the reception area had a drop-dead view of New York Harbor. Based on Alex's description of Lisa as a fierce, unrelenting warrior, I'd been expecting Glenn Close in *Damages*, but that wasn't the woman who stepped out from behind her desk to greet me. She was about five-three, slight in build, with a small heart-shaped face and fine brown hair. She had a pleasant, easy talking style with a hint of a Southern accent.

"So tell me again why you need a lawyer?" she said after I'd taken a seat across from her.

Kind of a funny question, considering I'd given her the broad outlines on the phone; but I guessed it was part of her technique to obtain a read on me. I went through everything: all the incidents, the advice the employment lawyer had volunteered, what Alex had seen, what we'd learned from Sharon. She was a good listener, nodding, watching me closely, and fielding questions at various points.

"Since you don't want to sue, what exactly would you want a lawyer to do?" she asked.

"Take my case to management. Hopefully, once they hear what happened to Sharon and acknowledge how similar it is to my situation, they'll be willing to find the botnet on my computer. That will prove I never did those searches. And then I want them to give me my job back. I'd love it if you could take this on." I was certain about hiring her. After almost an hour, I'd begun to sense the tiger crouching in her.

She nodded slowly, as if still deciding. *Please*, I thought.

"It's a challenging situation," she said, "but I feel this new information from the television reporter makes all the difference. I'd definitely be willing to take on the case."

I exhaled with relief.

"I need to put the issue of money on the table now," she added. "This isn't going to be cheap."

"Can you give me a rough estimate?"

"We're looking at about thirty hours of work on my part, and that's at seven hundred dollars an hour. I would also have to involve both an associate and a private detective I work with, an ex-FBI guy. He's easily another ten grand. And I'll need a retainer of twenty-five thousand. All of this is nonnegotiable."

It would take a huge bite of my savings, but I didn't have a choice. "Okay," I said, nodding. "What's the next step?"

"You've only one shot at going in there and making your case to this Potts fellow, so let's be sure what we have is as strong as possible. What Sharon is offering sounds good on the surface, but my detective and I need to sit down alone with her and evaluate her story, make certain she's trustworthy. My guy will also have to drive up to Albany and try to corroborate what she's saying."

Damn. That meant a slower process than what I'd anticipated. Also, though Alex and I had told Sharon that she'd be required to talk to people at the network, now I'd be adding a preliminary interview with a former FBI agent, which might spook her. And she'd have to make two trips to the city, not one.

Again, I didn't have a choice. Lisa's strategy sounded smart; I would just have to pray that Sharon wouldn't flinch. I assured Lisa I would try to arrange for Sharon to be in New York as soon as possible.

She walked me back toward reception and shook my hand. "I know this has been difficult," she said. "But I'll work hard to make it right."

I flagged down a cab and had the driver drop me a block from my apartment building at a small café. I picked a table at the back. Being out in public, especially in one of my "Brand Robin" dresses, could trigger renewed press interest, but I was sick of being cooped up in my apartment.

I ordered a light lunch and, for the first time in days, actually tasted the food. The last words Lisa had uttered kept running through my head: *I'll work hard to make it right.* This was the best I'd felt in days.

As soon as I returned home, I checked on the availability of the apartment my friend had stayed in. It was free over the next week. Then I phoned Sharon on her cell number. When she didn't pick up, I left a message saying I was ready to arrange her trip to Manhattan. I'd no sooner ended the call than I saw Bettina's name on my cell screen.

"Darling, how *are* you?" she said when I answered.

"Hanging in there. Have you discovered anything on your end?"

"Not very much, unfortunately. The Westport police have turned up nothing, so we still don't know who was skulking around that night. I'm coming up empty with Potts, too. I called him myself, on the pretense of trying to make him see the benefit of the sale, and he seemed truly shaken about you being gone. I know I told you he might be responsible, but I'm sensing now that he isn't."

"That's okay," I said. "I have other leads."

"Wonderful. What are they?" Pussyfooting wasn't one of Bettina's particular talents.

"I'll let you know as soon as I'm free to talk about them. Why don't I call you in a day or two?"

"All right. Just know I'm here for you."

At around five, I tried Sharon's cell again. Still voice mail. I couldn't help feeling a pinch of worry. Alex and I had conveyed on Saturday that the situation was urgent and that things might begin to move quickly. She'd said that was fine, that her job afforded her flexible hours. Maybe her office would know her whereabouts. I dug her business card out of my purse and tapped the number for the real estate agency.

"McLaren Realty," a woman answered.

"Hi, I'm trying to reach Sharon Hayes."

"Is it about a listing?"

"No, actually, it's a personal call."

"Well, I can give you her cell, I guess. You don't sound like a crazy person."

That was funny. "She's not coming into the office today?" I asked.

"Nope. Or tomorrow. She resigned this morning."

Panic welled in me. "Did she take another job?"

"I don't think so, love. She said something about heading to California."

Chapter 24

My stomach dropped. No, please, this couldn't be happening. Without her, I had nothing. The lawyer had made that utterly clear.

I sent Alex a text urging him to call me right after the show. Then I paced my apartment, my nerves on fire. What if Sharon was taking off not because she'd developed cold feet but because something had alarmed her? Vicky might have learned that Alex and I had made contact.

Whatever the reason, I needed to find her. Maybe the person who had connected Alex to Sharon had information.

My phone rang, and to my shock, I saw Sharon's name on the screen.

"Sorry not to ring you back right away," she said casually when I answered.

"No problem," I said, feeling my pulse slow. "I tried your office, too. They said you'd resigned."

"Yeah, big step for me. I absolutely hated that job, and after speaking to you and Alex, I found the guts to go in and quit first thing Monday. I'm making a fresh new start."

"The woman said you were moving to California."

Sharon laughed. "Oh, I just didn't want her to know my business. Besides, maybe I *will* go to California after I set the record straight."

"Speaking of that," I said, "I wanted to discuss your trip to the city."

"I'm ready," she said gamely. "I could even come tomorrow."

Lisa had indicated that Thursday morning at nine would work best for her and the private detective. I explained to Sharon about the need to meet with both of them, trying to make it sound like a simple matter of course. I suggested she take the train down on Wednesday, settle in at the apartment, and then I'd accompany her downtown the next morning to be sure she had no trouble locating Lisa's office. Fortunately, she didn't balk at any of it. Alex called five minutes after the show ended. "Everything okay?" he asked.

"I had a little scare, but it's taken care of. And the appointment with Lisa went well. Do you have time for me to fill you in?"

"Yes, and I have news, too. Just give me a chance to hop on the subway and get home. I'll call you from there."

"Do you want to come up to my place and talk here? We could have a bite to eat." I'd blurted it out without even thinking.

"Uh, sure," he said, "as long as it's no trouble."

I laughed. "No trouble whatsoever. I'll just call this place that delivers great chicken piccata. I'm one of those ruthless career bitches who never learned to cook."

He arrived thirty minutes later, carrying a silver wine sack. I led him into the kitchen where he opened the bottle of Italian red.

Over dinner, I brought him up to speed. When I told what had happened with Sharon and my initial fear that she'd been bound for parts west, he frowned.

"What's the matter?" I asked. "It was all a misunderstanding."

"I worry she's running hot and cold, that maybe she did think of bailing but then reconsidered. We need to monitor this."

"All right, I'm going to check out the apartment tomorrow. I'll be there when she arrives on Wednesday."

"That's smart."

"You said you had something."

"Yeah. I did some snooping and found out who's in Vicky's inner circle. As you'd expect, there's plenty of turnover on her staff, but there are a handful of people who've been with her for a while—the executive producer, his deputy, Vicky's assistant, and a personal publicist she pays on her own and who works on projects beyond what Ann's team handles. I assume they're all suffering from Stockholm syndrome."

"I'm pretty sure her assistant and the publicist were at my party. I saw them in the elevator with an older guy, balding."

"That sounds like her EP. All of them were in D.C. with her the night you were drugged, so I'm not sure who her confederate is."

"What about one of her senior producers, like the one who told Maddy about Vicky being tech-savvy?"

"I wondered about him. He went running to Mommy when Maddy asked him for help. But he's only been there three months. There's a big difference between kissing up to your boss and leaving someone a poison brownie on her behalf."

"Unless he didn't know the significance of what he was doing," I said. "After I started drooling on the air that night, he probably would have suspected that the brownie was the cause, and yet he may have been too afraid to come clean."

"Could be."

"Or," I said, my blood chilling as a thought took shape, "what if the accomplice is someone working on *Pulse*?"

Alex raised an eyebrow. "Any ideas?" he said.

"It would have to be a person with ties to Vicky, and I have no clue who that could be. Perhaps someone who once worked on her show. Or hopes to in the future."

"Okay, that'll be my next assignment: to suss out if anyone on our show used to be in her camp."

"Speaking of the show, can you believe I've never heard from Tom?"

"There's something weird going on with that dude. He's oddly detached these days."

"He hasn't figured out you're collaborating with me, has he?"

"I'm sure no one has a hint of that. Except for helping Maddy when I can, I've been minding my own business."

"Is she performing any better?"

"I think so. And she had this interesting idea about us tackling more crime stories. She did a whole analysis on how well those stories rate."

My mouth fell open. "I can't believe it," I said. "*I* did that analysis and turned it over to her for background."

"Pretty Machiavellian of her."

Though I had warned Maddy about contacting Vicky's producers, I'd never gotten around to saying I'd been told "hands off" in regard to the crime stories.

"Well, I hope she submits the damn thing," I said, pissed as hell. "It will bite her in the butt, just like it did me."

As I began to clear the dishes Alex joined in, and we carried everything to the kitchen. Loading the dishwasher, our hands brushed momentarily. I realized how strange it was to have him in my apartment, inches away from me. Only days ago, I'd been giving him instructions at work.

"I was going to bring you something chocolatey for dessert," Alex said, "but I figured your stomach would recoil at the idea."

"I'm afraid it will be years before I even look at anything chocolate again," I said. "Dove bars all over Manhattan can sleep soundly tonight."

He laughed. "Where did that brownie supposedly come from, anyway?" he asked.

Shit, I thought. I should have known that would be next. Wiping the countertop, I explained the circumstances and how I'd thought C. stood for Carter.

"Were you guys pretty tight?" Alex had said it easily enough, but I knew the question was loaded.

I sighed, turned, and faced him. "I should admit this now, because it will probably come out eventually. It's one of the things that hurt my cause last week. I had a brief fling with Carter."

Alex tipped his head back a little and parted his lips, as if a lightbulb had gone off in his mind.

"Was it obvious?" I asked.

"Not to me," he said. "But after I landed the job, I heard rumors that he was involved with a woman at work."

"We weren't seeing each other that long. It only started after my life began to unravel. And I'm going to plead temporary insanity."

He looked directly at me, those hazel eyes both curious and bemused. "From you, I'll accept the plea," he said. "But I can hardly blame Carter."

"Thanks," I said. I felt momentarily flustered by the comment and changed the subject awkwardly as I walked him to the door. But later, lying in bed, I realized how much I'd enjoyed his company over dinner. Thinking about him kept me from brooding about Maddy's sneaky move.

First thing the next day, I booked the rental apartment for the rest of the week and then walked the twelve blocks north to Ninety-third Street and Lexington Avenue to pick up two sets of keys. It was an attractive prewar building with a canopy, no door-man but a porter who came on duty at midnight for extra security. Classic in design, the apartment was decorated simply but elegantly, almost from the pages of a Restoration Hardware catalog: a sofa in laven-der linen, a pale leather armchair, and on top of the mantel, two carved wooden urn-like sculptures with finials on top.

On Wednesday morning I returned with a few basic groceries: coffee, OJ, bagels. I filled a bowl on the coffee table with tangerines and set a flat of grass on the mantel between the urns. It was a bit manic, I knew, but I kept hearing Alex's words in my head, that Sharon might be running hot and cold.

I was back before noon, waiting for Sharon. I'd offered to pick her up at Penn Station, but she'd insisted on hailing a cab herself. I figured that even with traffic, she'd arrive by noon. At 12:10, she still wasn't there, and I could feel my tension mounting. Then the buzzer sounded.

She was dressed in white pants, a pink top, a cotton sweater in a pink and yellow floral print, and big gold hoop earrings. She looked nervous but excited. I showed her around the apartment, poured us each a glass of sparkling water, and suggested we sit in the living room.

"Gosh," she said. "This apartment is gorgeous. I feel like I have my own place in the city."

I smiled. "When you were in local news, did you ever consider working at a bigger job down here one day?"

She shrugged. "I was probably pretty different from most of the people you've known in the business. I never thought of myself as ambitious—I just loved sports and kind of fell into work at the station through a contact my dad had. And then a funny thing happened. I was good at it, and the more I tasted success, the more driven I felt. I started to imagine making a stab at New York one day. Then, as you know, everything fell apart." She took a quick sip of water, her pink lipstick leaving an imprint on the glass. "What about you?" she asked. "I bet you always dreamed about coming here."

"Yes," I said. "Though initially, not with a plan to be in television. I wanted to make my mark as a print journalist. I started appearing on the morning shows to chat about articles I'd written, and almost instantly, I was hooked."

"Why did TV appeal to you so much more than print?" she asked.

"The pace, for one thing. The sheer thrill of being live. And there was something so, I don't know, *validating*, about being on television."

My reply surprised me. I'd fielded variations on the question numerous times over the years but had never responded that way. I wasn't even sure what I'd meant. "Do you have family up in Albany?" I asked.

"I was married for a while but divorced about five years ago. No kids. I'm seeing someone now, a nice guy named Hal. He's proud of me for doing this."

I checked if she'd like to grab a meal later, but she insisted she would be fine eating dinner alone, that from the cab she'd spotted a little restaurant nearby she wanted to try.

"I'm just going to pretend I'm Mary Tyler Moore tonight," she said, smiling. "If I had a hat, I'd toss it in the air."

"Sure," I said, "but stick close to the neighborhood. We don't want Vicky figuring out you're here."

"Right, I understand."

"About tomorrow. Because of traffic, we should allow about an hour to make it downtown. Why don't I swing by in a cab at eight?"

"No, no, I can manage on my own if you give me the address. This is important to me. I won't be late."

I didn't like the idea of her going on her own, but I wanted to keep the goodwill flowing and chose not to press the matter. I wrote out Lisa's address, thanked Sharon again, and said goodbye.

I headed home, stopping briefly at the Korean market to pick up a few provisions for myself this time. Walking down my block, I realized that my anxiety had subsided but not completely. Though I was pretty sure by now that Sharon was fully committed, I worried that Lisa would find some issue with her story that I couldn't predict.

Lost in thought, it took me a second to process what I was seeing as I neared my building: Ann was standing not far from the entrance, holding a huge bouquet of flowers. I felt a flash of fury at the sight of her, but I stopped when I reached her.

"Robin, please," she said. "Can we talk?"

"Uh, why don't we go around the corner," I said. "There's a Pain Quotidien, and we can talk there."

I left the groceries and flowers inside with my doorman, and we walked in silence to the café, where we found a quiet table at the back. After we ordered drinks, Ann leaned toward me. Blue-gray circles under her eyes betrayed that she'd clearly had a few sleepless nights herself.

"Robin, I don't deserve your forgiveness," she said, "but I'm asking for it anyway. I was a fool to doubt you."

"Why this sudden enlightenment?" I asked, letting the sarcasm drip.

"I've had a few days to think about it. I know you. I know you're not capable of doing any of those things, even if you were under stress."

"You were awfully certain a few days ago."

She pulled her hands together and brought them to her face, pressing them against her mouth. Her fingernails were unpainted and the cuticles ragged. I'd never seen her with anything other than a perfect manicure.

"I'm totally ashamed to admit this, but I let my desperation to protect my job color everything," she said finally, lowering her hands. "Potts knows we're friends, and I think I was afraid to look like I was partial to you. I went overboard to hear his side of things."

The waitress set two bowls of cappuccino on the table, and I looked off, absorbing Ann's words. "That's the last kind of behavior I would have imagined from you, Ann," I said, meeting her eyes again. "If someone had asked me to bet, I would have said you'd always put a friend first."

"And that's how I always saw myself," she said. "But I've let my financial concerns get in the way. Matthew handled our money, and it turns out he made a mess of things. Our only investment was the East Hampton house, and we can't unload it at the moment. I have nightmares about losing my job and being a fucking bag lady."

"Why didn't you ever mention this?"

"Partly because it's all so tedious. And partly because I was sure the house would sell. But I don't want this to be about my money woes. I want to make up for what I've done."

"Then start with the truth. Did you tell anyone details about my situation with Janice?"

"Absolutely not," she said. "Even when I thought those incidents from your past might be affecting you, I never breathed a word."

"Do you have any idea who did?"

"No, but I can try to find out if you want. I can talk to Potts."

I shook my head. "No, don't say anything to him. I've hired a lawyer, and we'll be making a presentation. If you speak to him, it could throw our plan off."

"Then tell me what I can do. I want to help."

"Okay, you can share relevant information you hear."

"I will," she said, nodding somberly. "I'll keep you abreast of all developments concerning you."

Despite my protests, she picked up the check, and we parted with her promising again to keep me in the loop. As I walked home, I felt several emotions wrestling inside me: anger, sadness, and regret. I wasn't sure the friendship could ever really be repaired.

"So your friend found you?" the doorman said as I collected the flowers and groceries. "She came by a couple of times looking for you."

She'd been persistent, then. Could I give her a second chance? I remembered what Jake had told me the other day, that I'd refused to even entertain the idea of forgiving him. Maybe that was a trait in myself I needed to face: a reluctance to forgive.

I ordered food in and ate alone. Later, I ran out and around the corner for a vanilla ice cream cone. I couldn't even bear looking at the chocolate in the case.

"You seem to be enjoying that," the doorman said when I returned.

I was. Thanks to Lisa and now Sharon, I had a sense the nightmare could end

I woke the next morning, thankful to see sun streaming in my window. Good weather meant that Sharon would have no difficulty finding a cab. Nine o'clock came and went. I pictured her telling her story, prayed that it sounded as plausible to Lisa as it did to me. At ten-fifteen the phone rang. Lisa's name was on the screen.

"So how did it go?" I asked.

"Not good," Lisa said. "She never showed."

"What?" I felt as if I'd just been shoved from behind. "Maybe she's lost. She wanted to travel downtown by herself."

"We assumed at first that she had trouble finding the place. That's why we gave her extra time. But we've tried her cell four or five times. No answer."

Sharon had bailed, just as Alex feared she might.

"Okay, let me head up to where she's staying. She might not have left town yet."

I flew out of the apartment, dressed in jeans and a tank top. I hailed a cab this time, on Madison Avenue, and was at the building in under ten minutes. I was crazed, but I knew that if Sharon was still there, I couldn't let my panic show. I had to calm down and reason with her.

I rang the buzzer twice, but no one answered. I wondered if she *was* lost. Maybe she'd taken the subway instead of a cab and was trying to find her way back from the far reaches of Brooklyn. There was no cell service underground. I let myself into the building, rode the elevator to the sixth floor, and hurried to the apartment. I knocked twice and, when Sharon didn't answer, opened the door with the extra key.

The first thing I noticed was her big yellow purse squatting on a table in the foyer. She was still here, I realized gratefully. But then I detected that the AC was off and the apartment was hot as hell. There was a smell, too, I realized. Something spoiled, like meat left a day too long.

I froze in place, scared. "Sharon?" I called out.

I forced myself to tiptoe into the living room.

One step through the doorway, I saw that something was wrong. The wall by the fireplace was spattered with brown droplets, as if someone had sprayed a drink there. I took two more steps, and my gaze was yanked to the floor.

Just beyond the lavender sofa, Sharon was lying facedown on the rug, dressed in the floral sweater she'd worn yesterday. Her body was saggy, lifeless, and one side of her face was mashed into the carpet. To the right side of her head was a dark half-halo of blood.

Chapter 25

I cried out and jerked backward, fear knocking me onto my heels. But I couldn't tear my eyes away. As I peered closer at Sharon, I saw a huge gash on the back of her head, clotted with dark, ropy blood. A few feet away, on the floor by the wall, was one of the urn-like sculptures from the mantel, lying on its side.

"*Sharon*," I called again, my voice strangled.

It was clear she was dead. Her right cheek was turned upward, and through strands of her long blond hair, I could see that her eye was open and cloudy.

The words formed in my head: She's been *murdered*. I stepped back. What if the killer was in the other room?

I spun around and staggered into the foyer. Flung open the door. I ran to the elevator and jabbed again and again at the call button, twisting my head every second to make certain no one had emerged behind me from the apartment.

From the elevator, I fled through the lobby into the street, and with my hand shaking hard, tapped 911 on my phone. "Someone's been murdered," I told the operator. "A woman. Send the police." It took me a second to remember the address.

"The police have been dispatched," he said. "Please stay on the line."

"I—I can't." I had to call Lisa. "But I'll wait outside."

"Ma'am—"

I hung up and phoned Lisa's office. When I told the secretary it was an emergency, she put me right through. My voice faltered as I told her the news.

"I'm on my way," Lisa said.

"What should I do until you arrive?"

"When the cops show up, be cooperative, but say as little as possible." I could tell by her breathing that she was already on the move. "If detectives get there before I do, explain that Sharon was about to make a statement in an investigation and that you've asked your lawyer to join you to help provide information. Do your best to avoid any press."

Next I texted a single word to Alex: "*Urgent.*"

In under five minutes, two uniformed patrol cops pulled up in a cruiser. I stepped forward and introduced myself. Briefly, I described the scene and turned over the key.

"We need you to come upstairs with us, okay?" the older one said.

I didn't want to go back up there, but I knew it wouldn't do any good to protest. I'd reported the crime, and they needed to keep me in their sights until I could be questioned.

We rode to the sixth floor with them asking for a few more details. As we stepped off the elevator, I pointed quickly to the apartment, a few doors to the left. The older cop whispered that I should go to the end of the hallway and wait there. As I retreated, I saw one of the cops touch his hand to his gun as the other unlocked the door and opened it. They vanished inside.

I leaned back against the wall, steadying myself. I felt my whole body being compressed downward, crushed by grief and guilt. I kept flashing back and forth between the Sharon of last night, so excited to have dinner alone in the city, and the Sharon lying on the floor with her head bashed in.

Had Vicky done this? Was she more ruthless and dangerous than I'd even imagined?

How would she have known Sharon was here? I recalled something Sharon had said to me about her boyfriend last night: *He's proud of me for doing this.* Though Alex and I had stressed to her the importance of guarding our plan, she'd obviously leaked it to her guy. And maybe someone else.

The corridor was stifling, as if there were no AC flowing through it. The foul smell from the apartment seemed to be seeping in my direction, and I kept fighting the urge to gag.

The two patrol cops reemerged. They took down basic info from me and then began going up and down the length of the hall; they looked in the room with the trash compactor and strung yellow crime scene tape across it. After they'd finished, one of the cops boarded the elevator, and the other walked back toward me. Detectives would be arriving soon, he said. Then he returned to the door of the apartment and stood guard.

I felt desperate to talk to Lisa. I wondered how I'd be able to connect with her. The cops weren't going to allow me downstairs yet, and they surely wouldn't clear Lisa to come up here. Discreetly, I sent her a text explaining where I was.

Two detectives arrived about ten minutes later, an older white male and a younger female, African-American. I could tell from her eyes that the woman recognized me, though she might not have known from where. After introducing themselves—Hogan and Stainback—they asked me a few basic questions and told me to wait. Then they snapped on latex gloves, slipped on booties, and entered the apartment.

For the next twenty-five minutes, I waited, feeling more and more frantic. A few people poked their heads out of their apartments, curious about the noise in the hallway, but they were told by one of the patrol cops to step back inside and wait for the police to come by. Soon another group of cops arrived, wearing jackets imprinted with CSU.

Finally, Detective Hogan appeared again and strode back down the hall toward me. "Ms. Trainer," he said, "we'll need you to stop by the precinct to make a full statement, but I'd like to ask you a few more questions here first, if that's okay."

"Of course," I said.

"Why don't we go downstairs and have a seat in the lobby. It'll be more comfortable."

"Thanks. I'd appreciate that." Cooperative, just as Lisa had advised.

There were two plaid armchairs against the far wall of the lobby, and Hogan gestured for me to sit in one while he took the other. Detective Stainback stood near my chair. Hogan tugged a notebook from his inside jacket pocket. Something about that notebook made everything more real. I could feel grief welling up in me. Sharon had come to my rescue, and now she was dead.

"I know this is upsetting," Hogan said. "But do the best you can."

He asked me to describe my relationship with the victim and how I happened to be at the scene. I kept it short and basic, as Lisa had recommended: who Sharon was, how I'd arranged for her to travel to the city to make a statement in an investigation, and how I'd hurried here when she failed to show for an appointment.

"What kind of investigation?" Hogan said. "Are we talking investigative journalism?" Stainback must have filled him in on who I was. I told him no, it was more complicated than that, and as pleasantly as I could muster explained that I would prefer to have my lawyer with me when I shared the details.

He shrugged, not pleased, and then moved on to questions about the crime scene: Did I touch anything, was the door locked or unlocked, was the AC off in the living room when I arrived, did I see anyone at all in the vicinity?

While we spoke, another vehicle arrived, and two men rolled a stretcher into the lobby and onto the elevator. It wouldn't be long before the press descended.

I kept slipping a look at my watch, praying Lisa would show.

And then there she was. I could see her through the glass half of the front door, dressed in a beige suit and standing next to a guy of about thirty.

"My lawyer is here now," I said, leaning forward. "I need to fill her in."

A look passed between the two detectives, one I couldn't interpret. Hogan announced that he'd like me to go to the precinct on Sixty-seventh Street as soon as possible and give a full statement. Detective Stainback, he said, would meet me there. I nodded in compliance.

As soon as I'd stepped outside, where a throng of people had gathered on the sidewalk, Lisa touched a finger discreetly to her lips in warning and then introduced me to her associate, Colin something. The three of us walked silently down Lexington Avenue for almost a block. People traipsed by in the heat, taxis flew down the street, but all of that seemed to be part of a parallel universe, a world I'd been accidentally dislodged from. When we neared the corner, I told the two lawyers that the police wanted me to make a statement at the precinct.

"Let's talk for a minute first," Lisa said, continuing to walk. "Could you tell how Sharon had been killed?"

I ran through everything I'd seen.

"Do you think the murder had just happened?"

I shook my head. "No. She was wearing the same clothes she had on yesterday, and there was a smell, like her body had been decomposing. It seems like she must have been killed yesterday evening sometime."

"I need to ask you," Lisa said quietly, "where were you last night?"

"What?" I said, coming to a complete stop. "You think—?"

"No, of course not, but the police are going to wonder."

"I was home," I said. "My doorman can vouch for me. I ran out once for ice cream, but I was gone just a few minutes."

"This isn't my area of law—and we may need to bring in a criminal lawyer at some point—but the first person the police focus on during a homicide investigation is the one who found the body. They may suspect there's something you're not telling."

I felt another jolt of fear. "What if Vicky killed Sharon but made it appear somehow that *I* did?" I said. "That's been her MO with everything else."

Lisa pursed her lips. I could tell my comment worried her. "From what you've said about the crime scene, it sounds like the murder happened in the heat of the moment, and so whoever did it probably didn't have time to frame you," she said. "You have nothing to hide, so just tell your story. I'll be in the room with you, so watch me, okay? I'll flash you a sign with my eyes if you're going somewhere I don't like. They're going to seem real sympathetic at first—lots of 'This must be very upsetting' stuff."

"Yeah, they've already done that," I said.

"Then they'll start to narrow their focus, press you more, ask for your alibi."

"Should I tell them about Vicky?"

"Yes," she said. "You're going to have to."

We hailed a cab and took it to the precinct. The situation unfolded the way Lisa had predicted. Stainback was there with a new guy named Nowak, who seemed the most senior of all the cops I'd dealt with. For a few minutes, they employed the feigned-concern-for-what-I'd-been-through tactic and then began to lob tougher questions. I willed myself to stay calm.

When I explained about Vicky and Sharon's connection to her, neither detective could disguise surprise. Though I hated dragging Alex into the investigation, I had no choice but to mention the role he'd played in locating Sharon.

"I've never had any actual proof that Vicky Cruz did those things to me," I said at the end, "but there was circumstantial evidence, and Sharon's story seemed to bolster it all. I had no idea I was putting Sharon in any danger when she came here. I just wanted to clear my name."

"In addition to you and Mr. Lucca, who knew Ms. Hayes was here in Manhattan?" Nowak asked.

"Her boyfriend apparently. Beyond that, I don't know."

They asked for Potts's contact info, and I wrote it out for them.

"There's just one more thing," I said. "Sharon was going to bring a photograph with her of a Barbie doll that she believed Vicky Cruz had left in her mailbox years ago. If you find it, could you give me a copy?"

Nowak said that he wasn't sure if that would be possible.

"Good job," Lisa said once we were outside. "I'm going to reach out to Potts now. I want to beat the police to it."

I said goodbye and, desperate to be home, headed toward Third Avenue to hunt down a cab. Within seconds, I could feel fear galloping up on me again. If Vicky had killed Sharon, did that mean my life could be in danger? I flashed on my experience in Westport, the silhouette on the curtain.

As soon as I was in the cab, I checked my phone. Alex had called three times while I was being grilled by the police.

"My God, this is awful," he exclaimed when I shared the details. "It's too big of a coincidence for it not to be related to your case. Vicky must have found out that Sharon was here."

"Do you know if Vicky was at work yesterday?" I asked.

"Yes, her show was live. I saw her on the floor once."

"She could have slipped out in the late afternoon. Or gone to the apartment after the show."

"Do you think she went there with a plan to kill Sharon?" Alex asked.

"The murder didn't appear premeditated. She might have stopped by, hoping to reason with Sharon, convince her not to go public. When Sharon refused, she could have become enraged and struck her with the first object she laid her hands on."

"I'm going to see what I can find out from a buddy in the DA's office."

"By the way, I had to give your name to the cops, Alex. I'm so sorry to drag you into this."

"Don't worry about it. Look, I need to book a guest for tomorrow. But I want to talk more about this later. How are you doing?"

"I won't lie, I'm pretty shaken. You want to come by after the show again?"

"Sure. Hang in there till then. And Robin? Be careful, okay?"

I practically stumbled into my apartment. As soon as I closed the door, I let the tears come. For Sharon. Each time I'd spoken to her, I'd been so caught up with my own cause that I hadn't focused on what she'd been through. She'd lost a job she loved, too. And been framed by an evil woman. And now she had died trying to clear her name and help me do the same.

Around four, Lisa rang. From what she could infer, she'd reached Potts before the cops. She said he'd listened intently and asked her to meet him at the University Club at eleven the next day.

I'd no sooner disconnected than the phone rang and I saw Ann's name on the screen.

"There's something going on," she told me. "Lots of closed doors, and Potts wants me on call tonight. I don't know if it has anything to do with you, but I thought you should be aware of it."

"Thanks," I said. "It might have to do with me. I can't reveal anything more right this minute."

"Do you want me to see what I can find out?"

"Um . . . yeah. But please don't bring up my name."

"Right. I'll be in touch if I hear anything."

"Okay. Thank you." I'd almost not uttered those last two words, but they'd slipped out nonetheless.

"You're welcome, Robin. I'm going to prove I'm not the person you thought I was a few days ago."

Alex arrived at 8:45, his face grim. Instinctively, we hugged as soon as he'd stepped through the doorway.

"Are you still reeling?" he said.

"It just keeps running through my mind on this horrific loop."

I led him into the living room.

"You hear from the cops?" I asked.

"Yeah. Thankfully, they let me drop by the precinct at around five rather than having them show up at work."

"It went okay?"

"Yeah, I think so. It was a little bit weird when they asked what I was doing last night. I know that's routine, but it's unsettling."

"Were they okay with your alibi?"

"I don't really have one. I went home after work, crashed on my couch, and never saw a soul."

"They can't for a second believe you were involved."

"It doesn't seem so. Mostly, they wanted to know background information. Why Sharon was here, why I was helping you, my thoughts on Vicky."

"It's *got* to be Vicky, right?"

"I would think so. Tell me about the crime scene, will you? So far I haven't been able to glean anything from my contacts."

"Lots of blood. Not only on the rug but arcs of it on the wall. There was a decorative urn lying on the floor, and I'm assuming she was struck with that."

"More than once, obviously."

"How do you know?"

"I was at plenty of crime scenes in my old job. If Sharon had been struck just once, the blood would have leaked from her head onto the floor. Blood on the wall means someone hit her at least twice. When you strike an open wound, it's similar to splashing in a puddle."

Cringing, I pressed my hands to my face. "I feel responsible. Like I beckoned Sharon to her death. And all for my job. She died because I wanted to get back on the air."

"Hey, don't think that way," Alex said, touching my shoulder. We were still standing in the middle of the living room. "Neither one of us ever anticipated anything like this."

"It's just all so horrible."

"Hey," Alex said again, pulling me into a hug.

"I'm also being selfish," I said. "With Sharon dead, I'm practically right back where I started."

"Let's not get ahead of the situation," he said. "We'll figure it out."

Instinctively, I leaned in to him even more and let my head drop on his shoulder. For a brief second, my anguish seemed to diminish. I drew back after a moment and was looking straight into his eyes. I reached out without thinking and touched Alex's cheek gently with my hand.

He lowered his face and kissed me softly on the mouth.

Chapter 26

I surrendered briefly to the kiss, then pulled back. There was no denying the truth. I'd liked that kiss, but it made everything too complicated.

"I'm sorry," I said. "It's just . . . right now. . . . I don't want any entanglements, Alex."

"I hear you," he said. "You have more than enough to contend with. Besides, I should let you get some rest."

"Promise me you'll do the same. Thanks to me, this has been a dreadful week for you, too."

"It's all been my choice. Call me if anything comes up."

As I closed the door behind him, I could feel that my neck was flushed.

I took a long hot shower after his departure, but it did nothing to quell how distraught I was over Sharon's death. Throughout the night, I tossed fitfully, sleeping only short stretches at a time. At moments, staring into the darkness, I thought of the kiss between Alex and me. I'm attracted to him, I realized. It had been sneaking up on me day by day. In the short months we had worked together, I'd always mentally acknowledged his appeal, but I'd tended to think of him as the guy the interns mooned over. He was five years younger than I was. A senior producer. And yet, a bond had formed between us over the past week and a half, and the sexual heat had intensified, like a brush fire fanned by a breeze.

But as I'd insisted to Alex, I couldn't go there now.

When I woke the next morning, there were a few seconds when I did nothing but relish the feel of cool sheets around my body. Then memories of yesterday rammed into me. Sharon murdered.

Coffee in hand, I raced through news sites, looking for anything I could find on Sharon's murder. The *Daily News* and *New York Post* both had fairly big stories—nothing like a bludgeoned-to-death blonde on the Upper East Side to titillate the public—but there was no mention of a suspect and thankfully no reference to me.

Lisa's meeting with Potts was at eleven. As the hour approached, that was all I could think about. At noon,

Lisa sent an email saying that, due to her schedule, she would be unable to talk by phone most of the day, but she was pleased with the way things had transpired. Potts and Carey had listened carefully, volunteered nothing, but asked for a follow-up on Monday. "They've clearly heard from the police and don't want to be on the wrong side of the issue," Lisa wrote. "Progress."

It looked like the situation might finally be shifting in my favor. Though it would be dumb to get too far ahead of events, I needed to at least consider what would happen if Vicky were arrested and the truth surfaced at last. There was a more than decent chance that I'd be offered my job again. I wondered if I was mentally ready for it. I'd have to interact with Carter every night. Have to work with people like Tom who'd never bothered to contact me. Certainly, my return would require a considerable PR initiative.

I would have loved to go for a run that afternoon. It had been days since I'd circled the reservoir in Central Park, my go-to method for de-stressing and clearing my head. But I didn't like the idea of being that far from home. Not after what had happened to Sharon.

Late in the day, Ann called. "I wanted to give you another heads-up," she said, her voice low, "though I suspect you may know this. A woman Vicky Cruz used to work with was murdered yesterday, and Vicky's being questioned by the police. According to her lawyer, it's just for background information."

So things were fully in motion. Of course, talking to Vicky was not the same as arresting her. I had no idea whether the police had discovered any evidence linking her to the homicide. "It's not just for background information," I told her. "There's a good chance Vicky murdered this woman."

"Is this related to your situation somehow?"

"Yes. The woman came here to help me clear my name."

There were several seconds of silence. I sensed Ann deliberating.

"I'm driving out to East Hampton tonight," she said. "Why don't you come with me? I'll have a phone glued to my head, but you can at least lie by the pool and try to relax."

Surprisingly, I was tempted. This way I'd be be privy to every piece of news Ann heard. It would also be a chance to see if we could repair the damage to our friendship.

"You sure?" I said.

"I'd really love to spend time with you, Robin. Please say yes."

"Okay, but I don't think I can pull it together tonight. Why don't I take the Jitney out there tomorrow morning?"

"Perfect. Just let me know which one you'll be on."

While I'd been talking to her, a call had come in from Maddy. I rang back immediately. After what Alex had revealed, I had a whole new view of my sweet little second cousin. But I needed her at the moment.

"You said to call if I heard anything," she said.

"Yes, what's up?"

"It just feels kind of, you know, tense around here."

"Because of the changes?"

"Partly. But it seems like more than that. Everyone's really on edge."

"Keep your ears open, and let me know if you hear anything specific."

"Of course, Robin. Do you want to grab coffee tomorrow?"

"I'm going out to Ann's place this weekend. Why don't I touch base on Monday?"

The one person I hadn't heard from today was Alex. I wondered if the awkward moment last night would impact the rapport we'd developed. I couldn't let it. I glanced at the clock in my kitchen. It was an hour before the show was due to go on. I sent Alex a text asking that he call when *The Pulse* was off the air.

It was nine o'clock by the time he touched base. "Wait till you hear this," he said after I shared news from my end. "Despite our warnings to be discreet, Sharon apparently told a few former coworkers that she was going to New York and why."

"How'd you hear this?"

"I reached out to that guy Nate in Albany, the one who connected me to Sharon. Needless to say, he was pretty upset with me. But he ended up divulging information."

"So one of Sharon's pals may have been loyal to Vicky and leaked the information to her."

"Exactly. Here's an even bigger bombshell: Nate talked to Sharon's boyfriend, Hal, who told him that he had a voice mail from Sharon early Wednesday evening saying that Vicky had called her, wanting to talk. The boyfriend tried to reach Sharon several times that night, but she never picked up. I bet the person who betrayed Sharon passed Vicky her cell number, too."

"Do you think Nate could have tattled to Vicky?"

"He's an older guy, and he seems pretty genuine. Says he thinks it was an editor at the station who'd always loved, in his words, working both sides of the street. He thinks she may have stayed in touch with Vicky and turned over the info to curry favor."

"Why would Sharon end up meeting with Vicky? Wouldn't she realize how dangerous that could be?"

Silence.

"You still there?" I asked.

"Yes. I was just wondering if Sharon might have been open to discussion."

"What do you mean?"

"What if Vicky offered to pay her to keep quiet?"

I groaned. "I don't want to believe that," I said. "And if Vicky was willing to pay Sharon, why turn around and murder her?"

"Maybe it was all a ruse to wrangle her way into the apartment. Or maybe Sharon ended up demanding more than Vicky wanted to pay."

I wasn't buying it. Even if it was true, I was still the catalyst for Sharon's death. I felt exhausted suddenly. "I probably should get to bed," I said. "I'll be away this weekend, but I'll stay close to my phone. There's bound to be news."

"You aren't going back to Westport, are you?"

"Not on my life. No, I'm taking the Jitney to East Hampton tomorrow morning. To stay with Ann Carny."

"Have a good weekend," he said. "I'll be in touch."

Thirty minutes later, he phoned back. "A lawyer pal called last-minute and invited me to Sag Harbor. Can I give you a lift out that way tomorrow?"

"Actually, that would be great," I said. A ride would make the trip far less of a hassle. Plus, it would guarantee a chance to make certain everything was smoothed over with Alex, that my pulling away from the kiss hadn't done any damage.

I texted Ann the update, and then fell into bed. Sharon was in my dreams that night, trying to say something I couldn't understand. When I woke with a start in the morning, I felt completely frayed.

Alex had said he'd pick me up at nine, and from there we'd exit the city via the Triboro Bridge. At about 8:45, as I finished my espresso, the doorman rang up. "There's a gentleman here to see you," he announced.

"Um, fine," I replied, realizing that Alex had made better time driving uptown than planned. "I'll be right down."

I hurriedly tossed sunscreen into my toiletry case, double checked that I'd packed running shoes, and rode the elevator downstairs.

"He's outside," the doorman said as I dashed through the lobby.

I stepped onto the sidewalk. Carter Brooks was standing right there.

Well, well, look who'd turned up? Like a bad penny, Aunt Jessie would have said. My body tightened defensively. What I didn't feel, I realized, was a hint of attraction to the man.

His eyes fell to my duffel bag. "I take it you were expecting someone else," he said with a half-grin.

"What is it you need?" I asked, ignoring his comment.

He was wearing a blue-and-white-checked button-down shirt and off-white flat-front pants. Hamptons-bound, too, I figured.

"I just wanted to see how you were doing. I've been thinking about you."

"Oh, is that right? I guess you were in such a tizzy about me passing out on-set that you lost my cell number."

"I'm sorry I didn't get in touch before now. I just wasn't sure of the best way to handle the situation. It's all been a big mess, as you can imagine."

"How dreadful that you were inconvenienced."

He raked a hand through his thick brown hair. "It's not about inconvenience, Robin," he said, lowering his voice as two people exited the building. "Potts was very insistent that I steer clear. He got wind of our relationship, and he wasn't pleased to say the least."

"Did you mention to anyone that you were seeing me?"

"Not a soul, so I have no freaking clue how we were busted. But trust me, I'm sorry I gave in to the pressure not to call."

Trust me. That was a laugh. "That wasn't the only reason you showed no concern, was it?" I said. "You hated the item that ran about me and the show."

He pulled back his torso slightly, obviously surprised that I'd gone there. "It wasn't only the item that got me. Tom let on that you were jockeying to play a bigger role. I didn't like how you were maneuvering things."

"For your information, it was Potts who suggested I play a bigger role, not me. And what was wrong with that?"

"Whatever. I just want us to be on good terms, that's all."

"Did you tell Potts that I was obsessed with Vicky?"

"Of course not," he said adamantly.

"And what about my past? Did you let him in on what my stepmother had done?"

"What?" he said, looking indignant. "Think what you want about me, but I'm not that big of a scumbag."

I bet that was what all the scumbags said. "I really need to head back upstairs," I told him. "Happy paddleboarding."

"Robin, wait," he said, reaching for me. "Like I said, I'm sorry. I'd like to work with you again. I hope there's a way that can happen."

I tugged my hand away and hurried back into the building.

Back in my apartment, I sat on my couch, trying to decode Carter's visit. The timing had to be meaningful. My best guess: that someone had hinted to him that I might be coming back to the show, and he wanted to be sure he'd put out any fires.

That could very well mean that Potts was seriously considering bringing me back.

Could I believe that Carter hadn't yakked to anyone about our hook-up? Somehow Potts had found out. And so had Vicky. Otherwise, she wouldn't have known to make sure the napkin with the brownie had been signed with a C.

Alex arrived on time, and he smiled as I slid into the car. He was wearing jeans and a T-shirt, and his facial scruff was a little longer than usual. I felt something stir in me at the sight of him. I thought of the kiss again, the taste of his mouth.

He'd made a coffee run before stopping at my place and he nodded toward the cup holders as we pulled away from the building. "Just black, right?" he said.

"Yes, thanks for remembering. You must be glad to be escaping the city, too."

"For sure. I don't even care about hitting the beach. I just want to read. I loaded about ten books on my iPad this summer, and I've hardly made a dent."

"Me, too. And summer for me was always about reading, just spending endless hours in the library stalls, searching for new books."

"They probably have a table named after you at the Oneonta Public Library."

"Oneonta?" I asked, surprised.

He glanced in my direction. "Isn't that where your aunt lived?"

"How did you know?"

"You mentioned it on the ride to Albany."

"Oh, right." But I couldn't recall doing that. As much as I'd loved my aunt, Oneonta had stood for banishment, so I rarely uttered the name. I wondered for the first time if Alex had nursed a crush on me at work and researched my background. That would explain some of his eagerness to help.

I sipped my coffee and stared out the window, wondering where Vicky was at the moment. If the police ended up arresting her, the news would explode everywhere.

Without planning to, I drifted asleep and didn't wake until I felt Alex gently jostling my shoulder. "We're almost there," he said. "Can you give me the street address?"

"Oh, wow, sorry. I feel like a baby, sleeping the whole way like that."

"Will you need a lift home tomorrow?"

"Thanks, but I'll probably drive back with Ann."

"Okay, I'll check in with you if I hear anything. I may even bump into you at some point. I think we're having dinner in East Hampton tonight."

There was no awkwardness as we smiled and said goodbye, but I detected a degree of reserve from Alex, clearly because of the line I'd drawn.

Ann opened the door to her house, dressed in a bathing suit with a blue-and-white-print sarong knotted around her waist and her hair pulled back in a low ponytail. "Welcome," she said. "I'm so glad you decided to come."

"Thanks, I really needed this."

In one split second, maybe because of the coconut scent from her sunscreen, I felt overwhelmed with a sense memory of other summer days spent with Ann, a few of them here at the house. There was so much to lose if I didn't forgive her. I had to try.

"Who gave you the ride?" she asked, peering over my shoulder. I turned and followed her gaze as the car nosed away.

"Alex Lucca from work."

"The producer?" She took my bag and led me inside.

"Mm-hmm."

She wrinkled her nose a little, as if she'd picked up a hint of something burning.

"What is it?" I asked.

"It's not a big deal."

"Come on, Ann. There's something."

"Okay, when he first started at the network a year or two ago, I fielded a weird call about him. A reporter from the *Daily News* fishing for info. Alex was in the DA's office, right? I think there may have been an issue when he was there."

I'd sensed from the beginning that Alex had misgivings about his ADA job. But it had seemed to be about him not finding law to be a good fit. "You have no clue what the reporter was getting at?" I asked.

"No. I contacted HR, and they said they'd checked references before hiring him, so I guess it couldn't be anything serious."

"Probably not," I said, but her comment felt like a branch snagging on my sleeve. It would be worth looking into.

"Why don't I pour you an iced tea," she said, changing the subject. "Then we can sit down and talk."

I followed her to the kitchen through a large living/dining area decorated beautifully with white ultramodern furniture offset by sisal rugs. With drinks in hand, we headed out to the patio. A swimming pool ran lengthwise behind the house, the bottom painted to make the water look Caribbean turquoise.

"Your timing's actually perfect," she said as we took seats at the outdoor dining table. "Five minutes ago, I heard from the personal assistant Potts uses on weekends. He wants me available for a call in the next hour. I bet it has to do with Vicky and that woman's death."

My body tensed. "If the police have already found evidence incriminating Vicky, this could blow up in a huge way this weekend," I said.

"Why in the world would Vicky kill her?"

"Because the woman was going to tell Potts that Vicky harassed her in ways similar to what was done to me."

Ann shook her head in shock. "You'll be *cleared*," she said, breaking into a smile.

"Ideally, yes."

"Robin, that's fantastic," she said. "You must be so relieved."

"She hasn't been arrested yet."

"It's not too soon to discuss how to handle the situation if she is. This is your comeback, and we have to be prepared, make sure we leverage the press the best way possible."

"I've been thinking about that myself."

"Let me see about lunch, and then we can discuss it."

A little while later, over salade Niçoise, she helped me sketch out a rough plan. For background, I ran through the experience of locating Sharon and enticing her to the city. It was painful to rehash it.

"I can tell it hurts," Ann said, "but this will make your comeback story even stronger—that you worked so hard to prove your innocence."

By one, Potts still hadn't called. I helped Ann clear the dishes and then settled into a wrought-iron lounge chair by the pool. The house was set in the middle of a former potato farm, and I stared out beyond the pool, across a field covered with purple and yellow wildflowers. Far off to the left I could see another modern house and, to the right, an older shingled one.

I tried to read, but my eyes skidded off the page. Surely by now, I thought, there had to be some news. After about fifteen minutes, I wandered back into the house.

Ann was standing in the living room, her iPhone pressed to her ear. She looked perturbed and raised a finger, indicating she'd be off shortly. "All right," she said into the phone. "I'll let you know if there are any inquiries."

I held my breath as she tapped the screen to end the call. "News?" I asked.

"It's not what we wanted to hear," she said. "Vicky *was* questioned about the murder. But she has a solid alibi for the entire evening."

Chapter 27

"I can't believe it," I said. "Maybe she paid someone to do it."

Even as I uttered the statement, I realized how off
it was. The crime had looked spur-of-the-moment, a
case of anger escalating into homicidal rage. Not some
paid killer's MO.

"Robin, I know you have good reason to believe
Vicky is behind everything," Ann said. "And I've
been so wrong to doubt you before. But wouldn't
it make sense to at least consider other possibilities
in this woman's death? Did she have a boyfriend?
Isn't the boyfriend usually the killer in these sorts of
crimes?"

I shook my head in dismay. "I don't know what to
think anymore." I pressed my fingers to my temples.

"Would you mind if I took a run right now? I could really use it."

"Not at all. I was just going to work out on the patio and then make a dessert."

I dug out my running shoes and laced them up while sitting under the front portico. Before I broke into a jog, I tried Alex's cell. It went to voice mail immediately, so I left a message.

I headed in the general direction of the ocean. My legs had been craving this, and for a while I let myself relish the sensation of my feet coming down hard on the pavement and the rush of air through my lungs. But before long, my thoughts were scrambling crazily, grabbing all my focus.

Vicky might have an alibi, but somehow she had to be responsible for Sharon's death; it was too big a coincidence otherwise. That meant she'd sent another person to the apartment, a cohort who was supposed to reason with Sharon but ended up striking out. After all, Vicky must have arranged for an accomplice to plant the brownie in my basket when she was in D.C.

Maybe, I realized, the person who had left the brownie had also killed Sharon. How was I going to solve the whole freaking puzzle? Two days ago I had allowed myself to believe that the situation was coming to a head. Now everything I'd banked on was like dust sifting through my fingers. If the police didn't find Sharon's photo of the Barbie, or refused to turn it over to me, I was back to square one with clearing my name. And Vicky was still at large.

Then I stopped in my tracks and replayed the words that had surged through my brain. *Vicky at large.* I was on a stretch of road with just a few houses, houses with empty driveways because the inhabitants were hanging at the beach. What if Vicky were trying to track me down this weekend and had determined where I was? For all I knew, she was the one who'd followed me to Westport.

I reversed course and headed directly back to Ann's, my legs pumping so hard they ached by the time I reached the house. Maybe this time I *am* being paranoid, I thought, reflecting under the portico. There was no way Vicky could find me here. Still panting, I walked around the house to the patio, where Ann was typing on her laptop at the table.

"Anything new?" I asked.

"Nothing so far, but the quiet is scaring me. Some reporter's bound to find out Vicky was questioned."

Then what? Would I end up part of the Sharon story, making my situation even worse?

I traipsed back to the guest room and tried Alex again, but it still went to voice mail. After changing into my bathing suit, I returned to the patio and plunged into the pool.

Just being in the water reminded me of my swim in Westport, my arms slicing hard through the water so determinedly. I'd started to find my way back that day, and I had to keep going.

I swam for thirty minutes, and afterward, despite my nap in the car, I slept again on the lounge chair. Later, Ann lit the grill to barbecue steaks for dinner. It was even hotter out than it had been earlier, so she suggested we eat in just our suits and robes, in case we wanted to take an evening dip.

She served the meal at eight, the outdoor table lit with candles in hurricane lamps. The food was fabulous, but I could only poke at it. I stared out at the darkening sky above the field. Why hadn't Alex called yet?

"Robin, I know this has been a setback," Ann said, pouring us each another glass of wine. "I'll help you, I promise. Tell me what I can do."

"There's one thing, but it won't be easy," I said.

"Spell it out."

"As you know, the Internet searches were done when Keiki was at her desk, but I've learned there's a way to do that remotely. I need to convince Potts to have an outside forensic firm examine my work computer. I was counting on Sharon's story forcing him to take that step. Now I have to do it without that."

"Okay, I'll talk to Potts," she said. "It will probably be better to wait until Monday, when I can do it face-to-face."

"He won't like you pushing on this."

"Tough. I'm not going to let you down again."

"Thank you, Ann," I said. It was clear she was doing everything in her power to undo the damage to our friendship.

I helped her clear the dishes and load the dishwasher and then carry the dessert plates out to the patio. She'd made blueberry crumble.

"Why don't we sit by the pool and have the crumble there," she said. "I was at that table so much of the afternoon."

It was dark out, the only illumination coming from the hurricane lamps and the light at the bottom of the pool. I looked across the field. I could no longer see the outline of the houses; only one of them had lights on. My fear returned, unbidden.

"Okay," I said hesitantly.

"What?" she asked.

"I just feel a little nervous tonight, with Vicky free. It's stupid to worry out here, but I can't fight it."

"I understand completely. Let's go inside as soon as we're done with dessert. I'll lock up after that."

We settled into two of the lounge chairs, the desserts set on a small table between us. "Actually," she said, climbing back out of her chair, "why don't I lock the front door right now."

As she went inside, my phone rang from the pocket of my robe. I dug it out, expecting to see Alex's name, but Bettina's was on the screen instead.

"Sorry to call on a Saturday night," she said. "There's something I need to share with you."

"Not a problem," I said, on full alert. "Tell me what's up."

"Remember that item we ran on the survey Potts commissioned, the one that raved about you?"

"How could I forget it?"

"The writer is this borderline-hysterical colum-nist named Natalie, and she called me out of the blue tonight. There's been some buzz about Vicky Cruz being questioned by the police in a murder investiga-tion, and Natalie was all in a panic that she might be swept into it somehow."

"But how?" I asked.

"Right after the item ran, Vicky apparently called Natalie, demanding to know who the source was. So the little fool ended up telling her. She claims she did it in exchange for other information Vicky had. Natalie has no idea if any of this is related to the murder inves-tigation, but she wanted to cover her ass with me in case it leaked out."

"What kind of information did Vicky share?" I asked, alarmed that info might be about me.

"Something vile about an executive at a totally different network, but that's not the part that's important. What I thought you should know, darling, is who leaked the original item to Natalie. It was your own PR person. Ann Carny."

For a few seconds I was too stunned to say anything. "Did Natalie have any idea why she did it?" I inquired, my voice lowered.

"Carny simply told her she was delivering a tidbit she thought Natalie would find worthwhile."

"All right, thanks. Let me try to get to the bottom of it."

I glanced back over my shoulder. From far off, I could hear Ann rummaging around the kitchen. I tried Alex's number once again. This time he picked up on the third ring.

"Hey," he said. "Sorry I missed your calls before. I was just about to phone you."

"I can't really talk now," I said, "but I need to update you. Are you going to be around later?"

"Everything okay?" he asked, his tone concerned.

"I just learned something pretty disturbing." There were footsteps behind me. "I'll call you back. I need to sort this out."

I dropped the phone back into my robe pocket as Ann reemerged onto the patio, carrying a fresh bottle of wine. On her way to her lounge chair, she scooped up our wineglasses from the table. Don't overreact, I warned myself. I needed to hear her explanation.

"Are you feeling too anxious to stay out here?" Ann asked, catching my expression.

"It's not that," I said, keeping my voice even. "Someone called with some very strange news."

"About Vicky?" she asked. Before she sat down, she leaned her chair on the back wheels and angled it slightly so she'd be able to see me better.

"About you, actually," I said. "You were responsible for that gossip story about the survey. The one I believe they so cleverly titled 'Cruzin' for a Bruisin' '?"

Ann forced a smile. "Okay, guilty as charged," she said. "I thought the survey was a chance to score a nice plug for you, but that moron of a reporter turned it into a Vicky-bashing item. I should have told you I planted it, but I felt too embarrassed when it backfired a little."

"You really thought that item would be *good* for me?"

"To have you presented as the rising star of the network? Of course I assumed it'd be good for you. I've always done everything to make you shine."

"But you knew Potts had accused me of seeming overly ambitious. That write-up surely didn't help my case."

"Potts talks out of both sides of his mouth," she said dismissively. "He likes keeping everybody's ego in check, but he also wants all the publicity he can lay his fat hands on."

She was trying to justify her motives, but her defense stunk.

"And didn't you consider how Carter would react to an item about me being the show's real star? He was furious." A thought took shape in my mind even as the words tumbled out. "Though maybe that's what you were actually hoping for. You were always so eager to make sure we didn't hook up."

"I was right, though, wasn't I?" she said. "Look at how that ended up hurting you with Potts."

I shook my head slowly, thinking. "It was more than you trying to protect my career," I said. "You seemed to dislike the sheer idea of me with Carter. What have you got against the guy?"

"I was looking out for you, Robin. That's what friends do."

You're not my friend, I thought. A friend wouldn't have shared the survey info. "Who told you about me and Carter?"

"No one," she said. She'd picked up the belt of her terry-cloth robe and was rubbing the end between her thumb and forefinger. "I figured it out on my own."

"Oh, come on," I said. "We hardly left a trail of bread crumbs through the forest."

"I'm not a fool, Robin," she snapped. "I'd watched all the back-and-forth on the air. And then one day in the hall, I could tell just by the way he looked at you. He was practically stripping your clothes off with his eyes."

A memory stirred. Carter talking about his ex-girlfriend, Jamie. She hadn't liked the way he'd looked at me, because deep down she was jealous as hell.

My brain was like a lock with the tumblers falling open one by one: Ann always warning me away from Carter; Alex revealing Carter had been sleeping with someone at work months ago; Ann's reluctance to meet men this year.

"You're involved with Carter, aren't you?" I said, shocked by the words even as I said them. "Or at least you were."

Ann looked off, deliberating, and then back at me, her gray eyes dark as slate in the candlelight. "Is that so difficult to imagine?" she said. "Just because I'm not all sexy and witty, like you are?"

"Of course it's not hard to imagine. You're a beautiful woman, Ann."

I felt a pang of sympathy, because she'd been wounded. And yet she'd planted the item to make Carter turn against me. "When did things start with the two of you?"

"In March, before you'd ever laid eyes on him."

"When the show was being developed?"

"Yes. Since Carter was going to be the linchpin, Potts wanted me to work with him. We couldn't keep our hands off each other. But with the launch, we realized we needed to cool things down for a bit. We had every intention of getting back. Until you decided you wanted him."

"What about Jamie?" I said. "Carter was dating her half the summer."

"I endorsed that idea," she said. "She was just a decoy. And then you had to go and wreck everything for me."

I thought I saw a tear swell in her eye. Carter, I realized, was an even bigger sleaze than I'd thought. He'd gladly let her groom him for bigger success and then strung her along.

"Ann, I never would have slept with Carter if I'd known you were involved with him," I said.

"Oh, please," she scoffed. "You don't expect me to believe that, do you? No matter what, you'd always feel entitled to bed the star of the show. You feel entitled to *everything*."

"Ann, that's not true." I was stunned by the harshness of her words. "I've never felt that way."

"Of course you do, Robin. It's always about you being on top."

"In case you're forgetting," I said, "I spent a year and a half off the air, with no one interested in hiring me. And the only gigs I was offered then were infomercials for juicers and mattresses."

"And you spent that entire time bemoaning your fate as if you'd been wronged. It's never enough for you. You snag the book contract, but you want that *and* a show. I help hook you up with the subbing gig, and you immediately start nosing around for what might be in development. The minute you caught a whiff of Carter's show, you started jockeying for the job. And *still* it wasn't enough. You had to fuck his brains out."

I'd never had a clue to her bitterness. It was like one of those scenes in a sci-fi movie when a character's face splits open and there's a hideous, snouted alien underneath.

And had it gone beyond pure resentment?

"Did you mention to Vicky that I was seeing Carter?"

"Why would I do that?" she said. Her expression seemed truly perplexed. "You know I loathe the woman."

"Someone clued her in," I said. "I ate the brownie because it appeared to be from Carter. As far as I know, you were the only one who knew about us at that point. Maybe you told her in order to stir things up, just like you tried to do with the item."

She stared at me, holding her head very still, as if afraid of jostling something free. I looked down at my plate, at the blueberries oozing beneath the crumbly topping. Ann, the devoted cook and baker. There it was—the truth.

"You left the brownie, didn't you?" I said, my heart pounding hard.

"Oh, please," she said.

"No, you did," I said. I shook my head, trying to make sense of it. "I told you at lunch that I'd heard Vicky talking about Ambien. So you made the brownie with it and left it for me. You knew I'd think it was one more of Vicky's dirty deeds. You didn't realize she was in Washington that night."

"All right, fine," she said, pure triumph in her voice. "But you'll never prove it."

"Why, Ann? Why would you hurt me that way?"

"Because I could stand you having almost everything in the fucking world, Robin, but not Carter, too. He was supposed to be mine."

I thought of the formula that had sprung into my head on my run: The person who left the brownie had also killed Sharon.

"You murdered Sharon, didn't you?" I whispered.

I wanted to snatch the words back but it was too late. Terror squeezed my chest, cutting off my breath. As Ann stared back at me, I tried to calculate the distance between my chair and the sliding glass door behind me. Would I have time to get inside and lock her out— or should I jump up and start to run? I thought of the houses so far across the field.

"You must be feeling frightened right now," Ann said, her voice flat.

"A little," I said. Calm, I warned myself. Don't freak her. "I also know how smart you are, and that you probably want to dig yourself out of this before it grows any worse."

She bent her head so I couldn't see her face. I knew she must be gathering strength, preparing to strike. My legs were limp with fear, but I slowly swung the right one off the chair, lowering my foot to the ground.

Ann glanced up. Tears were streaming down her cheeks. "I *do* want this all to end," she said softly. "I can't take it anymore. Can you help me, Robin? Please?"

"Of course," I said. I needed to keep the talk going. "Why don't we call someone? Not the police. But a lawyer, someone who can advise you best."

"Okay," she said. She wiped the tears away, using both hands. "I need someone who can understand and not hate me. You have to realize I didn't mean it. Everything—it just flew out of control."

"How did you even know about Sharon?"

"From Vicky. Someone from the stupid station in Albany told her that Sharon was headed to New York to expose what had happened years ago. Vicky didn't come right out and admit she'd done all those things to you, but she implied she did. Said you were too big for your britches. She told me I had to find out where Sharon was staying and talk sense into her. That day I brought you the flowers, I'd followed you to the building earlier, the one where Sharon was staying. I went back afterward and kept hitting buttons on the intercom until I found Sharon. I told her I was working with you and needed to talk to her."

"I don't understand," I said. "Why would you feel the need to aid Vicky?"

"She found out about the brownie. I don't know how, but she did. I was in a panic, thinking she'd go to Potts. Then I realized it was just going to be something she had on me and could use when she wanted. She wanted to make me her bitch."

"Did she also send you to Westport to check on me?"

"No. Carter took the night off, and I thought he was with you. Keiki knew where you were staying, so I drove there."

"Okay, I understand," I said. I could barely hear myself over the thumping of my heart. "I know how desperate you must have felt. Vicky made me desperate, too."

She started to cry again. "The woman's a monster. She told me that if she was caught, she'd bring me down, too, that I had to sort it out. I tried to reason with Sharon. I even offered her money, but she wouldn't listen. She told me to leave, that it was over for Vicky. I couldn't let that happen."

"A good lawyer will understand. I'll help you find the right one."

She took a deep breath and dabbed at her tears with the end of her belt. "I need tissues," she said.

"Just use your napkin," I said. I felt a new surge of panic.

She bounded up and quickly skirted around the back of her chair and then mine. I started to rise, but before I could move, she was behind me, thrusting her hands in front of my torso. I saw a flash of the belt from her robe. She had it stretched in front of me, and she pulled it toward me, pinning my arms and chest against the back of the chair.

"What are you doing?" I yelled.

She tightened the belt, and I could feel her tying it behind me.

"Please, Ann, no," I yelled. I tried wiggling to free myself.

She yanked the chair back on the rear wheels and began rolling it across the patio toward the pool. I swung my legs over the sides, trying to grip the ground with my feet, but I couldn't reach it. We were at the edge of the pool. I felt one more push from behind.

And then I was toppling over sideways into the deep end.

Chapter 28

The chair seemed to freeze on top of the water. I held my breath, willing it to just stay there. But then, quickly, it began to sink. I thrust my head up, gasping for air, and in seconds I was underwater, being sucked to the bottom of the pool.

I pressed my lips tight and struggled to free my arms. The belt was wet, and it felt like I was glued to the chair.

My lungs started to burn from holding my breath. I was going to die.

Then there was an explosion of sound and a force torpedoing through the water toward me. Someone had plunged into the pool. It's Ann, I thought. She's going to hold me down.

I could feel hands tugging on the belt. I was free suddenly, and the swimmer's arm was around my upper torso, dragging me through the water. My lungs were searing, desperate for air. Against my will, my mouth opened and filled with water.

Then I was above the surface and being hoisted onto the patio. I spat out water and gasped for air. A man was holding me. It was Alex. He was panting and dripping wet. He leaned me farther forward, patting my back. More water spurted from between my lips.

"Can you breathe okay?" he asked.

I couldn't answer. My throat felt raw, and I had started to shiver.

"Yes, I think so," I said finally. "Where is she?"

"Over there," he said, jerking his head. "She came after me, and I punched her. I knocked her out. I need to restrain her, though."

Alex scrambled up and ran across the patio. He tore off his belt and used it to secure Ann's wrist to the base of the grill. She started moaning, not fully conscious yet.

"Robin, where's your phone?" Alex called out. "Mine's ruined."

I felt for it in the pocket of the robe. "Ruined, too," I said. "There's a landline in the house. In the kitchen."

"Yell to me if she moves," he said.

As he ran into the house, I saw him glance up and scan the second story of the house. He disappeared inside.

My head was throbbing, as if someone were whacking it with a hammer. I wanted to lie back, but I didn't dare let Ann out of my sight. A minute later, Alex was back, talking to the 911 operator on the house phone.

"You don't remember Lisa's number, do you?" he said after hanging up.

"No, everything's in my phone."

"Okay, I'll figure something out. We need a lawyer for when we deal with the cops."

Alex found rope in the tool shed to better secure Ann. Next, he helped me out of the sopping wet robe and led me to one of the dining chairs, easing me into it, and draped a dry towel around my shoulders. He pulled up a chair next me. Haltingly, I described the circumstances and Ann's confession. She had come to and was thrashing on the patio, trying to escape.

"Stop or I'm going to punch you again," Alex yelled to her.

Five minutes later, two sets of cops from the town arrived. I related what had happened. Ann was screaming, demanding to be freed. They placed her in handcuffs, and two of the cops led her off somewhere. An ambulance arrived, and the EMTs examined me. They tried to pressure me into going to the hospital, but I insisted that I was okay. One of the cops said detectives would be there soon.

I rested my head on the table. My brain felt clogged with water, as if I were still in the pool. After a while I could hear Alex talking to someone, but I couldn't make out the words, and then a detective was sitting next to me, introducing himself. He was young, only in his thirties, I guessed. I quickly told the story, trying to make the shivering stop.

"Why don't I let you put on dry clothes," he said, "and we can talk more in a minute."

I staggered back into the guest bedroom, stripped off my bathing suit, and changed into jeans and a sweater. I grabbed my purse from the chair. When I returned to the patio, I saw that the overhead lights around the pool had been switched on. It was bright out there, like a photo shoot.

"They're taking us to the police station in separate cars," Alex said, approaching me. "I've found a lawyer to meet us there. You don't need to say anything else until he arrives, okay?"

Inside the car, my shivering began to subside, but I still felt shaken to the core. Ann was a murderer. She'd killed Sharon, and she would have killed me if it weren't for Alex. She'd been my friend for over four years, offering advice, sharing her home, sometimes just sipping wine by my side at a bar in our part of town, and I'd been blind to the resentment and rage that had been building in her. Was it because I was so caught up in my own saga, in my unrelenting drive to be on top again?

At the police station, I explained I needed to wait for my lawyer and was taken to a room by myself, with no idea where Alex was. I rummaged through my purse for a comb, blush, and lip-gloss and tried to make myself look less bedraggled. I still felt shell-shocked from what had happened, from everything I'd learned.

It was over an hour before the lawyer was ushered into the room. He was dressed in white pants and a navy blazer, looking as if he'd been interrupted mid-surf and turf at the yacht club.

"Butch Harrison, Robin," he said, thrusting out his hand. "Alex has filled me in to some degree, but why don't you take me through it."

I did, including the backstory. "Ann's going to deny the whole thing," I said at the end. "She'll say—"

"Don't worry," he said, raising his hand. "Alex saw her throw you in the pool. There's security video, too. Alex spotted the camera on the roof."

I closed my eyes, savoring the relief.

"Let's get your statement out of the way now," he said, "so you can go home."

Two hours later, Alex and I were together again, headed toward the house in Sag Harbor where he was staying. While I'd been interviewed, one of the cops had driven him back to Ann's to retrieve his car. Because of the high humidity, his clothes hadn't fully dried yet. "You're still squishy," I said, half-smiling.

"I know," he said. "I feel like a big sponge."

"Thank you, Alex," I said, overwhelmed with gratitude. "Thank you with every ounce of my being."

When we stepped inside the clapboard house on a side street in town, a man jumped up sleepily from the couch. He was fortyish, slightly balding, dressed in sweat-clothes.

"This is my friend Dereck," Alex said. "I've filled him in on the phone."

"I'm just glad you're both okay," Dereck said. "How did Butch do?"

"Excellent," I replied. "Alex said you were the one who convinced him to come to our aid. Thank you."

"The guy owes me a favor. Julie finally went up to bed, by the way. Want me to rouse her?"

"Nah, we'll fill her in at breakfast," Alex said. "Thanks for everything, man."

Alex said that he'd show me to my room and led me upstairs. I was exhausted, and my legs ached as I climbed each step. The bedroom was under the eaves, with a slanted ceiling, but that seemed comforting to me. Part of me wanted to crawl under the duvet and close my eyes; another part didn't want to let Alex out of my sight.

"Do you need anything?" Alex asked. "Tell me what I can do."

"Would you mind fixing me a cup of tea?" I asked. "I can't seem to shake these chills." They had started again on the drive from the station.

"You need something to sleep in, too," he said. He rifled through a duffel bag on the floor and handed me a soft gray T-shirt. He also pulled out fresh clothes for himself.

"I guess I've co-opted your bedroom," I said.

"That's okay. They have a daybed on the screened-in porch, and it's a great place to bunk down."

After he left, I changed into the T-shirt and slid under the covers of the double bed, propping myself up against the headboard. Briefly, I was overwhelmed with the terrifying sense that I was sinking all over again.

Alex was back in ten minutes, wearing dry clothes and carrying a mug with steam rising from the top. He set it on the bedside table and lowered himself onto the bed. I could feel the warmth of his body through the covers.

"How do you know Dereck?" I asked.

"Law school. He was older, but we hit it off. Thankfully, his home number was listed with 411."

I took a long sip of tea. Swallowing, I realized my throat was raw and sore. "I never asked you," I said. "What made you come to Ann's house?"

"Dereck, Julie, and I were eating nearby at someone's house. You sounded a little freaked on the phone, and I didn't like it. I knew you'd been worrying that someone at work had betrayed you, and I wondered suddenly if it was Ann. I just flew out of the dinner and swung by the house to check on you. I'll be honest. I invited myself to Dereck's this weekend because I was worried about you."

"I still can't believe it. If you hadn't come, Alex, I would have drowned. She would have cut the belt off and dragged the chair out of the pool and then told the police the next morning that she'd gone to bed, leaving me sitting out there. I'd had a couple of glasses of wine, and it would have looked like I'd stupidly taken a swim and died. Or even that I'd drowned myself because of the mess my life was in."

"Did you ever sense any animosity from her?"

"No, not really. A couple of times she'd seemed slightly annoyed with me, but I assumed it was because I was burdening her with so much." I picked up the edge of the white duvet and ran my fingers along it. "From what she confessed tonight, though, she'd been seething underneath for a while. It was probably fine when I was out of work and needy—she seemed so supportive of me then—but once I got the show, her resentment built, and it finally ate through any good feelings she had for me."

"She always looked so cool-headed."

I nodded. "Little things are starting to bubble up," I said. "Like the night of my book party, she had this kind of lame excuse why she could only pop in. I didn't think much of it at the time, but now I'm wondering if it's because she couldn't bear seeing me as the center of attention that night."

I tapped my hand to my mouth as another revelation hit me. "There's something else. That quote in the *Times* piece about my ambition being as naked as a porn star? I wonder if she was the insider who said that. She wanted to help me with the piece, but she couldn't stand that I was being profiled.

"And then once she found out about Carter," I added, "I had to be stopped."

Alex crossed his arms over his chest, thinking. His hair was still slightly damp, contrasting even more with that lovely luminescent skin of his.

"When I was in the police station," he said, "I flashed on something that happened when I about ten years old. My family used to rent a place on Cape Cod for part of the summer, and one year my sister and I put on a talent show with a bunch of kids. She had a great voice, and with every rehearsal, it was evident she was going to steal the show. One day she was rehearsing on this low porch, and one of the other girls, who was standing on the ground below, took a bite out of her calf. It was crazy—she didn't just draw blood, she left this whole row of teeth marks. A few adults came running over and kept trying to figure out if there'd been some kind of altercation, but even as a ten-year-old, I could see that this girl was consumed with jealousy of my sister. And you wouldn't have had a clue until then."

"I've felt jealous at times, like when I saw other women bag jobs I wanted. But nothing like that."

"There's one point I keep wondering about. How do you think Vicky found out that Ann had made the brownie?"

"I have a hunch she guessed it. Vicky apparently has an uncanny way of reading people. It's like she smells their weakness, senses where the soft underbelly is. Vicky found out from the reporter that Ann had leaked that item saying I was the show's real star. After that, Vicky knew Ann had something against me. When Vicky heard about the brownie, she knew *she* hadn't done it. So she guessed Ann had and let her think she had proof."

I felt my eyes grow heavy and closed them for a second.

"You need to sleep," Alex said.

"Can I ask you a question?" I said. "Why did you leave the DA's office?"

He cocked his head, puzzled. "What brings that up at this moment?"

"When I arrived at Ann's, she made a comment about it. I think she wanted me to be suspicious of you so I wouldn't be turning to you for help."

"There was a case that shouldn't have been tried. I was overruled, and it went to another ADA. The guy ended up with a ten-year sentence. After that, there was no way I could stay another day there. I left in a huff. I hated myself for not doing more to change the situation."

"Is that partly why you wanted to help me?"

He smiled. "That," he said, "and total infatuation."

I smiled back and set down the mug of tea. I reached for his hand, brought it to my lips, and kissed it.

Chapter 29

It was just before eight in the evening, a little later than when I'd arrived at the same spot two months ago. I was standing outside Bettina's apartment, though this time there were no festive party sounds pulsating inside.

It was ironic, really, as I thought of it, me all decked out that night in my fuck-you shoes. I should have known a pair of booties that pinched my feet like a son of a bitch couldn't be counted on for much.

I rang the bell, and Bettina's male Filipino housekeeper answered. He led me into the massive living area, gestured for me to take a seat, and asked if he could bring me a refreshment. I declined.

After he departed soundlessly, I rose and drifted over to the wall of floor-to-ceiling windows that faced west to the Hudson and the densely packed New Jersey waterfront. The vista was even more spectacular tonight than it had been the evening of my party; because it was fully dark out, lights twinkled fiercely everywhere.

"Please forgive me," Bettina said when she swept into the room a good ten minutes later. She was dressed in a deep-orange pantsuit, a nod to fall, and carrying what looked like a vodka on the rocks. "I had a call I just could *not* get rid of. No drink for you?"

"I'm fine, thanks," I said, turning from the window. "I have to ask. Is it as magical now as it was at the start?"

"What, darling? You're not inquiring about my sex life, are you?"

I smiled. "No, the view."

She shrugged. "I'm going to tell you a little secret, Robin," she said. "I appreciate my view, I do. I worked hard for it. Unfortunately, it's like going to bed with a gorgeous man. After a while, things become familiar, and some of the magic does disappear. Now, come talk to me."

We took seats opposite each other, she in a curved white armchair set on a Plexiglas base and me on the couch.

"It seems as if some of the drama is finally dying down," she said.

"Yes, a bit," I said. "For the first time in days, there were no reporters camped out in front of my apartment this morning."

"You said you had a question for me. I'm eager to hear and to help if I can."

I had called two days ago and requested a meeting. I knew my question would surprise her. But it was something I'd been mulling over for the past four weeks.

It had been a truly crazy month for me, and tough at times. Not just because of the trauma of East Hampton but because I was still wrestling with grief over Sharon's death and my failure to see the ugly mix of emotions I'd triggered in Ann.

She'd been charged that night with trying to drown me, and afterward the police in New York City had taken her DNA in conjunction with the investigation of Sharon's murder. The story had been everywhere in the press for two weeks but only the bare outlines: Ann Carny had tried to kill me. She had also allegedly murdered Sharon Hayes. The full details had yet to surface. Ann had been painted as a career girl come unhinged, and one of the tabloids ridiculously had made her a cautionary tale for chicks leaning in too far.

Vicky had been spared. So far, at least, there was no evidence linking her directly to Sharon's murder. Ann had tried to take her down, but it hadn't worked. Vicky admitted that she'd called Sharon but claimed it was only out of concern for her own career. Sharon, Vicky said, had tried to sully her reputation years ago, and she'd feared another attempt. She also said she'd shared her concerns with Ann, but she had no idea why Ann would try to become her avenger.

I'd retained a PR person to assist me, and he'd issued a statement saying very little but saying it well. I used the ongoing investigation as an excuse to be discreet; at least I was controlling the information.

The Monday after I returned from Long Island, Lisa Follett met with Potts and Carey. They agreed to search my computer and within days had found the botnet. During Lisa's frank discussion with them, a few more details emerged. It had been Ann who'd told Potts about my history with Janice, and she who'd revealed that Carter and I were involved. Ann always led me to believe she was working on my behalf when behind the scenes she was doing her best to undermine me.

Lisa found out that there'd never been a mystery suspect, as Ann had implied to me the night before I was axed. It had been her way of toying with me, cat-and-mouse-style.

On Wednesday, Lisa had yet another meeting with Potts. He conveyed that he planned to offer me my job back. Because of the impending sale of the network, the decision had to be run by others.

I should have been frustrated by having to wait longer, but I wasn't. I used the time to run and to think and to connect with a few old friends. And to talk to Alex. We walked together sometimes and ordered in food at my apartment, discussing what had happened and trying to make sense of it. I still felt overwhelmed by what he'd done for me. We both knew that a physical relationship was going to happen. Some nights it felt wildly erotic, sitting on the couch next to him and feeling the charge between us. But we were taking our time. I had work to do before I became invested in another romantic relationship.

After the Ann story hit and word began to gurgle up that I might be exonerated, I heard from a couple of people in management at the network. Never from Tom, though. Within days it came out that he was going to a bigger show at a whole other network.

Maddy called right after the weekend in East Hampton. She was all fluttery with her concerns. I arranged to meet her on Tuesday and told her I'd discovered that she was passing my research along as her own.

"Oh, I didn't realize I wasn't supposed to do that."

"Of course you did, Maddy," I said. "And until you can examine what you did and realize why it was wrong, I have nothing more to say to you."

I'd learned by this point that Alex was the guy she was so taken with. She had confessed her infatuation to him after the weekend, to his total surprise.

A few days after Ann's arrest, I arranged to meet with Jake. I told him I wanted to come downtown one night to pick up my boxes and asked if he'd order us a pizza. I knew the request floored him.

It was unsettling to spend an evening at the loft, sitting at the same pine table where I'd eaten so many meals as we laughed and talked. But I fought off my discomfort. I also forced myself to adjust to seeing Jake in reading glasses. I ate three slices of pizza, drank a beer, and related what had happened to me.

"I really appreciate you sharing all of it with me, Robin," he said.

"That's not the only reason I came down here. There's something else I wanted to talk about with you."

"Don't tell me this is one of those 'I've met someone I'm serious about' moments."

I laughed out loud. "No, not that. I wanted to respond to one of the points you made when I was here last."

"Okay."

"When things started to fall apart between us, I did owe you another chance, or at least an attempt at another chance."

"Look, I came down a little hard. I'm the one to blame for what happened."

"I'm not excusing your infidelity. But I did box you out in our marriage, particularly when I had my own show, and even before that. It pains me to admit this, but I was never all in during our marriage. It's not because I didn't love you. I can see now that I've always found ways to keep my distance in relationships. I don't want to sound all 'boo-hoo, woe is me,' but the truth is that my screwed-up past has gotten the better of me in my personal life."

"You were open to me about what you'd been through, Robin. Maybe I should have helped you cope with it better."

"That wasn't your responsibility. It was mine. And I'm sorry that I came into our marriage without having fully dealt with it. I'm going to do that now, though. Find a therapist." I smiled. "Maybe one who specializes in wicked stepmothers and stain phobia. And deal with it."

He nodded, picked up a pizza crust, and obviously deliberated finishing it before dropping it back in the box. "Does that mean making peace with your father, too?"

"Yes. But not in the way you might expect. I've responded to his calls and emails over the years because,

I think, deep down I was hoping he was on the verge of saying he was wrong to choose Janice over his daughter, who was still grieving for her mother and needed him desperately. But that's not going to happen. And I've decided the best thing for me to do is accept the reality and lose all contact with him. That's the only way I can truly move on."

"I hope I'm not part of the going-incommunicado plan. I told you I wanted to be there for you, and I meant it."

"I'm okay with that, Jake. I want to stay in touch. But I'd like to take it slow."

"Sure. Hey, somehow I've inspired you to eat a ton of carbs tonight, so I feel that bodes well for the future."

Two weeks later, the offer had come from Potts. My job back, along with an apology and a healthy raise, the latter probably as protection against my trying to sue his flabby ass off. Potts also made it clear that Vicky would be warned and watched. Unfortunately, the network had no grounds for terminating her before the end of her contract. "She's a nutcase, and they know it now," Lisa told me later that day. "But their hands are tied."

I'd thanked Potts for the offer and told him I'd like time to consider it.

I did think about it. Again and again. And that led me to Bettina's.

"Here's what I wanted to talk to you about," I told her. "I want to come to work for you again."

She made no attempt to disguise her total surprise. "I must say, darling, you've completely caught me off guard."

"It doesn't have to be a regular job," I said. "I'd love to consult again, like I did before. Maybe there's a project you can think of for me."

"Oh, there's plenty for you to do. There's even a job I'd give you in a heartbeat. But why aren't you going back to your show? Potts assured me he was rehiring you."

"He offered," I said. "I don't want to be back on that show."

"Darling," Bettina said, "do another show, then. Take some meetings and listen to the offers. If you want, I'll talk to Tony about an entirely different show for you once he buys the network."

"Thank you," I said. "You've helped me through this, and I appreciate it. But I want to take a hiatus from TV."

"You worked so hard to get back. Potts will be gone before long, and you won't have to deal with him anymore. And between the two of us, Vicky will be out once her contract is finished."

I couldn't go back to the network as long as Vicky was there. But it was more than that. If I wanted a career in television, it couldn't be for the same reasons I'd been involved up until now.

That night by the pool, Ann had been blistering in her comments about me, but she'd been right about one thing: I *had* spent a year and a half bemoaning being off the air. I was desperate to be the girl on the side of the bus shelter again. It wasn't simply because I loved the work. It ran deeper than that. My career had served a visceral need. When Sharon had asked why I preferred TV journalism to print, a word had slipped out of my mouth: I'd told her that for me, being on TV was *validating*. And it was. I'd felt that way from my first time on the air. I'd been more than happy as a print reporter, but as soon as I had a taste of being on-camera—as a guest on a show—I was hooked. It was like a drug, in some ways. It had tangled me up, made me push other things away. And my obsessiveness had hurt my marriage.

In hindsight, I could see that craving that role probably had to do with my father, with a need to feel believed and accepted.

At some point, I might be open to being back in the game. But only when I could do it because I loved the work.

"Would you want a full-time job?" Bettina asked.

"What I'd love for now is a freelance project," I said. "I promised my publisher that I would throw myself into publicizing the book for the next few weeks. Fortunately, this whole mess has really helped the sales."

"Why don't you give me a day or two to put together a proposal for you, and I'll be in touch."

"Perfect," I said, rising. I knew she must have evening plans, maybe a dinner at Positano or Pastis. "And thank you, Bettina. I'm very grateful to you."

"How is it going, anyway?" she asked. "I hope you've had people to lean on during this time."

"People like you, yes. And there's a guy I've started to see. He's the one who saved me in the swimming pool."

"What a sexy way to connect," she said, swinging open her front door. "I seem to only meet men at dreary dinner parties, and they're all eighty-five years old. Goodbye, darling, have a nice evening."

"Thanks again, Bettina."

"Remember, if you change your mind, I'll make sure you're back on the network in a millisecond."

"Maybe someday," I said.

Acknowledgments

O ne of the parts I enjoy most about writing a book is doing all the research for it. That's where you really get to play detective. I would like to thank the people who so generously helped me gather information for *Eyes on You*: Barbara A. Butcher, chief of staff at the NYC Office of Chief Medical Examiner; Susan Brune, Esq.; David S. Rasner, Esq., partner at Fox Rothschild, LLP, and co-chair of its family law practice; Ronald S. Katz, Esq.; Dr. Mark Howell, psychotherapist; Danielle Atkin, freelance TV producer and writer; Brad Holbrook, former news anchor; Tom Miller, information security manager; Andrea Kaplan, president, Andrea Kaplan, PR; Caleb White, police officer; Ted Lotti, deputy director of corporate security, the Hearst Corp.

I'd also like to thank my awesome agent, Sandy Dijkstra, who has been with me for thirteen books now, and although that's not a lucky number, with Sandy I always feel like I've hit the jackpot; Sandy's fab team, including Elise Capron, Thao Le, and Andrea Cavallaro; my terrific book editor, Carolyn Marino, whom I'm thrilled to be working with now; Emily Krump of William Morrow, who was always there when I needed her; Rachel Elinsky, the associate director of publicity at HarperCollins and a dream to collaborate with; Katie O'Callaghan, the associate director of marketing at HarperCollins, who has given me a bucketload of help and great advice; and the fabulous Kathy Schneider, associate publisher at HarperCollins, who has always had such faith in me.

About the Author

Kate White, the former editor-in-chief of *Cosmopolitan* magazine, is the *New York Times* bestselling author of the standalone novels *Hush* and *The Sixes* and the Bailey Weggins mystery series. White is also the author of popular career books for women, including *I Shouldn't Be Telling You This: Success Secrets Every Gutsy Girl Should Know*. She lives in New York City with her family.

www.katewhite.com

THE NEW LUXURY IN READING

We hope you enjoyed reading
our new, comfortable print size and found it
an experience you would like to repeat.

Well – you're in luck!

HarperLuxe offers the finest in fiction and
nonfiction books in this same larger print size and
paperback format. Light and easy to read, HarperLuxe
paperbacks are for book lovers who want to see
what they are reading without the strain.

For a full listing of titles and
new releases to come, please visit our website:

www.HarperLuxe.com